Wyatt's

WAY

Wyatt's WAY

BY

LEXI POST

Cover design by Bella Media Management
Formatting by Bella Media Management
Cover photo: Period Images

Print ISBN: 978-1-949007-23-7

Excerpt of *Christmas with Angel* © 2015 by Lexi Post

WYATT'S WAY
Last Chance Series, Book 7

By Lexi Post

After the loss of his grandfather, Wyatt Ford is homeless and rudderless when he lands at Last Chance Ranch with the last of their horses. His mood is anything but pleasant, so when he inadvertently hurts the feelings of the sweetest woman in town, he's determined to make it up to her. But she has a backbone, which attracts his full attention, and he finds himself willing to go the extra mile for her. That is, if she'll let him.

Alyssa Parker, Ms. Parker to her third-grade students, has a strong moral compass, a strict code about only dating locals, and a goal to purchase her very own home. Her interest in Mr. Ford is fleeting…until he comes to her rescue. Just when she thinks her cowboy hero seems too good to be true, she discovers his biggest fear, one that looms large between them.

Wyatt knows letting Alyssa go is the right thing to do for her, but it's the worst move he could make for himself. It means tackling his past on his own. But even if he comes out a winner, what good will it do him if he's lost the woman he loves?

For updates, sneak peeks, and special prizes, sign up to receive the latest news from Lexi http://bit.ly/LexiUpdate

Acknowledgments

I want to thank my husband, Bob Fabich, Sr., for all his patience on the days when I'm buried in writing, revisions, and edits. He knows I'd rather spend the time with him and is always there when I've finished.

Thanks to my awesome sister Paige Wood, who keeps my stories on the right track with ruthless precision in the nicest way.

I couldn't have come up with this story if not for the ever-present help of my critique partner, Marie Patrick. Thank you, my friend.

For telling me stories about Meeko and Kentucky (yes, real horses), I thank fellow author Kayce Lassiter. You really know how to tell a story, lady!

A special thank you to Lexi's Legends, who helped with so many of the names and details that I needed for Wyatt's story. Specifically, thank you to Diane Scott, Teresa Fordice, Evelyn Nore, Penny Brosze, Patricia Way, Charlene Whitehouse, Stephanie Hale, Rochelle Ireland, and Alison Pridie.

And I can't close without saying thank you to Lisa Fishback, KC, Beth Cotter, and Cathy Christensen for taking a final look to make sure this story was ready to go.

Author's Note

Wyatt's Way was inspired by Lewis Carroll's book, *Alice in Wonderland*. In this children's story, Alice falls asleep on the banks of a stream and dreams about following a rabbit down a rabbit hole then growing larger and smaller. She meets many characters including the White Rabbit, a Hookah Smoking Caterpillar, a vanishing and reappearing Cheshire Cat, a Mad Hatter, a Dormouse, a March Hare, a Mock Turtle, a Gryphon, and of course, the Queen and King of Hearts. The story is about a child's attempt to navigate the adult world, which makes no sense to her.

The lack of logic to this dream story can be disturbing, so what better basis for a nightmare? And Wyatt has plenty of those based upon Carroll's story. But can he figure out what they mean? Is his tie to his past too strong to live in the now? Can illogical thought and coincidence make sense in the real world? How will they overlap when he meets his own Alice? And if the two are not compatible, which will win, and at what cost?

Chapter One

Canterbury, Arizona

Mid-August

Opening the door of the vet office, Wyatt Ford halted. He expected it to be like the one they had used for High Mountain Ranch, clean, sterile, with a hollow echo inside concrete walls. This felt like walking into someone's home. To the left was a waiting area with comfortable chairs accompanied by small tables. In a quick glance, he noticed two floor lamps and a bookcase with children's books on the lower shelves as well as more adult books higher up.

To the right, an older woman sat behind a wooden counter that looked like it might have been a hotel desk from the 1800s. "Cowboy, if you just need to come in from the heat, feel free to have a seat but do close the door. Ms. Parker is likely feeling a bit cramped."

"Yes, ma'am." Quickly, he shut the door, only to find a woman sitting behind it in one of the comfortable chairs. She wore a short-sleeved, flower-print dress that looked to be lilacs and a pair of off-white heels. Her profile showed straight golden hair pulled back in a clip and a slightly upturned nose, but she didn't look at him, her gaze focused on the hallway at the end of the waiting area.

"Welcome to Canterbury Tails. How can I help you?"

He took off his hat and focused on the older woman. "I'm here to talk to the vet. Last Chance Ranch sent me."

She patted her dark-colored hair, the white roots showing. "Now, I'm sure the ranch didn't send you. Was it Cole, Riley, Trace, Whisper, Logan, or Lacey?"

If she'd meant to impress him, she'd succeeded. "Riley O'Hare, ma'am. She wants the vet to come out after dinner."

"Well, you just take a load off, and I'll let Miss Jenna know you're here."

"*Miss* Jenna?" Did the ranch have a female vet?

The older lady stood and gave him a stern look. "That's right, *Miss* Jenna. She's not only the vet for that spread, but she's Logan Williams fiancé, so be sure you don't go jumping to no conclusions about her expertise if you want to keep your job at the ranch."

He shook his head confused by all the connections and the woman's tone. "No, I wouldn't ma'am."

"That's Ms. Richards, to you. Now, go set."

He'd obviously just messed up again. *"You need to show you're worth the trouble, boy."* He heard his grandfather's words as clear as if he were standing right next to him. It had barely been four weeks since the old man had a heart attack and up and died on him, leaving him homeless and rudderless. No wonder he could still hear the deep raspy voice from too many cigarettes clearly in his head. But if there was one thing he'd learned after fourteen years of living with the old coot, it was that ninety-five percent of the time, he was right.

He needed to complete this errand and show those at Last Chance that he was worth the trouble, even if he wasn't sure he was. He moved to the chair farthest from the tall woman who was already there. Sitting down, he leaned his elbows on the chair's arms and studied the reception desk, staying silent. He didn't want to say the wrong thing, which had become a new habit in the last month.

But he couldn't help glancing over to sneak a peek at the woman also waiting there. She wasn't petite, yet there was something very soft and feminine about her. She was girl-next-door pretty. Wholesome and kind looking. Everything about her invited him to chat.

He snapped his gaze back to the desk. It was best he kept to himself. Ever since his grandpa passed, he'd felt like he was standing on the edge of the Grand Canyon and the slightest breeze would push him over. Uncomfortable in his own skin, he'd screwed up at Last Chance multiple times while trying to help and had blurted the wrong things to piss off half the people associated with the place.

"Is one of the horses sick?"

The question caught him unawares, and he started from his reverie to look at the woman in the flowered dress. "Miss?"

"I asked if one of the rescue horses was sick?" She gave him an empathetic smile, her light brown eyes shiny from a watery sheen.

"Ah, no. Just new horses. Every horse that comes to the ranch has to be examined by the vet." Something that had annoyed him. As if his horse Tundra wouldn't be in perfect health. That had started his unwelcome to the ranch.

He tried to stay focused on the conversation with the woman. He even liked her voice. "Two new ones arrived this morning."

She cocked her head slightly. "Poor things. I haven't been to the ranch, but I've heard they are wonderful to poor abused, neglected, and unwanted horses. Have you worked there long?"

Yeah, he'd heard that too, but he'd insisted on staying a couple weeks to be sure his grandfather's horses would be well taken care of. It wasn't as if he had anywhere else to go. "No, Miss. I'm just visiting for a bit."

She nodded as if that made all the sense in the world, when he knew it didn't. He wasn't related to anyone on the ranch except maybe the horses. It still infuriated him that he couldn't afford his grandfather's ranch even with the money left to him. It was his home, but the family insisted on selling it. Resentment burned strong in his gut.

"I brought in a chinchilla. Her name is Miss Piggy, after the Muppet. She's not doing well. I think she may have eaten something she shouldn't have."

He yanked himself from his angry thoughts. "A chinchilla? I didn't know they could be pets."

She smiled. "Oh, yes. They are very educational, too." Her smile faltered. "I just hope the children won't be too upset if she doesn't make it."

As he'd learned the hard way, life and death went hand and hand, with no concern as to how people would feel about it. He shrugged. "If the pet dies, it will be a good lesson. They might as well learn sooner rather than later that everything dies."

The woman's light eyes widened before she looked away to Ms. Richards, who stood at the entrance to the waiting area, a frown on her face.

"Ms. Parker. You can go down to examine room two. Dr. Jenna has looked over Miss Piggy and wants to confer with you."

Though Ms. Parker wasn't looking at him, he could see a tear in the corner of her eye as she rose. "Thank you, Connie."

Connie Richards gave Ms. Parker a kind smile and took her hand, giving it a squeeze. "Dr. Jenna is the best. You know that."

Ms. Parker nodded silently as she continued down the hall.

As soon as the sound of a door closing reached them, Ms. Richards rounded on him. "What were you thinking?"

Surprised, he sat back. "What?"

"I heard you." She advanced on him, mimicking his tone. "They might as well learn sooner rather than later that everything dies." She halted two feet away. "Could you be any more callous? The woman is already feeling guilty and heartbroken and you rub salt in the wound? What rock did Cole find you under?"

Every word she spoke stabbed him with guilt. Hell, he'd done it again. He hadn't meant to be so unfeeling. Why had he said that? "I apologize, Ms. Richards. I didn't mean to say the words out loud."

Her hands found her hips as she stared down at him. "Oh, so just thinking it would be good for third graders to learn that the pet they have loved all last school year is dead and they should get used to it is okay?"

He shook his head. "No ma'am." He felt like a sixteen-year-old all over again being dressed down by his grandfather. He was acting like the sixteen-year-old he used to be, too, instead of the thirty-year-old man he'd become. Or he thought he'd become. What was wrong with him?

She threw her hands up and stomped over to her desk. "Well then, I suggest you apologize to Ms. Parker as soon as you're able because that poor woman has to tell at least twenty children next week that their pet died."

He stared at her. Twenty children? Finally, what Mrs. Richards said about third graders clicked. "She's a teacher."

"Of course, she's a teacher." The woman eyed him. "Exactly how long have you been at Last Chance."

He rose, holding his hat with both hands. "A week. This is my first day in town."

The woman looked him up and down. "Well, young man,

there's a few things you need to know about living here. First, Canterbury and Wickenburg are small sister towns despite being spread out, and the ranches surrounding these towns are well known. Second, we all care about each other here and look out for each other, so if you're thinking of staying, then you better make it up to Ms. Parker. She's the sweetest, most kindest woman you're going to meet in all of Canterbury."

She paused to study him from the top of his head to the toe of his boots and back. He got the feeling she found him lacking.

"And third, you better lose that attitude, real quick, unless you like being a pariah."

He nodded, afraid if he said anything, he'd just make things worse. Why had he said that to Ms. Parker? He knew better. He wasn't the ass he'd made of himself. At least he hoped he wasn't.

"Now, you get on back to the ranch. Dr. Jenna said she'll be over after she picks up Logan and Charlotte. And you tell Annette I'm expecting her to be at Ollie's tomorrow for our lady's lunch."

"Yes, ma'am."

"And say it nicely, will you?"

"Yes, ma'am, I will."

She stared at him a moment longer then waved her hand. "Now shoo, I've got work to do."

Happy to be getting out of there, he opened the door quickly only to be brought up short by an old man with a German Shepard. Backing up so the two could enter, he waited until they were inside then quickly slipped out.

Jogging down the steps to his truck, he couldn't help cringing. His grandfather would definitely have something to say about his behavior. He halted on the second to last step. But that wasn't going to happen. His grandfather was six feet under and now there was no one between him and the yawning abyss. No one to keep him from sliding back down the rabbit hole.

Shaken more than he cared even to admit to himself, he continued to his truck, barely keeping from stepping into oncoming traffic as he headed for the driver side door. Shit, he better keep to himself and away from other people until he could get his equilibrium back…if he ever could.

Alyssa Parker pulled into the driveway of her father's house, thankful it was finally Sunday. It had been a rough week between preparing for a new school year, losing Miss Piggy, and the unfeeling cowboy from yesterday. The cowboy was probably her biggest stressor only because of her own expectations.

When he'd sat down, she couldn't help but notice how large he was. He was one of those few men who could make her feel small. Most cowboys were slim, but this one had meat on his bones as her mom used to say about her dad. He had dark hair, a strong nose, and a bit of scruff about his jaw and chin. But what had taken her breath was when he'd looked at her. His turbulent green eyes had her melting inside.

Then she'd had to ruin the effect by striking up a conversation with the insensitive jerk. She should have known better. Her first impressions of men were always wrong. Now what she needed was some of her dad's homemade banana and chocolate chip pancakes and a little advice about pets from a man who actually cared about them.

Opening the door of her old practical sedan, she stepped out into the heat of the morning only to be confronted by a squawking grey goose. "Oh shush, Gerti. It's only me."

The goose honked a couple more times then waddled around the vehicle to check for any strangers. Her dad was the only one in town, that she knew of, who kept geese for watch dogs instead of the usual canines.

He'd bought the ten acres of land when he was twenty years old and had built the sprawling adobe ranch house with his own two hands. He wouldn't propose to her mom until it was finished. Alyssa loved growing up on the outskirts of town. Unlike a real ranch, her home had been eclectic with an odd assortment of animals over the years and her friends had loved visiting.

Thankful she'd only wore her tank top, jean shorts, and cowboy boots, she opened the back door of her car and grabbed the paper grocery bag and the small plastic bag from the seat. Closing it with her hip, she started toward the arched wooden door at the front of the house only to be accosted by one of the goats. "Shoo." Turning her back on the animal like a pro-football running back, she made her way past the tackle to the door.

Stepping into the air-conditioned foyer, she leaned back to shut out the heat. "Good morning, dad!"

"Did you get the glue?"

She walked through the open living room, her gaze going to the view through the floor to ceiling folding glass doors that spanned the full twenty-four feet. She never grew tired of the scene of dirt yard, out buildings, desert landscape, and the pines beyond. Passing through the wide arch into the kitchen, she inhaled deeply. "No wonder the goats are circling. It smells heavenly in here."

Her father lifted four pancakes from a skillet, opened the oven, and added them to the pile on a plate inside. "Honey bacon. It was on sale."

She set the two bags on the counter peninsula then walked over to give her father a kiss on the cheek. "You had me at bacon."

He chuckled. "I had you the minute you walked in the door. Wash your hands and sit."

She grinned. She was thirty years old, but her father never stopped thinking of her as his little girl. "What did you need the glue for? I thought you had super strong glue in the garage."

"I do." He pulled the plate of pancakes out and placed them on the kitchen table on the other side of the peninsula. The plate of honey bacon was already the centerpiece. Then he reached over and pulled the coffee pot from the coffee maker on the corner of the counter and poured them each a cup.

She dried her hands and took her seat before lifting her cup to her lips to inhale. "This smells like, hmm, mocha?"

Her dad grimaced. "Yeah."

She laughed. "Let me guess, Ms. Davis is now selling coffee flavors at the office."

"That's why I try to avoid going into the office. But the project manager keeps calling these stupid meetings to make sure we're all on the same page. You'd think I'd never built a house before." He speared two pancakes and plopped them on her plate.

She took a sip of the coffee. "Well, this is a lot better than the scented candles she was selling last winter."

"Hmph." He took four pancakes for himself before passing her the bacon. It was hard to believe he'd be retiring at the end of the year. Just like he looked at her as his little girl, though she was hardly little, being taller than him, she always viewed him as a rock steady man that not even a monsoon could blow over.

But the fact was, he was balding on the back of his head and his stocky frame did have a bit more weight. Still, his arms, mostly bare in his t-shirt, would be the envy of any young man from the gym. Of course, it was an *early* retirement.

Taking four strips, she added them to her plate. She cut a

large piece of her dad's famous pancakes and stuffed it in her mouth. As the banana and chocolate flavors mixed with the fluffy buttermilk sweetness, she moaned. "I think this is my favorite flavor that you make. I will never ever grow tired of these."

"You better not. It's the only way I can get you to come visit me."

She coughed. "Excuse me? You are always welcome to visit me, you know."

Her dad stuffed a big helping of pancakes into his mouth to avoid answering.

It wasn't like they lived that far from each other. They were in the same town, but he disliked what he called her "cube," her second-floor apartment. He never understood why she'd moved out of the sprawling ranch, even after he'd scared away her third boyfriend.

Taking another bite of her favorite breakfast, she chewed. Soon, she hoped to be moving out of her one-bedroom apartment. She was saving for a down payment on a house. If she'd calculated correctly, she was pretty close. "Will you come visit me when I buy my own home?"

Her dad took a sip of his coffee and frowned, looking at the cup as if it was from some alien planet. It appeared that mocha coffee wasn't his favorite. "If you just bought a nice piece of property, I'd have built you a house that was worth visiting already."

She stifled her groan. It was an old refrain. There was no way she would let her father take on building her a house when he was working a fulltime job. That was just too much. He wasn't in his late twenties anymore like he had been when he built his current home. "You're about to retire from building. It's time to enjoy life."

That got her another "humph" as he filled his mouth with more pancakes.

They ate in companionable silence. After finishing her plate, she looked longingly at the remaining pancakes. She really shouldn't since she'd eaten bacon too. Though she'd taken after her petite mom in looks, she had her dad's stocky frame. Her mom called it "big boned." She called it, "always needing to diet."

"Allie, just have some." Her dad lifted the pancake platter and set two more on her plate before taking the last three for himself.

"Dad, I had bacon today. You know I'm trying to keep my weight down." She actually hadn't gone down since the beginning of the year, but she hadn't gone up either.

He shook his head as he finished chewing before he spoke. "That's crap. You have good muscle on your bones, and you need to feed that if you want to keep up with those hellions you try to teach." He gestured with his fork. "Aren't you starting school tomorrow? You need to have three good meals and a good night sleep."

Unable to resist the aroma coming from her plate, she drizzled syrup over the stack and cut into it. "You're right. I'll need my strength for the first day of school. Speaking of, I need your advice."

Her dad put down his fork. "If it's about that computer guy, I say let him go."

She sighed. "No, not about that. I already dropped him two weeks ago."

"Good. There was something not right about him."

She silently agreed but didn't want to get into it. "No, it's about Miss Piggy's death. Do you think I should just bring in a new pet to the class or let the students have some input?"

"Hmmm, how old are they again?"

"They're nine. I have third graders this year." She took another bite while her father pondered her question. She'd tried making his pancakes, but there was a secret ingredient he wouldn't divulge.

"I think you should let them be part of the process. When we run into a problem at the site, I always ask my guys for input on how to fix it. It makes them more motivated to do a good job."

"I understand that, but these are children."

He waved his fork and shook his head as he chewed. When he swallowed, he responded. "Doesn't matter. They'll be more interested and be more involved in caring for it. Remember when I brought home the peacock and you were afraid of it? But when I asked you if you'd like a llama or a pig, you took care of that cranky old llama until the day she died."

She laughed. "Good point. Sally wasn't that cranky, only around men."

Her dad chuckled. "Especially around that city dude you dated when you first moved out."

"You mean, Earnest?"

"Yeah, Ernie. He didn't like that animal spitting on him one bit. Got all his fancy clothes dirty. What'd he expect coming out to a ranch."

"Dad, he was trying to impress you." She couldn't help smiling at the memory.

"Oh, he left a lasting impression, that one."

She shook her head as she rose, her plate completely empty and her stomach full. He was the reason she'd decided it was time to stick to only local men. She picked up their dishes and walked around the peninsula counter to the sink. "At least he was better than the cowboy I ran into at the vet yesterday."

Her dad wiped his mouth with his napkin. "A cowboy left you with a bad impression? That surprises me."

"Surprised me, too."

"Was he rude?"

She thought about the conversation they'd had. "Not rude, just very unfeeling. Silly me for thinking a handsome cowboy would have a heart."

"What did he say?"

She could tell she had her dad's full attention now. The thought of sending her dad to Last Chance to straighten out the cowboy filled her with glee. "He said my students would have to learn sooner rather than later that all things die."

Her father pushed back his chair and crossed one foot on his other knee. "Well, that's true."

She stilled. "Dad, I was there with Miss Piggy not knowing if she was going to make it. I think a little sympathy was called for, don't you?"

"Of course. I'm just saying what the man said was true." He held up his hand as she opened her mouth to protest. "But I agree one hundred percent that he should have shown a little sympathy."

"Thank you." She ran the sprayer over the dirty dishes, possibly a little harder than was called for.

Her dad put his hands behind his head. "Do you have any ideas for involving your students in the animal selection?"

Happy with the change of subject, she shrugged. "No. I wasn't even sure if I would involve them until just now."

"I believe those flat wooden silhouettes of animal heads you made a few years back are still in the garage."

"I forgot about those." They were only about two inches thick, but each was very distinctly the animal she'd wanted. She could check on those and make sure he hadn't peeked at the project she was working on for his retirement present. Using his garage and tools made it hard to keep it a surprise, but she had it covered with a blanket and bungee cords.

He waved toward the kitchen slider. "I still have that wood in the barn if you need to make more. What animals were you thinking?"

She set a rinsed dish in the dishwasher. "I'm not sure. Probably the usual, rabbit, guinea pig, hamster, gerbil, chinchilla, ferret, hedgehog."

"What about turtles, iguanas, and snakes? You don't want to forget the boys."

She dropped the utensils in the dishwasher and closed it. "Nope. I'm the one who'll have to care for it during the breaks, and I want something cuddly that won't scare Snowdrop."

Her father rose and walked into the kitchen. He started taking the corn out of the paper bag she'd left on the counter. "That rabbit still have the run of your cube?"

"It's an apartment, Dad, and yes." She opened the small bag with the glue and post-it notes. "You never told me what the glue was for."

He didn't face her. "I broke something, what else? Need to glue it back together."

"What broke?"

"What is this, twenty questions?" Her father strode to the far side of the kitchen and threw the paper bag in the trash.

It was such an odd response, she couldn't let it go. "Dad, what did you break?"

He came back, dragging the trashcan with him. "I broke the picture on my nightstand. Must have hit it in my sleep. Happy?"

Oh, that was the picture of her mom, him, and herself at the Grand Canyon. No wonder he was so touchy. He loved that picture and the memory. It wasn't long after it had been taken that she died.

Alyssa moved to the stool on the other side of the counter, searching for a change in subject. "What are the post-it notes for?"

Her father stopped husking the corn and huffed. "They are to remind me of all the blasted paperwork I have to do before I leave Gila Bend Construction. I feel like I've got a part-time job with this whole retirement thing. It would be easier to just keep working."

That was not going to happen according to the company. It still made her angry they were forcing him out, but they had given him a sweet package. "I'd be happy to help if you need it."

He went back to shucking the corn. "I thought you were going to check out those wooden silhouettes of animal heads. I can tell you right now, there is no chinchilla or ferret for sure."

"Oh, right. Where did you say the wood was?" She jumped off the stool, ready to get to work. She already knew what she'd have the students do to vote on their favorite animal.

"It's in the barn, on the left. You'll need the ladder as it's up in the loft. Didn't really think I'd be using that wood again any time soon."

"That makes sense. Your jigsaw still in the shed or have you used it recently?" He always kept the tools he was using in the garage.

He set the last bare corn on the counter and moved the trashcan back. "It's still in the shed. It's a blasted furnace out there. Make sure you work in the garage."

"Will do." She left the kitchen and went outside through the garage. The triple digit heat hit her like a convection oven. Striding across the dirt yard, she made a beeline for the barn, slipping inside before the goats could catch up. At least she no longer had to outrun child-hating peacocks.

Chapter Two

Wyatt held Kentucky's head as Riley soothed the salve over the gelding's leg. The poor animal, half Thoroughbred half Quarter horse, was what was called a "wobbler" and could never be ridden, but even worse, he had a knack for hurting himself.

He wasn't used to being around horses with unhealthy quirks. The other horse, Meeko, that came on the same day from a different place wouldn't let them near him. Dr. Jenna had tried, but he was having none of it. Even feeding him had become a dare.

While Meeko would as soon as cause them injury, Kentucky seemed focused on injuring himself. "Is that going to ever heal?"

Riley wiped her hands on her jeans, never one to be particular about how she looked. She was tough. He learned that the minute he met her. She rose from her crouched position and set the jar of salve on the beam at the top of the stall. "It would if he'd stop licking this stuff off. You'd think it was made of carrot juice. Grab me a Telfa pad and some gauze from the tack room."

He patted the horse and carefully let himself out of the stall to get the requested materials. After being at Last Chance almost two weeks now, he felt like a fool for being so anal about Gramps' horses before he arrived. He owed Garret, Riley's man, an apology. It felt like apologizing was all he'd been doing lately, and there was still another he hadn't made yet.

Grabbing the supplies from a cabinet in the tack area, he moved into the stall again and handed them over to Riley. "Didn't Dr. Jenna say to leave the wound open?"

That got him a scowl from the red-haired ranch hand. "Yeah, but that was before we realized Kentucky has a death wish – death by infection."

He couldn't argue with her there.

"Keep him pre-occupied while I wrap this."

"Sure." He gave the horse a pat on the side to get his attention. "Hey, Kentucky. What do you say we have a man to man talk here."

Riley coughed, from the dust or his conversation, he didn't know nor wanted to know.

"This licking at your wound isn't smart. I know you can't resist, but you have to dig deep down and find the will to. Trust me, I know what that's like and it's not easy. If you do this again, I'm going to have to tie you so you can't reach that leg. I know you wouldn't want that. It's never fun being restricted. But if you do resist and leave that bandage alone, I promise to reward you with, um, a song. How's that sound? You behave and let yourself heal and I'll sing to you every day. What do you think?"

He paused, waiting for the horse to look away, but Kentucky's ears were trained on him as was his gaze.

"Oh, I see, you're wondering if my singing will sound like caterwauling. Well, I have to say I'm insulted you would even have that thought. You just go ask Tundra or Guinness or Blaze if I don't sing right well. Just don't talk to Lady. She's a princess and has no use for this lowly cowboy."

The horse continued to give him his full attention.

Glancing down he could see Riley was just finishing up the

wrapping. He let out a heavy sigh. "I see where this is going. You won't believe it till you hear it. Fine, I'll sing, but I don't need no heckling." He cleared his throat then started singing *Let it Be*.

He was through the first verse before Riley interrupted.

"Okay, Wyatt. I think we get the picture. He'll let it be and you've got a great voice. Now if your bribe works, we're all set, but if not…" She reached up and took the jar of salve off the beam, we're going to need more of this." She handed it over Kentucky's back for him to take.

"You want me to go to Dr. Jenna's and get more?" He'd been waiting for just such an opportunity.

She put her hand on her hip. "Well, I don't expect you to find more around here."

"Right." He nodded. "Kentucky, remember what I said while I'm gone." He moved around the horse and once more left the stall. "Do you need anything else while I'm in town?"

Riley shook her head. "No. Just get back here by two. I've got to meet Garret at the paint store by three."

He checked his watch. He had plenty of time. "No problem." Striding out of the barn, he threw the jar in the air and caught it as he headed for his truck. It had been a week since he'd been a jerk to the teacher Ms. Parker at the vet and he finally had a chance to apologize.

Jumping into the front seat, he set the jar in the console. Checking the address he'd looked up days ago, he plugged it into his GPS before pulling out. He was in such a rush, he almost backed into his box trailer with all his belongings that was sitting under the mesquite tree next to the dirt parking area. The near miss had him taking a deep breath.

Putting the truck in drive, he drove down the dirt road toward the main highway that would bring him to Canterbury and in particular the elementary school there. He always took responsibility for his actions, at least since he'd come under his grandfather's care, and knowing he still had to apologize to Ms. Parker was bothering like a burr in his boot.

Cole Hatcher, part owner of Last Chance, hadn't said how long he could stay, but he found working with Riley and the others who dropped in to help with the horses had given him something to do. Their crazy schedule, or lack of schedule, had him wishing he could organize them, but this wasn't his ranch.

Of everyone who came and went, he got along best with Annette, Cole's grandmother. He just felt comfortable around the older woman and her husband, though her husband was rarely around.

Pulling into the parking lot of Canterbury Elementary school, he stepped out of his truck and strode to the entrance. A man in uniform greeted him and required he state his purpose. He kept it simple, no need for everyone in town to know why he had to speak to Ms. Parker.

Once in the main office, he started to sweat, despite the cool air-conditioning. Memories of waiting for the principal to see him and pass judgement on whatever he'd done this time flooded him. He had to force himself to remember that in his final high school days while under his grandfather's care, he'd never had to see the principal once. Moving to that new school had been like wiping the slate clean, as well as himself, except the one time.

"Mr. Ford, you wanted to see me?"

Lost in his trip down memory lane, he started at the sound of her voice. He rose from the chair, his hat in his hands as he looked into her amaretto-colored eyes. He didn't remember them being so pretty. He must have been half-blind last week.

She wore a royal blue short-sleeved dress that buttoned down the front and was belted at the waist. Her thick golden hair was tied back in a low ponytail. He wasn't sure if it was the dress, but her hair looked brighter than he remembered.

"Mr. Ford? I need to get back to my students. Did you need something?"

"Yes, I…" he looked around the office to find at least five pairs of eyes on them. He lowered his head to whisper. "Is there someplace we can go that's more private."

Her eyes widened as if he asked the impossible.

"Perhaps outside?"

She seemed to think about that a moment then finally nodded. "Yes. This way." She walked out one of the double doors to exit the main office and led him down a hallway to a side door.

He couldn't help noticing the sway of her hips. The more he saw of her, the more he liked her, but he'd made a terrible first impression.

As they stepped outside, he donned his hat against the bright sun. A few paces away from the door, she halted and faced him, crossing her arms over her chest. "So, how can I help you?"

He knew he'd been a bit insensitive but had hoped she'd not thought much of it. From her stance and her tone, she had definitely thought about it. "Ms. Parker. I came here to apologize. I didn't mean to be so oblivious to your emotions over your pet."

"My classes' pet."

"Yes, your classes' pet. Miss Piggy. I understand that it's hard to lose a pet. I'm usually not so rude."

"Then why were you?" There was no softening in her eyes or tone.

And wasn't that the question? It was something he'd been asking himself since the moment he'd come to town. "My only explanation is that my thoughts were unpleasant when we had our conversation, and I'm afraid I let that color my reactions. For that I'm sincerely sorry."

"Apology accepted. Have a good day, Mr. Ford." She dropped her arms and brushed past him to return to the building.

Stunned and not a little confused, he whirled around. "Ms. Parker?"

She halted but didn't turn around. "Yes?"

He strode to where she stood and walked around her to face her. "I know it's hard to believe, but I don't normally act like that." He rubbed the back of his neck. He was making a mess of this. "Is there something I can do to make it up to you?"

She looked past him at the building then returned her gaze to him. "No. I'm good. Now, if you'll excuse me, I need to return to my job."

"Right, yes. I understand. I appreciate you accepting my apology."

Her stern look softened for a moment as she cocked her head slightly. "Is there something you need from me, Mr. Ford?"

In other words, why the hell was he still standing there bothering her when she'd accepted his apology. It was a good question, but one he had no answer for. "No, not at all. Thank you for your time." He lifted the brim of his hat an inch and gave a quick nod.

She studied him for a moment longer then hurried away.

He turned to watch her as she strode to the door and disappeared inside the building. Her ponytail fell to her waist. Exactly how long was her hair? He shook his head at the stray thought. He might as well walk around the building to his truck. No need to further disturb the school personnel.

Movement at the bank of windows to the right of the side door caught his attention. There had to be at least fifteen young faces staring out of those windows, all smiling at him. Not sure what that was about, he waved.

A couple waved back before their attention was caught by someone in the room and they all scrambled from sight. It appeared the school didn't get many visitors if he was a prime attraction.

He remained on the grass and strode along the building, finally turning the corner toward the front entrance. The feeling of being watched caused him to look behind him.

"Well, this must be a really small town." In the glass doors of the main lobby were at least six women. Two smiled at him but the other four went back to talking among themselves. He shook his head at their odd actions. How big was the school anyway?

Unlocking his truck, he jumped inside and started it up. From what little he'd seen, the area was filled with cowboys, so why was he such a strange sight? He pulled out of the parking lot and continued up the highway toward Dr. Jenna's.

Before he'd arrived at Last Chance, it hadn't even occurred to him to find out anything about Canterbury or Wickenburg because he was busy with funeral arrangements, laying off good men, and packing. It appeared the sister towns were both small in population and large in land. But that didn't bother him. Many towns in Arizona were like that.

So why did he still feel uncomfortable about what happened with Ms. Parker. She said she accepted his apology, but it wasn't enough. Something was seriously wrong with him.

Stop talking to yerself and focus on what matters. He grinned as his grandfather's words drifted through his mind. He could always count on the old man to get him out of his head and back to reality. His mood dimmed. But his reality sucked with his home and his anchor gone. Now who would remind him to stop talking to himself?

He pulled into a parking space not far from Canterbury Tails. Maybe he just needed to put his behavior toward Ms. Parker aside. He'd apologized, and she'd accepted his apology. That was that. He still had a couple of people back at Last Chance he needed to prove his worth to, as Gramps told him, so he'd focus on that until he left to wherever he would go.

With the empty jar of salve in his pocket, he opened the door to the vet office. Stepping inside, he quickly shut it, Ms. Richards admonition from last time still front and center in his mind. But Ms. Richards wasn't at the desk. In fact, no one was in the waiting area.

Taking off his hat, he took a seat. Maybe she was out back.

He didn't have long to wait before the older woman breezed in from outside. "Lunch is served!" When there was no response, she looked around. "Oh, you're back."

He rose. "Yes, Ma…Ms. Richards."

"Hold on. I want to talk to you." She turned away and briskly disappeared down the hall.

Looking at the door, he briefly thought of leaving, but Riley needed the salve for Kentucky, so whatever scold Ms. Richards planned for him, it appeared he'd have to accept it.

The click of her heels coming up the hall proved she was in a hurry to speak with him, or at him, whatever the case might be. She walked behind the counter and sat as she dumped her purse on the floor and a brown bag on the desk in front of her. She motioned with a set of pink finger nails. "Come over here, Mr. Ford."

Another thing his grandfather always said was there was no use borrowing trouble, so he put a smile on his face and approached. "It's Wyatt, Ms. Richards."

She froze for a minute as her drawn-on eyebrows lifted. "Really, well, then Wyatt it is."

Her return smile had him breathing a sigh of relief. Quickly, he took the initiative. "Riley asked me to pick up more of this." He reached into his upper right pocket and brought out the jar, setting it on the counter.

She turned it to face her. "Didn't she just get this three days ago?"

He nodded. "Yes, but Kentucky has decided it tastes as good as carrots."

Ms. Richards sighed as she shook her head. "They do get some odd ones at that ranch. I'm sure Dr. Jenna can fill it, but right now she's on her lunch break, and I don't want to disturb her. She works so hard."

"I understand. If you like, I can come back later."

"Yes, that would be good. Come back in a couple hours."

"I will. Thank you." Anxious to get out of there, he was just about to put his hat on when she slapped her hand down on the counter.

"Not so fast, Wyatt."

So close. "Did you need something, Ms. Richards?"

"I sure do. Now you set yourself down over there. We need to talk. Just let me get this bowl of chili from Ollie's uncovered, and you can keep me company while I eat my lunch."

Damn. So much for escaping. "Of course. I'd be happy to." He walked over to the waiting area and took a different seat than last time. Anything to keep the woman from talking about his past behavior.

She came out from behind the desk with an insulated bowl, a spoon, and a napkin. "Ollie's makes the best three alarm chili this side of the 17. The Black Mustang touts that it has the best based on one of those city magazines, but what do they know?"

"I trust your judgment on that."

She gave him the side eye. "Since when did you get all charming like?"

He forced himself not to grimace, but he refrained from responding since anything he said would just lead back to his last visit.

She popped the lid and steam rose. She inhaled deeply. "Yup, the best chili ever." Sticking her spoon into the hot mass, she held it over the bowl but didn't lift it to her mouth. "So, Wyatt. Did you apologize to Miss Parker?"

Though she stared at the spoon, he could feel her entire attention was on him. "Yes, I did."

"Good." She blew on the spoon before lifting it to her mouth and closing her hot pink lips around it. "Hmmm, I swear I'm as addicted to this as an addict to pills."

No, she wasn't, but he didn't plan on getting into a debate about that. He understood what she really meant.

"Did she accept your apology?" This time, Ms. Richards stared at him as if she knew it wasn't that easy.

He wasn't sure he wanted to share any details with her. His gut was telling him she had ulterior motives, maybe town gossip? "She did." He shrugged as if it didn't matter much.

Ms. Richards' painted brows rose. "Really? Just like that?"

The woman was definitely not telling him something. "Yes. Why wouldn't she?"

"Because that sweet woman is as tough as cow leather when it comes to doing the right thing. She teaches her students that words are worthless, except when they hurt, and only actions show a person's true intentions."

As the older woman daintily consumed another mouthful, he pondered that. Was that why he felt as if there was something missing? That she'd forgiven him too easily for his offense? "Maybe because I went to the school and apologized, she felt that was true action." That must be it.

"That's not it." Ms. Richards shook her head as she let

another spoonful of chili cool. "No, she wants to see if you really meant it."

He jerked his head and frowned. "What? She doesn't even know me."

"Exactly. She's measuring your worth as a man. That can only mean one thing." The woman chose that moment to fill her mouth with chili.

He waited impatiently. When she swallowed, he asked the obvious. "What does it mean?"

Ms. Richards rose. "Hold that thought." Walking behind the counter, she picked up a water bottle and brought it back with her, setting it on an end table. "Well, sugar. I forgot to make sure Dr. Jenna had a cold drink." Walking out of the room, she returned with a can of cola and started down the hall.

Well, hell. Just when he thought he'd find out why Ms. Parker's quick forgiveness didn't sit well with him, the woman decided to walk out.

That's what he should do. Return in a couple of hours, pick up the salve, and go back to Last Chance. He could waste the time checking out the Black Mustang. Garrett had told him it was a bit off the beaten path, but a good place for a drink, a sandwich, darts, pool, or for watching the game. That's what he should do.

Then why was he still sitting there anxiously waiting for the receptionist to return? His grandfather would have a guess, and probably be right. But it wasn't as if he could ask him.

The clacking of heals on the hardwood floor told him his chance to escape had come and gone. Ms. Richards appeared and grinned. "You're in luck. Dr. Jenna said she'd have the salve ready in a few minutes."

Why did he get the feeling the sudden change in time frame had nothing to do with Dr. Jenna and everything to do with Ms. Richards?

The woman returned to her seat and picked up her lunch. "This should be cool enough to eat now. So where were we?" She scooped a spoonful into her mouth as she looked expectantly at him.

Though his gut told him this woman remembered exactly what they'd been talking about, he answered because he really wanted to know what she'd figured out. "You said that the fact Ms. Parker is measuring my worth as a man, a man she doesn't even know, can only mean one thing."

"Oh, yes, of course." She pointed at him with her plastic spoon. "It means she wants to know more about you but isn't sure if that's a good thing or a bad thing."

"What do you mean?"

Ms. Richards took another bite before answering. "It means, she's going to wait and see if you follow-up your words with actions. If you do, she'll make an effort to get to know you, and if you don't, she'll forget about you. That means the ball is in your court. What are you going to do?"

"Me?" It had to be female reasoning, which he wasn't very experienced with since it had just been him and Gramps and ranch hands, all men, for fourteen years. Sure, he'd dated, even had a couple relationships, so to speak, but he'd not been very good at understanding female reasoning. That had all started when his mother had decided he was too much trouble and dropped him off at his grandfather's, letting the old man raise him while she raised his two sisters.

"Yes, you." Ms. Richards pointed at him again with the spoon. "You need to do something for her. You have to admit, being as callous as you were when she was so worried, requires more than a simple apology."

And there it was, his crime laid out in the light of day for the two of them to pass judgment on. It wasn't pretty.

"What should I do, send her flowers?" Women always liked flowers.

"No, not for Miss Parker." Ms. Richards put the lid on her empty container. "No, she's not that easy. Sure, she's pretty on the outside, but her inside is more complicated. She'd want something related to the incident. If it had been Snowdrop, a nice little burial at her dad's place would be appropriate, but Miss Piggy was a class pet."

Now he understood. He also understood where Miss Parker might be coming from, and why he'd felt let down when she accepted his apology. It needed to be more to make up for what he said. "What about a gift certificate to a pet store for the new class pet. I'm guessing she'll get another." His stomach tightened at a thought. "Or was she so broken up, she can't bear the thought of another pet?"

Ms. Richards rose. "I like the way you think. That's an excellent idea. And no, she wasn't so devastated that she's not getting another pet. I heard it from Mrs. Heestand that Ms. Parker is letting the class decide what kind of pet." She walked back to her desk and stuffed the empty container in the brown bag then tossed it into the trash.

"Mrs. Heestand?"

Ms. Richard's nodded. "Yes, she's Mr. Heestand's wife. He teaches first grade and overheard Ms. Parker in the teacher's lounge telling another teacher that she'd made a wooden voting grid for the kids to decide on what type of animal."

His neck muscles suddenly felt tight. His instincts had been right. Ms. Richards was a town gossip. Now there was little doubt that his conversation with her would probably reach Ms. Parker's ears before he had a chance to follow through. He almost didn't want to for just that reason, but he needed to for his own sake. He was messed up enough without adding to it. His plan was to whittle down the people he had to prove his worth to, not rachet them up.

"I'll go fetch that salve for you, and you can be on your way. There's a family pet store just a mile west of us. It's a little out of your way, but since your truck is facing that way, you wouldn't have to make a U-turn. The store will be on your left."

He rose, feeling like he'd been manipulated but not able to pinpoint exactly how. Since it served his purpose to follow through on the plan, he'd just go with it. Then he'd be down to just two more people he needed to make things up to…that was if he could get out of his own head and stop pissing off people he spoke to.

"Here you go." Ms. Richards walked into the waiting area and handed him a full jar of salve. "I'll put it on the Last Chance account. You have a good day."

"Thank you." He gripped the jar in his hand and set his hat on his head, anxious to leave. He had the door open and was halfway through it when an older lady approached carrying a cat in a carrier.

The animal was obviously too heavy for her. He offered to take the cat in. When she agreed, he brought it inside, set it on a table and quickly exited. Next time, he'd find another way to be helpful on Last Chance. Someone else could stop at the vet's if anything else was needed.

Chapter Three

At the sound of the bell signaling lunch, Alyssa sighed. "Okay, remember your manners, walk don't run." She might as well have been talking to Snowdrop. Her students rushed out of her classroom as if they couldn't wait to get away from her. It may not be true, but sometimes it felt that way.

Today, it didn't. She was relieved to be able to escape the barrage of questions she'd received ever since walking back inside after meeting Mr. Wyatt Ford. She hadn't even known his name until the office told her he wanted to see her and she saw him sitting there.

But her students had them married with two children already, one particularly sweet girl thinking that six children would be best.

As she pulled her purse from her desk drawer, she could still hear her students.

Is that your boyfriend, Ms. Parker?

Of course it's her boyfriend, stupid. Why else would he come here? You think it's her plumber.

He's not a plumber, he's a cowboy.

You don't know that.

Uh-huh, do to. He had a cowboy hat on and he walks like a cowboy.

Cowboys don't walk no different than anyone else.

Do to.

Do not.

Do to.

Do not.

Ms. Parker, what will your name be when you marry the cowboy?

She'll still be Ms. Parker? Right, Ms. Parker?

Is he a good kisser?

Ms. Parker and the cowboy sitting in a tree. K-I-S-S-I-N-G. First, comes love. Then comes marriage, then comes Enrique in the baby carriage.

Hey, Ms. Parker, Jose called me a baby.

If the name fits.

I think Ms. Parker is going to live on a ranch and have lots of babies because she likes kids.

You like kids, Ms. Parker? Is that why you're a teacher?

She won't be our teacher anymore. Please Ms. Parker, don't have babies until I'm in the fifth grade, okay?

Ms. Parker isn't having babies. She's going to have horses.

Don't be an idiot. Humans can't have horses. They're too heavy for the stork to carry.

I think he's handsome. Do you think so, Ms. Parker?

My brother's a cowboy.

Ms. Parker, I think you should have six babies so you can teach them all at the same time like you teach us.

Striding to the classroom door, she quickly stepped into the now empty hall. Maybe if she left the scene of the crime, she could get rid of all the haunting voices.

Thankful she didn't have cafeteria duty, she headed for the teacher's lounge. A little adult conversation was just what she needed right now. Who knew a lone man could disrupt her entire class for hours?

Granted he was a handsome man, as Lydia had so kindly

pointed out. And he did sound sincere. But he'd said it himself. He was just visiting.

Stepping into the teacher's lounge, she hadn't even closed the door before her arm was hooked into Mrs. Langley's and she was being pulled to a table.

She set her purse down just before she was yanked into a chair and forced to sit or fall on the floor.

"Okay, spill." The thirty-two-year-old brunette with the angelic face looked anything but angelic.

"Spill? Spill what. I haven't even had lunch yet."

"Come on, Lyssa. Don't hold out on me. Who was that drop dead gorgeous hunk of cowboy you were talking to on school grounds?"

"Martina Langley, what were you doing ogling a man?" Exasperation combined with shock made her tone a bit harder than she meant it to be.

Marty waved her hand. "I'm married, not dead."

"But you have your own cowboy to look at."

"Doesn't mean I can't enjoy the view." Her rich throaty laugh caused a few others to look their way.

"Shhh, everyone doesn't need to know I had a visitor."

Marty's eyes rounded. "You're kidding, right? Everyone in the whole school knows. What they don't know is what you talked about. How dare you be keeping such an hombre a secret from me."

Her stomach clenched as if she'd swallowed plaster of Paris, and it had suddenly hardened. "I'm not hiding anyone. I don't even know him."

"Oh, chica, it's not bad news, is it? Someone from your padre's company?" Marty's hand clasped hers. "You can tell me. I'll help in any way I can."

Jiminy Cricket. "Nothing's wrong. He's not from dad's

company. He just came by to apologize. I ran into him at the vet's last week and he was rude, so he came to apologize. Honestly, I didn't think I'd see him again, and from my first impression, I didn't want to."

Marty let go of her hand and squinched up her face as if she'd just eaten spinach, or what she referred to as nasty green vomit. "How can that package of hotness not make a good first impression?"

"Because…" she stopped. Marty had a point, Mr. Ford's first impression was very, very good. He was tall, dark, handsome, and a cowboy, and she'd assumed he'd be understanding as well, which is why she started the conversation. And here she was telling her students not to judge a book by its cover. What a hypocrite. "Actually, it was his second impression that upset me."

"Fair enough." Marty leaned forward across the table again. "What did he do?"

Being completely honest, she relayed the conversation exactly as she remembered it and waited with bated breath for Marty's reaction. Her father's response wasn't what she had hoped, so this validation was greatly needed.

Marty sighed. "I have to agree with you. He was callous and lacked empathy." She shook her head. "And I had such high hopes for you."

Confused, she lowered her brows. "Don't tell me you were thinking like my students and already had me married to him with six children."

"No, no, of course not." Marty grinned. "I was thinking three children."

Exasperated, she stood. "Really? I'm getting my lunch."

Marty laughed loudly. "I was only kidding."

Walking to the refrigerator, she ignored her friend. She was only thirty-years-old. Why did people keep thinking her only goal in life was to find a man? Her goal was to buy her own home. She didn't even need children because she had plenty at work and could still go home and enjoy the peace and quiet. Grabbing her leftovers from the fridge, she closed the door and brought them to the counter.

Marty bumped her hip with her own. "Relax. The gossip about you and him will die down in about a month."

She glared as her friend snickered. Unfortunately, what she said was probably true. Not much out of the ordinary happened at Canterbury Elementary. Having a stranger come to the school that no one in town knew was bound to be the topic of conversation for a while.

"Has your class chosen a pet yet, Ms. Parker?" Mr. Heestand stepped up next to her to pull a paper plate out of the cabinet.

Thankful for a distraction, she smiled at the older man. "Not yet. I'm giving them until next Friday to decide. Right now, the Ferret is winning, but three days ago, it was the rabbit, so I have no idea what we will end up with."

The man unwrapped his sandwich and placed it on his plate. "Well, I think it was simply genius to allow the students to see each other's votes and have time to change their own over time. Are you having conversations about the pros and cons of each?"

"I am. I found a number of children's books in the library that speak to each animal, so we are reading and discussing."

The man pulled a napkin from the pile on the counter. "A great learning experience. Did your class have anything to say about the gentleman who came to visit you this morning?"

She gritted her teeth to keep her smile steady, happy when the microwave dinged, letting her know her lunch was ready, and she could look away without being rude. "Oh yes." She put all the exasperation she could into her voice. "They had far too much to say on that subject." She pulled her plate out and looked the man in the eye. "I'm hoping after recess they will have forgotten and we can get back to learning."

The man was either clueless or chose to ignore her signal that she didn't want to talk about that subject. "I doubt that. Quite interesting that he would come to your place of employment. I haven't seen him in town. Is he a relative?"

To her relief, her stomach growled, and she smiled apologetically. "If you'll excuse me. I better get some food in my stomach or I won't be able to hear myself teach." Without another word, she left the counter and turned toward her table.

There were now three other teachers sitting there. Maybe she should go back to her classroom to eat.

Marty sidled up to her. "Don't be chicken, chica. Better to brave the lions in their den than wait for a surprise attack."

She swallowed hard. "You'll be my wingman?"

Marty laughed. "Always."

She took a step closer to the table and Marty grabbed her arm again. "But you will owe me."

She stiffened. "What?"

"The Black Mustang, next weekend, dancing and karaoke. Promise?"

Relieved that was all her friend wanted, she nodded. "Promise."

~~*~~

Wyatt hitched Cyclone up to the new wagon. The Clydesdale was a little shorter than his own Percheron Cross, and not as broad. From what he'd heard, the animal had to be lugging something every fourth day or he started destroying things. It was hard to believe as he stood stock still for the harness.

"Is that going to work?" Riley strode out of the barn and over to where he'd just laid the reins on the padded seat.

"It fits him perfectly."

Riley jumped up in the driver's perch. "Good. I'm hoping a ride down the road will make the big guy happy. We're running out of stuff for him to haul."

He opened his mouth to suggest an idea he'd had earlier in the week but closed it. Riley was always telling him she wasn't the boss and didn't want to be. From what he'd seen, no one had that responsibility except Cole, and he was always at the firehouse. It was an odd way to run a ranch, but it was an unusual ranch.

"Wish me luck."

He stepped back. "Good luck."

Riley snapped the reins and Cyclone headed out of the yard to the dirt road that eventually led to the highway.

Shaking his head, Wyatt strode to the ranch house and up the three steps to the porch. There was an uneven flow to the horse rescue ranch. Riley took care of things three days a week. The other four days were under the auspices of whichever relative was available. Cole or his two cousins, Logan and Trace. Every time the disorganization got the better of him, he reminded himself that he was just a guest and on borrowed time.

Then there was Whisper, Trace's wife. She was supposed to be an animal whisperer. Like Riley, she was tough but easy to get along with as was Dr. Jenna, who had insisted on checking out his horse as well. Tundra wasn't usually excited by vets poking around, but his big horse had been surprisingly docile. Lacey, Cole's wife, reminded him too much of one of his sisters Shaine, very girly girl and a bit bossy, making it harder to know what to say.

Closing the thick wooden door behind him to keep the

cool air from escaping, he dropped his hat on the banister ball of the staircase to the second floor and strode down the hall to the large kitchen in the back. Based on the smells coming from that direction, he'd guess his favorite female at Last Chance was baking…again.

As he turned the corner, he caught Annette closing the oven door, one hand on her lower back. She was still slim and active, so much so that everyone forgot her age. He didn't. He'd learned at least that much from his grandfather's death. "Hey beautiful. What smells so heavenly?"

The silver-haired matriarch of the family turned at the sound of his voice. "Me, of course." She smiled tiredly as she pulled out a chair and sat.

"You've got that right." She shouldn't be working so hard. "What you need is a tall glass of iced tea." He moved to the cabinet and pulled out two glasses.

"You're a sweetheart. I've been so busy making these peanut butter chunk chocolate cookies for Charlotte's birthday party, I forgot about drinking."

After filling the glasses with ice and tea, he put one in front of Annette and set one down across from her before taking a seat. He'd met the outgoing soon-to-be three-year-old and doubted that she would even know that her grandmother slaved over homemade cookies for her birthday party. "You need to take a break."

Annette sighed after a few sips. "I will when I finish these."

At seventy-something, she reminded him of his grandfather and was just as stubborn, but he'd learned over the years how to deal with that. "I can do that."

Her eyebrows rose over her glass as she pulled it away. "You?"

"Are you saying you don't believe I can bake?" He squinted

one eye at her, making sure to sound insulted. "Even after I made those ribs last Sunday? You know, the ones I caught you eating again around midnight?"

"You do have a point, but ribs on the grill, no matter how delicious, are not the same as baking cookies."

He crossed his arms and leaned back in the chair. It had been fun cooking for the whole family. It had reminded him of when they did their monthly barbeques at High Mountain Ranch. "You doubt me? I am a man of many talents."

A sly smile formed on the older woman's face. "Yes, I hear that you can sing, too."

Heat rushed to his face. He usually didn't sing in front of people, but he'd felt comfortable with Riley. He should have known it'd get back to Annette. "Only to horses."

"Now that's different."

He shrugged. "Had a horse who wouldn't calm down during monsoons. I was out in the barn one night and started singing to pass the time. When she calmed down, it became habit."

"Your secret is safe with me." She winked before taking another sip of tea. "Did you sing to the cattle you raised, too?"

He shook his head. "They preferred their own singing. Besides, half the time they were out in the back pasture. You have as much space here as we did, though configured differently. Have you and Cole ever thought of fencing in the whole valley?"

"Actually, me and Ed did have a fence at the other end, but after we sold off the cattle, it rotted away." She pointed at him briefly. "You have a lot of good ideas. Why didn't your grandfather add you to the deed of High Mountain Ranch or put you in his will?"

With anyone else, he would have refused to answer, but Annette was different. "He had planned to. He just never got around to it. His will was the one he and my grandmother had made up, and she died before I was even born." He sighed. "I should have pushed it, but it was his ranch. As much as it was my home, it felt wrong to harp on it." Though mentioning it once in a while couldn't have hurt.

"I understand. Some people think they still have time to get to those pesky details taken care of. Ed and I changed ours when we added Cole to the deed of Last Chance. How old was your grandfather?"

He took a gulp of the cold ice tea, still kicking himself for not realizing his grandfather's age. Men just didn't talk about that stuff. Finally, he put down the glass, but he couldn't look at her. "He was ninety-one."

"Well, knock me over with a raindrop! And you didn't think to suggest he update his will?"

He couldn't meet Annette's eyes. "I didn't realize he was that old. He was still out there with the rest of us, roping and herding cattle, loading them up, hauling feed." He finally looked at her. "He acted like you, as if he was still young."

Her eyes widened in surprise before she waved his comment away. "I'm more than ten years younger than your grandfather." She wagged her finger at him. "And don't even think about asking."

He grinned. The thought had crossed his mind, but he knew enough not to do that. "I'm guessing not a day over fifty-eight."

"You're a silver-tongued devil is what you are, Wyatt Ford. I'd have to have been a baby when Cole's mother was born. Seriously." She took another sip of tea, but there was a faint blush to her cheeks.

Yes, he did enjoy Annette's company. She was like the grandmother—

The oven timer dinged.

"Allow me." He rose before she could think of getting up.

"Fine, but I'm watching you."

He chuckled as he grabbed the oven mitt and pulled out the cookie sheet and set it on the stove. Picking up the next one filled with chocolate cookie dough balls on it, he placed it in the oven. Then he washed his hands and proceeded to scoop balls of dough onto a cool cookie sheet.

"I guess I underestimated you…again."

He looked over his shoulder at her. "Not exactly. You did the hard part. I wouldn't know where to begin to make the dough."

She laughed. "Now there you go being all up front and honest."

"Only with you." He blew her a kiss over his shoulder.

She remained silent as he finished adding balls to the sheet based on what she had done with the one in the oven. He learned fast.

When he finished, he took his seat again. Riley didn't need him, and he might just as well help Annette. It wasn't like he had anything else to do. "I was wondering. When Logan finishes repairing their barn, he said he'd be taking Macey and Lucky. Does he plan to take Cyclone?"

Annette shook her head. "No. He doesn't have enough work for the horse to do. I'm not sure even with that new wagon if we'll have enough to keep that animal happy."

"Maybe with the wagon you could start offering hayrides in the fall. It would give the big guy something to do."

Instead of shaking her head, or better yet, nodding in agreement, Annette's chin tipped up slightly as her blue gaze intensified. "You've though quite a bit about this." She paused, making him not a little uncomfortable. "What do you want?"

He jerked his head. "You mean for Last Chance?" He could think of a dozen ways to improve the operation.

"No. I mean what do *you* want in life?"

The question, in addition to her stare, caught him unawares. What he wanted was his grandfather and his home back, but that was a five-year-old's wish, for a child who didn't know any better.

What his adult self wanted was for the pain in his chest to stop. He couldn't imagine living with the gaping hole in his heart where the most important person in his life used to be. The thought of that had him wanting to do anything to make it go away. Unfortunately, he knew exactly what would make it stop and make him not care, and that scared the hell out of him.

Forcing himself from looking into that abyss, he focused on the older woman's eyes, her curiosity and concern evident in her pale blue gaze. He shrugged as much to release the tension that had built up in his shoulders as to emphasize his answer. "I don't know."

And there it was, out on the table, so to speak. The crux of his problem. "My grandfather left me some money. It wasn't enough to buy the ranch, and I don't exactly have a long work history since I just ran High Mountain Ranch with Gramps. No one would give me a loan."

He'd tried to convince his mother and her two brothers that he could pay them the proceeds from the small operation, but they just saw dollar signs based on how much the property was worth. A developer would pay big bucks for it, according to the realtor his uncle found.

"Basically, I'm homeless and my inheritance won't last forever. I guess you could say I've just been swept away in the flood waters of a Sonoran Desert wash."

Annette sat back and folded her arms. "I know it's only been about a month, but you might try switching your outlook."

He raised his brows, unsure what she meant. "How?"

"Instead of looking at your life as if it's just gone up in the flames of an uncontained wildfire, which, by the way, could have resulted in the same outcome, you could look at being swept away by flood waters as being washed clean and starting fresh with no baggage, no limitations, and endless possibilities."

He couldn't quite get his mind to grasp the concept. When he became an adult and his grandfather gave him the choice of heading out on his own or staying at High Mountain, it had been as he'd said, a "no brainer." After that, the thought of doing anything else had never entered his mind. It looked like it was time it did.

Before he could respond to that, the timer rang. He grinned as he rose. "Saved by the bell."

"Humph."

He could feel Annette's gaze on him, but he focused on the chore of making cookies. It was much easier than thinking of an unknown future.

"All I'm saying, Wyatt, is give it some thought. It won't come to you in a minute or even an hour. It kind of creeps up on you over time and when you aren't expecting it, you suddenly recognize it for what it is and you know. You just know."

The absolute confidence in Annette's voice had him turning. "You sound like you're speaking from experience."

She smiled as she slowly rose from the table, her hand on the back of the chair as if that helped. "I am. Sometimes, like myself, you get to go through the process a few times in your life."

Why did he get the feeling that she and Ed were in the process of a new beginning? It had to be his imagination. They were in their seventies. Ed was happy with his golfing and hunting, and she adored her great-grandchild. They lived on a beautiful spread with family all around. It seemed like a pretty nice life to him.

Annette patted his arm as she moved past him. "I'm going to take a nap, but if you tell anyone I did, I'll deny it."

He chuckled. "Your secret is safe with me."

"Yes, I guess it is." She walked to the doorway and stopped. "Think about what I said Wyatt. Think about it a lot." With those words, she disappeared around the corner.

He waited until he heard her bedroom door close then returned his attention to spooning cookie dough.

Maybe that was his answer. If he could focus on a new future, it would keep his past at bay. It worked when he'd been dumped at High Mountain Ranch, maybe it could now. But then his path had been set for him. This time he'd have to find his own. He just hoped he could before the need to escape his current losses drove him in another direction.

Chapter Four

"Come on Lyssa, you know you want to."

Alyssa shook her head. "Marty, there is no way you will get me up there alone."

"Fine, we'll all go. What do you say, chicas?"

Just her luck, the other three women with her and Marty had been drinking all night and were happy to make fools of themselves. Meanwhile, as the designated driver, she would get to fully experience the humiliation of singing in front of the crowded Black Mustang bar.

The next half hour was spent choosing a song. She didn't plan on actually singing. Lip syncing should do the trick.

She glanced over toward the pool tables for the fifth time. The Canterbury firefighters had one of the tables. She recognized a couple of them. They came to school every Christmas season with Santa. The kids loved Mason, who she was pretty sure was still stuck in his own childhood. He let her students climb all over the fire truck and himself.

Lieutenant Clark was the other man she recognized. He wasn't quite as brawny, but a little taller. He'd been promoted just before last Christmas, and she was happy to chat with him about it when she ran into him in the grocery store. Last she heard he was single, and she wouldn't mind getting to know him, but they didn't exactly end up in the same places very often. Dare she go over and strike up a conversation?

"We're up next! Come on, ladies."

Maybe after her lip-syncing debut…if she didn't die of mortification.

Marty herded them all closer to where the karaoke was set-up. The current singer was just getting started and it was clear she'd done it before. The slender brunette barely looked at the monitor.

Alyssa scanned the room, thankful none of her students' parents were in the crowd, though she did recognize another teacher from Canterbury Elementary. No harm there, especially because she wasn't drinking and from the way he was laughing, she'd guess, he'd had more than a couple.

There was nothing wrong with her having fun on a Saturday night, but she was always careful just in case. She loved her job, and it was a small town as far as population. The Black Mustang was miles away from Canterbury center and occupied a slice of desert in Wickenburg. Still, word traveled faster than a dust devil.

The door to the bar opened and in walked Mr. Wyatt Ford.

Alyssa froze. "Fudge."

"What?" Marty leaned in to hear her better.

"I have to go out back." She pointed to the restroom.

"Well, hurry. We're almost up."

She gave her friend the thumbs up, thankful that Marty had enough drinks so she wouldn't realize there was no way to hit the restroom and return in time.

Quickly, Alyssa strode toward the ladies' room, right past the pool players. She smiled as she and Clark made eye contact and she gave a little wave as if she just realized he was there before she ducked inside.

Son of a Biscuit. She walked to the sink and washed her hands. Now what was she going to do? Did Wyatt get her thank you card yet for the gift certificate to the pet store? No, it couldn't have made it that fast. He had no idea that she had found his gift very thoughtful. He'd proven beyond a doubt that his rude behavior was more the exception than his norm. Of course, that meant she was back to thinking about how handsome he was.

She dried her hands and pulled her fingers through her hair. Her cut-out shoulder lavender top was a bit wrinkled, so she tried to smooth it down over her jeans, but that didn't help. Since she didn't like having to keep track of her purse when going out, she had no lipstick, no hairbrush, nothing but her wallet.

She stopped all movement. What was she making a fuss about? Wyatt was just visiting. It's not like she would get to know him better. So he'd gone from being a handsome jerk to a thoughtful visitor. So what? She placed her hands on her hips. "Lady, you need to get a grip."

"You and me both." The voice from one of the stalls surprised her.

"Sorry, just talking to myself."

A stall door opened behind and a very tall dark-haired woman came out dressed in a black silk, sleeveless buttoned-down top and black leggings. She looked like Wonder Woman dressed incognito, definitely not like a woman who needed to get a grip.

The woman stepped up to a sink. "I kind of figured that, but I'm in the same boat."

"You're interested in a man you just met but don't know anything about him except he's just visiting the area?"

The woman stilled, turning green eyes as bright as Wyatt's

on her. "What are you, a mind reader. That's exactly my dilemma, and then some."

Alyssa laughed. "I guess it's not the first time it's happened."

The woman dried her hands then reached out. "My name's Mackenzie. People call me Mac. I'm a security guard over at Poker Flat Nudist Resort."

It was Mac's place of employment more than her job that surprised Alyssa. The woman looked like a superhero from a Marvel movie, so she fit the security job part to a T. "It's nice to meet you Mac, I'm a teacher at Canterbury Elementary. My name is Alyssa. People call me, well, whatever makes them feel comfortable."

Mac's dark eyebrows lifted at that before her gaze became very focused. "You look more like a Lyssa to me."

Wow, that was what all her friends called her. "That works." She hooked her thumb over her shoulder. "Is the man you're interested in out in the bar?"

"No, I came here to clear my head. You?"

Clear her head? In a noisy bar with sports on the televisions, karaoke being sung by good and bad singers alike and a couple of pool games going on? "Unfortunately, or fortunately, yes he is."

Mac grinned. "If you like, I can help."

As if Mac didn't already have her attention, her comment solidified it. "Help? How?"

"You can introduce me to your man, and I'll ask all the usual questions like where are you from, how long are you staying in town, what do you do for a living. That way he doesn't know you're interested and you get the information you need to make the decision. It's easy for me since I have no stake in him."

Her man? He was hardly *her* man. She wasn't even sure if she wanted to know him. No, that was a lie. She did. The day at the vet office when they first met, she had started the conversation because he looked so down. At the school all he'd said was that his thoughts were unpleasant. She wanted to know what they were. Her woman's instinct was telling her those thoughts would reveal a lot about him. But what good would it do to know him when he was leaving town? It was best to remain ignorant. "Thank you for the offer, but I think I'll just wing it."

Mac shrugged her shoulders. "Suit yourself. If you change your mind, I'm sitting at the bar getting drunk."

"Uh, is that such a good idea?"

"Usually, I'd say no, but since I'm trying not to break a vow I made, it's the only thing that I think will stop me." Mac dropped the paper towel in the trash can by the door.

That sounded serious, and her focus quickly shifted to Mac's problem. "Is there anything I can do to help you?"

Mac opened the door, the loud music spilling into the small room. "Unless you've got a shot to make me allergic to men, I don't think there's anyone who can help. Got to figure this out on my own." With that, she slipped back out into the noisy bar.

Alyssa shook her head. She must have heard wrong. It sounded like Mac wanted to be allergic to men. Confused, she looked at herself in the mirror one more time. It really didn't matter what she looked like. She was who she was, and she was pretty happy with who she was…minus twenty pounds.

Stepping to the door, she cracked it open to listen to what song was being sung. It wasn't what Marty had chosen, so she was safe on that account. She exited the bathroom and started past the pool games when Lieutenant Clark called her.

Happy for the distraction, she weaved through the two tables to get to the area that was a bit more lighted than the rest of the place. His light brown hair was very, very short, as if he'd asked for a buzz cut but the barber didn't quite dare. He was also clean shaven so either he didn't have much of a beard or he had shaved before going out. He was dressed in a crisply ironed olive-green button-down shirt and blue jeans, the jeans the only casual thing about him.

"Ms. Parker, how are you?" His gray eyes lit with his welcoming smile.

"I'm good. How is your new position? Have you settled into it?"

He chuckled. "The question is, have the rest of the men become used to me in it yet. It can be a difficult transition to have a peer promoted over you."

She hadn't thought of that. Her current Vice Principal had been promoted from teacher, but since she didn't know him well, that dynamic hadn't occurred to her. "I hope it's not too difficult."

"They'll get used to it. I did when my captain first made lieutenant."

She didn't begin to understand the positions in the fire department, so she simply smiled.

A yell from the other table distracted him and he frowned.

When he seemed to have forgotten they were conversing, she decided small talk was in order. "I've never seen you here on a weekend."

It worked. He brought his attention back to her. "It all depends on our shifts. They change depending on a lot of factors. It's very complicated."

"I imagine it is. Is that one of your new duties?"

He shook his head. "No, that's Cole's job. He's our captain." He glanced over his shoulder.

She followed his gaze and found not only the man he referred to but Wyatt Ford standing right next to him. They were talking, so she quickly returned her attention to Lieutenant Clark. Now she had a choice to make. Did she go over and thank Wyatt for the gift certificate, or simply go back to Marty? She glanced toward her table and found the women now doing shots. Obviously, she wasn't missed.

"I'm sorry, I didn't mean to keep you from your friends."

Quickly, she gave him her undivided attention. "Oh, you aren't. I'm their designated driver, so I wouldn't be doing shots with them right now anyway."

"Good point." He looked over at the pool table where the firefighters were playing. Only two balls were left on the green surface.

"Do you need to play?"

His turned back to her. "Not yet. When they finish this game. I was glad I spotted you here. I was wondering if I could come by the school, after classes let out, of course, and get your advice. Cole has put me in charge of all the school safety visits. I had some ideas on how to make them more interesting but would appreciate your opinion on whether they are age appropriate and see if you had other ideas I could build upon."

Flattered, she nodded. "Of course. I'd be happy to help. What day?"

"I haven't looked at next week's schedule as I'm on tomorrow, but I'll call you and let you know when would work."

If this was an excuse to spend time with her, she had to admit it was well done. Now he'd need her phone number to call her.

"Clark, you're up." The firehouse captain set his hand on Clark's shoulder, making the man appear smaller.

"Okay, Cap. Let me introduce you to Ms. Parker. She

teaches at Canterbury Elementary and has agreed to take a look at my ideas. Ms. Parker, this is Captain Hatcher."

The larger man smiled. "Call me Cole. I'm only 'captain' at the firehouse.

"And I'm Alyssa." They shook hands. Despite his bulk, he didn't squeeze too hard.

Cole spoke to the lieutenant. "Clark, try to take Mason down a peg if you can. He gets obnoxious when he wins too much."

"My pleasure." Clark started to leave but almost walked into Wyatt. "Excuse me."

Wyatt gave her a smile that had her reserve melting. "Ms. Parker."

Cole Hatcher's eyebrows rose. "You know Alyssa?"

She nodded. "We met the other day at Dr. Jenna's."

Wyatt had the grace to grimace. "Yeah, I was a bit of a jerk."

"But he made up for it." She didn't want Cole to think his guest hadn't apologized. "Thank you for the gift certificate. That was very thoughtful." There, she'd said it, and he'd receive the card in a day or two. They were done. She just wished they didn't need to be. There was something vulnerable about the tall, dark hunk that made her take notice.

"You're pissing off strangers now?" Cole's question caught her attention.

Wyatt, for all his size, seemed to shrink. "I told you I shouldn't leave the ranch. Is your wife still mad at me?"

Cole shrugged. "Lacey will get over it. She seems overly sensitive lately. Don't worry about it."

"Hatcher, we have a problem here." The shout came from the pool table.

"Excuse me. It seems the girls need help…again."

As Cole left, Alyssa became acutely aware that she was alone with Wyatt. "It doesn't sound like you're enjoying your visit."

The look she'd seen in his eyes at the vet's returned. "It's not a vacation."

"No?" She let the question hang. Wanting to know, yet not wanting to know.

"Someone very important to me passed away, and I'm making sure the horses are taken care of."

Her heart immediately opened with sympathy, but the logic in her brain halted that. "Horses?"

He shook his head. "I understand your surprise. Last Chance is a quality ranch. I didn't know that at the time. I've just been overthinking things too much lately."

Okay, now she was completely confused, but maybe that was for the best. He said 'very important person.' If he'd lost a girlfriend or wife, he would need time to heal. That could very well be why he kept upsetting women. She vaguely remembered something from one of their teacher continuing education trainings about people lashing out after the loss of a loved one.

Being away from the environment that reminded him of his loss could be helpful. "It sounds like Last Chance is the perfect place for you to be then."

At her comment, his gaze lost focus and his brows furrowed. Then he looked straight at her and gave a quick nod, his smile appearing. "Now that you mention it, I think you're right. Yes, Last Chance is where I belong now."

His reaction seemed a bit overboard for her statement, but he was back to smiling, so she wasn't going to question it. "Then I'm glad you're there. I—"

"Coming through. Move aside. Woman about to vomit

here." Marty brushed past her with one of the other women she'd come in with headed for the rest room.

Alyssa squinched up her nose. "That's someone from my group. Since I'm the designated driver, I better get back to my table. I have a feeling we'll all be leaving very soon."

"I understand." A slight smile still hovered about his lips as if he'd been in a similar situation. "It was nice seeing you again…Alyssa."

A vaguely familiar fluttering in her stomach started as he called her by her first name. That wasn't good. "Thank you again for the certificate. Enjoy your stay at Last Chance." Without waiting for a response, she turned and quickly made her way back toward the table, skirting the pool players who were intent on their game.

This time, she needed to ignore her usual empathetic nature. Wyatt Ford may be reeling from losing someone, but he wouldn't be around long enough for her to help. Actually, she had no idea how long he would be in the area or where he was from.

She slowed, scanning the people at the bar. She caught sight of Mac, who appeared to be joking with the bartender. Maybe she should have taken the woman up on her idea.

At that moment, Mac looked at her as if sensing she was being stared at. The woman raised her glass and winked.

She smiled and nodded then mouthed the words "Good luck."

Mac acknowledged the sentiment and drank to it.

For herself, she didn't need any luck. She'd dated men from Phoenix, or the "city" as her father referred to it, and that could be no more than a thirty-minute drive, but it still didn't work.

She loved her job and soon would be buying her own home. She was staying put. For all their disadvantages, Canterbury and

Wickenburg were home. No matter where Wyatt Ford was from, it wouldn't be close enough. He may have the most charming smile this side of the Colorado River, but someone else could spend their time coaxing it out of him.

Better that she see where her friendship with Lieutenant Clark might go. He wasn't going anywhere, except up the chain of command. She admired people who enjoyed their job, and he obviously did.

Happy with her decision, she reached the table. Patiently, she corralled the women into going to the bar to pay their tabs as she watched the restrooms for any sign of Marty. Though her gaze may stray on occasion to the dark-haired cowboy, that didn't keep her from her resolve.

~~*~~

Wyatt rode Tundra down the dirt road from the main house toward Cole and Lacey's. His horse was happy to be out in the early morning air, even if the temperature was fast approaching three digits.

For himself, he was both excited and nervous. *It sounds like Last Chance is the perfect place for you to be then.* Alyssa's words the night before had sparked an idea, but he wasn't sure how it would be taken. At this point in his life, he had nowhere else to go, so why not stay on at the ranch? His main concern was what the family would think about that.

"Whoa." Wyatt pulled Tundra to a halt. "Quickly, he dismounted and led his horse to the small corral to tie him up. He patted the gray speckled white beast on the side of his neck. "I may be right out if I'm rejected, so wish me luck." His horse just stared at him as if he was an idiot. "Right."

He forced himself to jog up the five steps to the wide wrap-around porch on Cole's new two-story home. Both vehicles were parked outside, so that had to mean Cole was there. What was the worst that could happen? Cole could tell him to pack his bags. That wouldn't be the end of the world.

But it could. His memories just wouldn't leave it alone. That his dreams last night had been uncomfortably fantastical proved how close he was. If he had no place to go and no purpose along with the emotional pain living in his chest, he knew exactly where he'd end up.

He knocked, the sound loud in the early morning stillness of the valley.

The door opened and a bright-eyed Lacey stood there in white tank top, white short-shorts, and white tennis sneakers, her pale blonde hair up in a clip. Her petite stature belied her control over the whole ranch.

Lucky for him, she smiled. "Wyatt, what a pleasant surprise. Thank you for the lily bouquet. You didn't have to do that."

Based on how angry she had been at him for scaring her horse, Angel, when he'd first arrived on the ranch, he'd thought he'd be sending bouquets for a month to make up for it.

He doffed his hat. "I wanted you to know, if I had known, I would have never gone in your barn."

She waved off his comment. "It really wasn't your fault. I've just been overacting to things lately. Will you forgive me for my hissy fit?"

Was that one of those questions women asked where there was no right answer? "I completely understand being protective of a horse. Just ask Garrett. I actually gave him a list for taking care of Gramps' horses for the ride to Last Chance." He grinned sheepishly. "Is Cole available?"

She stepped back, opening the door fully. "I'm sorry, here

you are standing out there in the heat, and I'm letting all the cool air outside. Come on in."

He stepped into the cool entryway, the new-house look and smell very evident.

"Cole! Wyatt's here." Lacey yelled up the curved stairway then looked at him. "Come on, I'll pour you a cup of coffee."

He'd been up for hours and already had his morning coffee but wasn't going to refuse. Following her into the open-concept white kitchen, he squelched a smile at how much it reflected Lacey's personality, as far as he'd seen. Everything was white. The kitchen window even had white curtains with yellow daisies, but it had a nice view of the base of the mountain. There was even a small dried-up stream that ran between the hill the home sat upon and the walls of the valley.

"Cream and sugar?"

He shook his head as he stood at the giant white marble island in the middle of the room. "No thank you. Just black."

She grinned as she set the mug of hot coffee in front of him. "I should have known."

"Should have known what?" Cole strode into the kitchen wearing a pair of plaid shorts.

Lacey turned at the sound of her husband's voice. "That Wyatt would take his coffee black like you do."

Cole lowered his head and kissed his tiny wife on the cheek. "And did you know that I left a surprise for you on the bathroom sink?"

Lacey's brows lowered. "There was nothing on my sink this morning when I got up."

"There is now."

The woman's light brown eyes practically glowed golden before she brushed past him. She stopped at the edge of the kitchen and looked back. "Excuse me, Wyatt." With that, she practically ran out to the entry toward the stairs.

Cole chuckled. "We won't see her for a while. What's up? Did I forget that we were supposed to meet today?"

Not sure what he'd just witnessed besides what he felt was a very intimate moment for the couple, Wyatt cleared his throat. "No. I just had an idea I'd like you to weigh in on."

"Oh, good. Lacey or Riley would have my head if I forgot another meeting. Let me just grab some coffee." Cole pointed to a set of sliding doors to the left. "We can sit outside and talk undisturbed."

Determined to follow through with his plan, he nodded before striding outside to a covered patio. Half the area was still in cool shadow as the sun had not risen very high yet. In the shade, there were a couple of lounges and a mosaic table with chairs. He pulled out a chair and set his coffee down. Beyond the patio was a large flat area that had been staked off in an unusual shape. A future pool maybe?

The slider opened and Cole strode over. "What is your idea? Is it about the ranch?"

"Yes."

As Cole sat, his smile disappeared and he stiffened. "There's a lot we can do here, but I do have limitations."

Hell, just what he'd been worried about. *If you don't ask then the answer is always a no.* His grandfather's words to him when he was still a teenager nudged him onward. "My idea or rather ideas were to see if you'd be willing to hire me fulltime. If I could stay at the main house, I wouldn't need a large salary."

Cole just stared at him with wide green eyes much darker than his own.

In that moment, the thought of Cole rejecting his idea had him wanting it more than ever. "I think there's a lot I could do to make this ranch even better, like fencing in the valley, streamlining the adoption process, and maybe even offering hayrides in the fall."

With no movement from Cole, he continued. "I have a lot of experience running High Mountain Ranch, so it's not like you'd need to train me. I've been working a ranch for fifteen years. Granted it was a small cattle ranch, but we had a lot of horses. And if you're worried about Riley, we get along fine. I have no problem taking directions from her. That woman knows her stuff."

He shut his mouth on his next sentence. He was rambling. He'd never had to apply for a job before except as a grocery bagger when he was fifteen. He wished Cole would say something. What the hell was he going to do now?

"Yes!" Cole's hand slapped down on the table. "Yes. Yes, to everything." The man was smiling ear to ear.

The change was so sudden, he wasn't sure if he would now be working for a crazy man. He gave Cole the side eye. "Are you sure? You didn't seem so a moment ago."

Cole laughed than took a sip of his coffee before putting it down and focusing his attention on him. "I was just surprised. Garrett had said he thought you were just going to stay a few weeks to make sure your family's horses were well taken care of. Otherwise, I would have offered you a job the moment you stepped foot on Last Chance."

That didn't clear anything up. "I don't think I understand."

"I keep forgetting that you're a stranger here. You fit in so well."

He held his hand up. "I don't think pissing off Lacey, Trace, and Riley proves that."

Cole chuckled. "You just irritated them. It's not a deal breaker. Believe me, we get on each other's nerves a lot worse."

"Will the others be 'irritated' if I'm around all the time?"

"Not a chance. They'll be relieved. I'm not sure if you noticed, but we have no fulltime hands. The only reason we're functioning right now is because everyone steps up, but as you have noticed, many of us have our own places to take care of, and other jobs to attend to. I was beginning to worry that I wouldn't be able to keep the place simply because of the lack of ranch hands."

"I know a few men from High Mountain that might consider moving out this way if you need more than myself."

"Not right now. Let's see if we have enough work for you, but I'm definitely open to it. With Whisper's financial trust for the horses, finances aren't the issue." Cole leaned forward. "But we aren't a great addition to someone's resume. A lot of ranchers think I'm nuts for having established this place." He sat back and lifted his coffee. "On the other hand, animal lovers and the state and county animal services departments are grateful we're here."

Wyatt studied Cole as the man looked past him at nothing in particular. "And you? Do you wish you'd never started a horse rescue ranch?" When he first arrived, he'd been very skeptical, but after a couple of weeks he was a total convert. Cole's answer suddenly meant more to him than he first realized.

"Not a single day goes by that I'm not proud of this place. I think I may have started it because of my mother's dismissal of any horse that wasn't perfect, but it became my calling." Cole shrugged. "I guess saving things is in my blood."

As Cole sipped his coffee, Wyatt found himself reflecting on his own impetus for being at Last Chance. In a serendipitous way, he felt as if this was his last chance as well. This position would give him the stability he needed to stay on the straight and narrow, as his Gramps called it. He'd feel even better about it if he had someone like Gramps who would enforce that.

The slider opened and Lacey practically skipped out to them. She made a beeline for Cole and wrapped her arms around his neck. "Thank you."

The man's grinned widened. "I'll be the one thanking you tonight."

She immediately gave him a tap on his shoulder and straightened. "Cole Hatcher, behave. We have a guest."

"Not a guest, a fulltime ranch hand."

"What?" Her head whipped around. "Is it true, Wyatt? Tell me he isn't just pulling a prank on me."

Surprised but pleased that Cole's wife seemed happy about it, he relaxed for the first time since arriving on the ranch. "It's true. In fact, I can start as early as tomorrow."

She clapped her hands. "This is the best day. I'll get the paperwork together."

"I thought you were heading to the grocery store for that Saltwater Seaweed snack." Cole raised his brows at Lacey.

"Oh, I forgot. I really wanted that."

Wyatt jumped at the chance to help speed the process along. His pessimistic side was still having a hard time believing he'd landed the position so easily. "I can run to the store for you if you want to take time getting everything together."

Lacey smiled at him. "You know that's not one of the duties."

He rose. "I know, but I'm still a guest and happy to help."

"Excellent. Thank you."

He started for the sliding door.

Lacey stopped him. "Wait. Will you stay at the main house or get a place in town? I'll need to know for the paperwork."

"There's plenty of room at the main house." Cole offered. "Of course, that would be up to my grandparents."

To live on a ranch again, a ranch he cared about, was more

than he'd seen coming. "I would be happy to live in the main house if Annette and Ed will have me."

Lacey strode by him. "Great. I'll call and see if it's okay and get the paperwork started."

He jumped ahead and opened the slider for her.

"We'll have you officially on board by next week."

He followed Lacey inside and closed the door. "Next week?"

She nodded as she filled a cup with coffee and turned toward a door he hadn't noticed before. "It will take that long for the background check to come back. It's just a formality. Don't worry. We'll have you working sooner than later."

He froze. Background check?

Lacey stopped after opening the door, proving she had her own home office. "When you get back from the grocery store, I'll need a copy of your license and another form of ID, unless you have a passport?"

He shook his head, his voice stuck in his throat.

"No problem. Just bring me two IDs. And thank you. You don't know how much we need you here." With a wide smile, she turned and disappeared into the room.

He forced himself to put one foot in front of the other. Was his past about to bite him in the ass? Just when he'd found a place to work, would his record be the final undermining of his balance on the cliff?

Opening the door, he strode outside into the hot sun. The hope he'd experienced for a few short moments shriveled up and died. Walking to his horse, he untied the reins from the corral fence. Resisting the urge to hug his only constant companion through all of this, he stepped into the stirrup and threw his leg over. "Tundra, I think we're screwed...again."

This time, the horse shook its head as if he completely

disagreed, but he knew in his gut things were not going to go as smoothly as he'd hoped.

Chapter Five

Not finding any seaweed snacks of any kind, Wyatt exited the grocery store empty-handed and stopped on the sidewalk to wait for cars to slowly pass so he could cross into the parking lot. Thanks to his height, he was able to scan the lot to find his truck while waiting.

At that moment a blue, double-cab pick-up truck turned down the wrong way into an aisle. Movement closer to the store end of the aisle caught his attention. Damn, a dark sedan was backing out. He couldn't look away.

The truck rammed into the back half of the sedan.

"Holy shit! Did you see that?" The teenager standing next to him pointed at the wreck.

"Yeah." He watched as the driver lowered his window and started yelling. What an asshole. He was clearly in the wrong. "I suggest calling 9-1-1."

"Really?"

He looked down at the kid. "Really."

The teenager's expression of excitement increased as he dialed faster than an Indy driver.

The traffic all stopped as everyone's attention turned to the scene. He took the opportunity to cross the street and head up the aisle, intending to stand by his truck and interfere if things got too heated before the police came, but just then, the driver of the sedan stepped out, clearly shaken.

"Alyssa." He was too far away for her to hear. As he strode closer, the twenty-something in the truck started to swear.

"Why don't you look where you're going, you idiot. Look what you did to my truck! You're going to pay for that."

Alyssa's back straightened. "That's doubtful, considering you ran into my car."

The man jumped out and looked at his front end. His hands went up and expletives flew from his mouth. "Listen, bitch. You clearly backed out when I had the right of way. You may not care about your old piece of junk, but this is a hundred-thousand-dollar truck. Parts are expensive."

As the man started toward Alyssa, Wyatt picked up his pace so he could come up behind her for support. As he got closer, he could see she was trembling. The bastard.

But instead of backing away, Alyssa took a step toward the man and pointed her finger. "The fact that you're stupid enough to spend so much money on a truck and then drive the wrong way down a parking lot aisle is all on your head. I suggest you own it." She paused to take a breath. "Is that alcohol I smell?"

The man stopped in his tracks.

Wyatt would have smiled if he wasn't so worried. He came up next to her. "Are you okay?"

She turned. Her face said she was on the verge of tears, whether from physical pain or the trauma of being hit or even anger, he didn't know. What he knew was the confrontation had gone on long enough.

He didn't wait for an answer. With the sound of a siren slowly getting louder, he stepped around her and towered over the man. "I suggest you get out your registration and insurance. Or is it your daddy's truck?"

The man's eyes widened before his brows came down and his face flushed red. "Who the fuck are you? This is none of your business."

He didn't do it often, but he was well aware his size could intimidate anyone with a set of brains. Taking a step closer, he crossed his arms. "I'm a witness."

The man was smart enough to take a step back, but he shrugged. "That means you can tell the police she caused the accident." His look turned sly. "That is if you tell the truth."

If was supposed to be an insult, the man's statement failed. It meant nothing coming from the source. "I always tell the truth. And..." He pointed to the row of people standing in front of the store now, all looking at them. "And so will they."

The man turned and stared, clueless about how busy the store was on a Sunday morning.

"Now, I'm going to see if Ms. Parker is hurt." He scowled as the man returned his attention to him. "You better hope she's okay." He spun around and strode back to where Alyssa sat in the driver's seat of her car facing out, her feet on the ground and a tissue in her hands.

He crouched down before her. "Are you hurt?"

She shook her head then nodded. "I don't know."

But she still trembled, which worried him. He didn't want her going into shock. He took her free hand in his. "It's going to be okay. *You're* going to be okay. When the ambulance comes, I want you to go with them."

Her eyes widened, but she didn't argue. "I've never been in an accident before."

He gave her his kindest smile. "Then I guess I'll have to teach you what to expect, right?"

She nodded, attempting a pathetic smile.

A second distant siren could now be heard, which told him there was probably an ambulance already in route. "From the sounds of it, the police will want you to explain what happened. Can you do that?"

"I can, but there's not much to tell. I checked behind me. No one was coming down the aisle, so I started to back out." Her voice intensified and her eyes glistened. "I even looked the other way. The wrong way, but he wasn't in sight."

He squeezed her hand. "I know. I saw the whole thing, and so did a number of other people. You just tell the police what happened from your standpoint and they will gather the rest of the information from the witnesses while you go in the ambulance."

She nodded, using her Kleenex to wipe her eyes. "Thank you."

"I'm happy to help. I'll come to the hospital once I'm done giving the police my statement. Is there anyone you need to call?"

Her eyes widened. "Oh, my father. He's expecting me for Sunday breakfast." Frantically, she turned and pulled her purse onto her lap. "Where's my phone? It's not here." Her voice rose with panic.

He laid his hand over her two. "Slow down. There's no rush." He heard the siren stop as the police must have turned into the parking lot. "Did you have it in the car or your purse?"

"Of course. It's in my cup holder. I don't know what's wrong with me. I'm never forgetful."

"It's okay. You're shaken. You have never been in an accident before. It's normal."

She turned and grasped her phone in her hand. "Will they wait?"

He looked over his shoulder to see an officer getting out

of his vehicle. "Go ahead. Tell your dad you're okay and to meet you at…" He had no idea where the hospital was or its name.

"Sonoran Heights Hospital."

He smiled. "Yes. Go ahead. I'll talk to the officer."

She quickly hit a button on her phone. "Hello, Dad?"

He rose and faced the police officer, ignoring the sweat pooling between his shoulder blades. The last time he'd spoken to an officer, he was barely sixteen and his sister had called the cops on him. Forcing himself to remain calm, he walked toward the man.

The policeman turned at his approach. "Are you the owner of this car?" The older man held himself stiffly, his face stern as he quickly sized him up.

"No, sir. This is Ms. Parker's." He glanced at the name tag, Sgt. Valdez.

"Ms. Parker?" The sergeant's brows lowered in concern. "Is she okay?"

That he was worried put Wyatt more at ease. "She's shaken. I told her to take the ambulance when it arrives and get checked out."

Sgt. Valdez nodded. "Yes. My grandson is in her class. He'd be very upset if she was hurt." He scowled. "Did you hit her vehicle?"

"No, sir." He pointed to behind the man. "That young man with the blue truck did."

He turned to look. "So I see."

Wyatt hoped he'd talk to the owner of the truck, who was taking pictures of the damage with his phone.

But the officer turned back to him. "Then why are you here?"

"I'm a witness. There are a few more in front of the store, including the teenager who called you. When I saw it was Ms.

Parker, I came over to help. She's never been in a car accident before."

Sgt. Valdez, who had looked toward the store entrance then back at him, sighed. "Probably more witnesses than I need. Who are you? I haven't seen you before."

"I'm Wyatt Ford. I've been at the Last Chance Ranch for a few weeks now." That was a bit of an exaggeration, but close enough.

"Oh, Captain Hatcher's place." He nodded. "I'm Sgt. Valdez."

Movement behind the sergeant had Wyatt taking note. "Sir, I think the man who hit Ms. Parker is thinking of leaving."

"What?" Sgt. Valdez spun around and strode toward the blue truck. "You! Step out of the truck."

Happy for the reprieve, he returned to Alyssa two steps away and looked down at her. Her shaking seemed to have stopped, so that was a good sign. "Is your dad going to meet you?"

She looked up at him, her eyes still a bit watery. "Yes. Thank you for all your help. I'm sure the last thing you needed to get involved in while visiting Canterbury was witnessing an accident."

"I'm glad I was here to see it." Looking over her car, he noticed the ambulance making its way through the parking lot with lights flashing. He held out his hand. "Come, your ride is here."

She stood and swayed a bit.

He grasped her other shoulder. "Don't move too quickly. They aren't going anywhere without you."

She gave him a half smile for his comment. "No, I suppose not."

Seeing that Sgt. Valdez was still busy with the other driver, he slowly walked her out between the cars. The ambulance with

Canterbury Fire Department emblazoned across it stopped and two paramedics jumped out. While one opened the back doors, the other strode to them and took her other arm.

"Ms. Parker, are you okay?"

"Hi, Maddox. I think so. But Mr. Ford said I should go to the hospital and get checked out. I've never done this accident thing before."

The dark-haired man smiled. "No problem. We're experts. I'll have Mason let Sgt. Valdez know where to find you. You can answer his questions at the hospital."

"Okay." Her voice was meek, far different from when she faced off with the other driver.

Wyatt's protective instincts ramped up even higher. But at the open doors to the ambulance, he released her into the care of the two men. He had to tamp down the urge to jump in and go with her.

They sat her on a gurney and started taking her vitals. As one moved to close the doors, she stopped them.

"Wait. Is Mr. Ford still there?"

The man called Maddox halted. "Yes." He opened one door wide again.

She looked out at him. "I hate to inconvenience you further, but would you be willing to take the shopping bags in the backseat of my car with you?"

Pleased to be of help, he lifted the front of his hat. "I will bring them to you."

She gave him a full smile this time, proof she was feeling better…at least until she eventually stiffened up. He'd been in an accident before. No matter how minor, sore muscles were bound to happen.

"Thank you." She gave a little wave and with that, Maddox closed the door, and the ambulance left the scene.

"Mr. Ford, if you don't mind?"

He tensed at the sound of the sergeant's voice. Time to tell the truth about the accident and keep it at that.

~~*~~

Alyssa watched one of her father's new ostriches strut across the backyard. She'd already named this one. She had "Diva" written all over her. As for the other two, she hadn't decided yet.

The sound of a silverware drawer slamming in the kitchen had her turning her head. "Ouch." She couldn't believe how stiff she was already. "Everything okay in there, dad?"

"I'm fine, I just closed the drawer with my hip because my hands were full. Relax."

Relax? That's all she'd been doing since he drove her straight to his house from the hospital. She'd barely had time to slip into a pair of old gray sweats and an extra extra-large t-shirt she kept in her old room before he practically forced her into the recliner she'd bought him last Father's Day. She moved her fingers over the controls to add more heat to her neck area.

When she'd bought the warming, cooling, massaging, and lifting recliner for her dad, she never thought she'd end up using it. She'd ordered it online and it came in pieces. Assembly was supposed to take an hour, so she'd planned on three, but this one had only taken her forty-five minutes, the drawings actually matching the chair parts.

She frowned at her father's old recliner across the room. Even though he used his new gift, he refused to get rid of his old, holey one. At first, she thought he only used his old recliner, but when he got her settled in the new one, she could faintly smell his cologne. That had her wondering. Her dad didn't wear any scent to work, and except for darts one night a week, she didn't see him using it very often.

"Here you are." He brought a steaming bowl of spaghetti in bolognaise sauce on a tray.

"Dad, I can walk. Put that on the kitchen table and I'll come in." She hit the button to bring her feet down. "I need to move."

He held his hand up as if he could halt her. "No, you need to rest."

She rose, barely stifling a cry as her back protested. "If you must know, I have to go to the bathroom."

He had opened his mouth to argue and quickly shut it.

"Besides, I need a change of scenery." She pointed at Diva who at the moment was preening at her reflection in the floor-to-ceiling glass folding doors."

"That bird is so full of herself, she's going to explode."

She chuckled. "I'll be in the kitchen in a moment."

It took her longer than a moment, but she managed to make it into the kitchen before her dinner had cooled much. Taking a seat, she breathed in her father's homemade sauce. He had learned to cook along with doing laundry, cleaning, and grocery shopping after her mother died. He always said anything worth learning was worth mastering. He'd mastered some of each. "This smells heavenly."

Her father grinned. "It tastes even better."

That was so like him. Rolling a forkful of spaghetti, she blew on it just to be sure then took a mouthful. "Hmmm." It had been so long since she had her dad's sauce. She might come over every Sunday for breakfast, but since she moved out, it was rare she made it over for dinner.

"Good, huh? Just think if you were living here, you could have that twice a month."

"Dad, are you trying to bribe me with food?"

"Did it work?"

She shook her head very slowly since her mouth was full of more wonderful spaghetti and sauce.

He shrugged. "It was worth a try. Don't know what I'm going to do with myself after this retirement thing."

His forced retirement at only fifty-five seemed to be more on his mind now. Though the company was giving him an amazing severance package, including health benefits, he was fighting it.

She didn't blame him. All he knew was construction. "What about being a consultant?"

He waved his fork like he would swat someone with it. "They want people with these newfangled programs. I'm being put out to pasture because my perfectly good skills are worthless to them."

It was so hard for her dad to keep up in his industry. Even at thirty she had to work to stay abreast of the latest teaching techniques and philosophies. "What about doing something you always wished you had time for?"

He swallowed another mouthful. "Like what?"

She rolled her eyes at him. "Now how am I supposed to know what you always wished to do?"

Frowning at her, he stuffed his mouth with more spaghetti.

Gertie and her entourage started squawking like the sky was falling and her father rose, setting is napkin next to his plate. "I bet it's that damn coyote."

"Isn't it a little early for a coyote? The sun is still up."

A knock at the door had her turning her head. "Ow."

He scowled at her. "I'll get the heating pad."

"Just get the door. I'm fine." It was probably just a neighbor who had heard about her accident. She'd had to call Marty to take care of Snowdrop since her father refused to let her leave. Between Marty and all the witnesses, the entire town would know by now.

Taking another bite of dinner, she pondered her father's retirement dilemma. She could ask around at school to see what some of the other teachers' parents had done.

"Who are you?" Her father's rude comment had her listening carefully.

"I'm Wyatt Ford. Your daughter asked me to bring these to the hospital today, but by the time I was done giving my statement and finding the hospital, she'd left."

A flutter in her stomach had her rising slowly.

"Are you the son of a bitch who hit her?"

"Fudge." She turned her whole body to face the kitchen opening. "Dad! He's not the one!"

"Then who is he?"

"Sir?"

"He's the one who helped me!" She started to walk slowly in that direction. What had she asked him to bring her? She had her phone, thanks to him, and her purse. The whole day was a bit of a blur. The muscle relaxers the doctor had given her obviously made her brain fuzzy.

Lower voices continued, and she couldn't hear what was being said.

Wyatt appeared in the opening to the kitchen filling the space with his stature and presence.

Her heart sighed at the sight of her cowboy hero. "Oh, hi."

"I brought your bags." He lifted the two plastic shopping bags with one hand. Condensation on one of them caught her eye.

"Oh no. I forgot about the ice cream."

"Ice cream?" Her father walked up behind Wyatt. "Just

don't stand there, son, come in and have a seat. I've got plenty of spaghetti."

Suddenly conscious of her old gray sweat pants and overly large t-shirt, she moved back toward her chair as Wyatt set the bags on the counter. "Sir, you may want to put the ice cream in that bag in the freezer."

Sitting slowly, she studied the bag. "How can it not be melted?" It had been all day since she'd left the grocery store.

Wyatt walked around her toward the other side of the table. "After Sgt. Valdez was done with me, I went to put the bags in my truck and noticed how wet it was. I rushed to the hospital, but after I discovered I missed you, I returned to the store and explained the situation. They were happy to give you a new half-gallon, and I believe they may have added a get-well cake also."

"They sure did." Her father lifted the cake out of the bag. "We'll have this tonight."

As Wyatt took a seat, she looked at her father in question.

"I invited the man to dinner. It's the least I could do after all he did for you today."

She turned her head slowly to Wyatt and smiled. "You're in for a treat." Suddenly, she realized he knew where to find her. "Wait, how did you find us? I can't imagine the hospital would give you this address."

"No, but the man at customer service who let me switch out the ice cream figured if you trusted me with your groceries, you would trust me with your address. By the way, he said to get well soon."

She looked to her dad, who shook his head. "Mr. Reynolds. Good man. Big gossip."

She agreed, but since he'd wished her well and added a cake, she wouldn't hold it against him.

"How are you feeling?" Wyatt's gaze subtly roamed over her.

It wasn't an unpleasant experience. "I'm stiff and sore, but the doctor said that would go away in a few days."

"So, no broken bones or anything?"

At her father's sudden intake of breath, she turned her head quickly. "Ow. Dang it. Don't worry Dad, I wasn't hit that hard. I told you, I was just backing out, barely moving."

Wyatt spoke. "Yes, but he wasn't moving slowly when he hit you."

"Allie, is there more to this than you're telling me?"

She slowly turned to give Wyatt a scowl. "My dad is worried about me. I don't think we need to make it out as more than it is, do we?"

Wyatt's green gaze shifted as he realized what was going on…finally. "No, we don't, but it's good that you have a father who cares so much."

Now that was an odd thing to say. "What do you mean?"

"Yeah, what do you mean?" Her dad sounded affronted as he brought a steaming plate of spaghetti piled higher than his own and set it down before Wyatt.

"I mean just that it's great that Alyssa has you."

Her father frowned as he took his seat again. "Why wouldn't she?"

Suddenly, she understood. She'd missed the cues, so used to reading children's telltale body language. Wyatt had none as if he didn't care that his father hadn't been there for him. "Dad." She placed her hand on her father's arm. "I don't think Wyatt had a dad who cared much." She faced Wyatt. "Right?"

He nodded as his mouth was full of spaghetti. He didn't reply until he'd enjoyed the mouthful. "Mr. Parker I've never had such flavorful sauce."

"Don't Mr. Parker me, son. Just call me Roy."

Wyatt stilled. "Roy then." He swirled his spaghetti onto his fork. "Thank you for inviting me to dinner. This is even better than Annette's sauce." He rushed to add to his statement as if he'd just uttered a blasphemy. "But please don't tell her I said so."

Her dad beamed. "Of course not. I rarely run into Mrs. Benson anyway. You were saying your father didn't care about you. How can you be sure? Sometimes we just show it in odd ways. That's what Allie says."

She swallowed hard at her father's misunderstanding of the situation, but before she could intervene, Wyatt answered.

"He didn't show anything. He got my mother pregnant and left. I'm afraid she doesn't have very good taste in men as it happened with two others, so my sisters didn't have any fathers around either."

"It sounds like your mother was better off without them then." Her father studied Wyatt. "Then who taught you the cowboy ways? You obviously have them."

Though her dad was being a nosey busybody, she was too interested in the answer to stop the interrogation.

Wyatt's whole body seemed to stiffen, and she glimpsed that look in his eyes that she'd seen in the vet's office.

"My mother's father. She sent me to live with Gramps when I was sixteen. Best thing she ever did for me."

She couldn't let that pass. "You mean because she gave you a male role model?"

He moved his gaze to her. "No. Because it saved my life. I was a teenager who lived in a bad neighborhood. Sending me to High Mountain Ranch out of the city, and to Gramps himself, straightened me out." A sad smile curved his lips. "The old man was tough as leather and as ornery as a wild burro. It was shape up or, actually, there was no alternative."

"For a man you admire, it seems a bit disrespectful to call him old." Her father, who thought of himself as younger than his fifty-five years, was obviously bothered by the term.

Wyatt looked him straight in the eye. "Gramps liked that better. He felt it gave him permission to be an as—jerk. He was ninety-one when he died."

That's who died? Now she understood. "I'm so sorry. It must have been hard to lose someone who was so important to you."

"Yeah." Wyatt took another mouthful of spaghetti and chewed slowly, clearly not willing to talk about it.

She understood. Losing a parent, so-to-speak, was like a blow to the chest, at least it had been for her.

He looked at her, the pain of loss clear in his green gaze.

She squeezed his hand before picking up her fork again. As Wyatt had so rudely put it the first day she'd met him, everything dies. How odd that she would think of that again.

Luckily, her dad took that moment to turn his attention. "What kind of ice cream did you buy, Allie?"

She grinned. "You're favorite, of course. Cherry vanilla."

Her father, who had cleaned his plate, rose. "I'll clean up in here. Allie, you should go set in my space-age recliner again. I see you wincing."

"Of course I'm wincing. I was just in my first car accident. That doesn't mean I'm helpless. I can help you clean up."

Her father gave her his don't-you-talk-back-to-me look and she gave in. "Fine. I wonder what you would have done if I hadn't bought you that chair."

"I can help you clean up, Roy." Wyatt rose and picked up her empty plate and his.

Her dad's eyes widened before he recovered. None of the men she'd brought home to her father had ever offered to help in the kitchen. Then again, she didn't bring Wyatt home. He more or less followed her home. She liked that idea better.

Rising, she groaned. How could her muscles have stiffened up so much in so short a time?

"Thank you, son. But I'd prefer if you helped my daughter back into my recliner."

"Yes, sir."

Wyatt missed her father's frown at being called sir, but she didn't. Dad really didn't like being called sir. It made him feel old.

"May I?" Wyatt offered her his arm with a wink.

She accepted it, and they walked very slowly back into the living room.

Wyatt pointed to Diva who had settled down on the patio after the sun had set and was sound asleep. "You have an ostrich?"

She barely remembered not to nod. "My dad just got three ostriches. I've named that one Diva."

"Is your dad an expert on birds?" He let her arm go as she lowered herself into the cooled recliner.

"Now, he might be." She chuckled as she remembered the variety of bird species they'd had over the years in addition to the mammals. "He just likes having unusual pets."

He pointed toward the front door. "You call those geese pets?"

She turned the heat back on and looked for her pills. "You mean Gertie? She's more noise than bite. It's Alfred you have to watch out for."

Scanning the room, she found her prescription bottle on the end table next to her dad's old recliner where he'd left them. "Could you hand me my prescription on that table?"

Wyatt turned toward the table and swiped up the bottle. "Pills? You're taking pills?" His voice had suddenly become loud.

89

"Yes. The doctor at the hospital prescribed them."

He stared at the bottle in his hand, but it was clear he wasn't reading it. "You could get addicted."

Something was definitely not right with him. "They're only muscle relaxers, and very mild ones at that."

"Too many—"

"Wyatt." She used her teacher voice with him. The one she used when one of her students was starting to escalate. "I haven't had one in over eight hours." She put her hand out. "Now bring them here or I'll have to get up, and honestly right now, I don't want to get up."

Her tone of voice must have seeped through because his head snapped up. "Right." As if moving by rote, he handed her the bottle.

"Thank you. Is something wrong?"

As if suddenly aware of where he was, he shook his head and took a seat on the couch next to her. "You'll be sore for a few days. I checked out your car before they towed it away. I think your rear axle might be broken."

"My car? I forgot about my car." How could she have forgotten about her car? She'd have to get it fixed. "Do you know where they towed it to?"

"No, but I'm sure Sgt. Valdez would know."

"An axel is going to be expensive, right?" She tried to remember how much extra she had in her checking account. She didn't want to touch her savings. That was for her future house. She was too close to meeting her down payment goal to take anything out of there.

Her father strode in with a glass of water. "It's time for your medicine."

She opened the pill bottle. "Dad, how much would it cost to get an axel on my car fixed? Do you know?"

"Axel? Who said anything about an axel? If your car's axel is broken, you were hit harder than I thought."

She swallowed the two pills before replying. "So that's bad?"

Her father took the glass from her. "Actually, Allie, you're going to need a new car."

Wyatt nodded. "But it may be a while to get money from the insurance company. When I left, the man who hit you was still trying to claim it was your fault. He's going to fight this." He smiled encouragingly. "But don't worry. There were too many witnesses. You'll get the money eventually."

"But I need a car now." She felt tears welling. "A new car will cost too much."

"What about your insurance? You can get a rental." Wyatt's addition to the conversation had her and her father looking at him before they both shook their heads.

"It won't help her." Her dad looked ready to punch someone.

"Why won't it help you?" Wyatt's question just made her want to cry more.

"Because, since my car is old, I only had liability coverage on my insurance to save money. I want to buy my own house so I've been saving every penny I can. If I have to buy a new car or even rent one, it has to come out of my pocket and that means…" She couldn't continue. Years of sacrificing gone all because some idiot hit her. She'd planned to start looking next month. Depending on the car she bought, it could be another year now.

"Bastard." Her father headed back toward the kitchen.

"Hey, don't cry." Wyatt lifted a tissue from the box on the end table between them and handed it to her.

She took it, feeling like an idiot.

"Listen, what's important is that you're okay. If you had backed out any farther, he would have hit your driver side door and you would still be in the hospital right now."

She sniffed. He made a good point. "Thanks. I know I should be grateful. I'm just not myself right now."

"You're right." He rose. "I should go. You need your rest."

She nodded, too messed up to think straight.

He started toward the front door when her dad walked in with two bowls of ice cream. "Where you going, son?"

Wyatt halted. "Thank you for your hospitality, but I don't want to impose any longer. Alyssa needs her rest."

"Yes, she does. It's been quite a day. You'll have to come back again for dessert. Are you in town much longer?"

Wyatt looked at her before returning his gaze to her dad. "Yes. I've asked for a permanent position at Last Chance."

Her father's eyebrows rose. "That's great to hear. I'll expect another visit from you in the near future then."

"You have my promise." Wyatt gave her father a smile and continued toward the door.

She lost sight of him but the sound of the door closing, and Gertie squawking, let her know he'd left.

"Nice fella." Her dad handed her a bowl.

She stared at it unseeing, her vision blurred. She needed to just not think right now. As she told her students, tomorrow was another day with endless possibilities. Picking up her spoon, she dug into the cold ice cream and forced herself to focus on the flavor and not on the huge disappointment filling her future.

Chapter Six

Wyatt sat on the porch sipping his coffee as the sun's rays started to lighten the sky. He couldn't sleep. The uncertainty about being able to stay at Last Chance and be a part of the quirky team had him strung tighter than a sprung snare.

It didn't help that he worried about Alyssa, but without her phone number, his only way of finding out how she was would be to visit her. It had only been three days since he'd seen her. She needed rest, not visitors. Unfortunately, his unease about both situations started his chaotic dreams again. It was as if the chaos he feared took over when he slept, jolting him awake when he tried to control it all.

"Damn stupid rabbit." His voice breaking the silence of the morning sounded eerie, like his dreams. Ever since his mother had read *Alice in Wonderland* to his sisters, his bad dreams had one constant in them, a white rabbit. Sometimes it talked. Sometimes it had fangs in a mouth big enough to swallow a man whole, and sometimes it trailed blood over everything.

The sound of a truck approaching had him setting down his cup. He listened as it came closer, coming up from behind the house. Maybe Cole had an early shift.

The lights shined on the dirt road out of the ranch before

the pickup came into view and pulled alongside the porch. When the window came down, he was surprised to see Lacey.

"Just the man I wanted to see. I've got something for you." She turned toward the empty passenger seat.

The coffee he'd just drank felt like mud in his stomach. This couldn't be good. Maybe the background check had come back, and they wanted him off the property. He rose and walked down the three steps, forcing his feet to move to the driver side window.

When Lacey held papers in her hand, her serious gaze on him, he silently cursed to himself. "What's this?" He forced his voice to sound calm as he took the folder.

"Just the final paperwork for your position here. You know, the usual benefits sign-ups."

Stunned, he frowned. "The background check came back okay?"

"Yeah." She cocked her head. "Why? Wasn't it supposed to?"

He'd stepped into it now. "Well, I did get into a little trouble when I was a teenager." 'Little' wasn't exactly the right word, but only one crime wasn't much.

She rolled her eyes. "Haven't we all. Nothing showed up, probably because any mistakes we make while under eighteen are sealed."

Sealed? That hadn't occurred to him. Having taken care of his younger sisters while his mom worked, he'd never thought much about the difference between being a minor and an adult. In other words, he had a clean slate. His new position, new home, and new community also meant starting over. And what about Alyssa?

"Wyatt, hey Wyatt." Lacey's waved her hand outside the window.

"Sorry, I was already thinking about my future here."

She dropped her hand on the door frame. "Speaking of your new position. It doesn't start until Monday, but I could really use your help today. I've got no one who can come in to feed and exercise."

"I'm at your disposal." He lifted the brim of his hat a couple of inches off his head.

She smiled for the first time since arriving. "Good. Then you should know that Whisper is coming down to talk to Meeko."

"Is she going to try to discover why he's being so ornery?"

Lacey nodded. "Yes, but she can't stay long. If you could feed and water and—"

"I know the drill."

Her shoulders slumped. "Thank you. I need to beat the traffic into Phoenix for a doctor's appointment before coming back up here to go to work, and Cole is sleeping after his last shift. If you need anything…" Her voice trailed off as if she wasn't sure what to tell him.

He put his hand on the top of the cab. "Go. I'll handle whatever comes up. If I get stuck, I'll call Riley. She may give me an earful, but she'll answer."

"You're right. I better get going."

He tapped the truck and stepped away.

As Lacey's truck headed down the dirt road, a heaviness lifted off his shoulders like the dust her tires kicked up. He turned and ran up the steps. Grabbing his coffee, he took a gulp of the now warm liquid and strode into the house. Annette would be up soon, and he wanted to get a fresh pot going for her and Ed, who for once, didn't have an early tee time.

Once he'd finished his coffee, he was striding back outside toward the barn. It felt good to be needed. No, wanted. He was wanted here. Little did he know when he'd discovered Last Chance Ranch on the internet as a home for Lady, Guinness, and Blaze, that it would become his, too.

Then again, he hadn't expected his own mother and her siblings putting High Mountain up for sale and leaving him without a home either. His step slowed as he entered the barn. He still resented the fact all they could see were dollar signs. They and Gramps didn't have a good relationship because he told it like it was with no flowery words at all. It could be hard to take when he criticized, but it also meant the accolades, when they came, meant so much more.

He missed the old man more than he could ever admit to anyone. He'd been the first adult to really care about him. The pain in the corner of his chest where he tried to keep it began to seep out, encompassing his heart. He came to stop in the middle of the barn, unable to move, reliving scenes from working on the ranch with Gramps.

A nicker from Kentucky snapped him back to the present. Would the gut-wrenching loss ever stop hitting him? He forced himself to stride forward. "How are you today? No new cuts I hope." He stroked the horse's nose as he scanned him for any new abrasions. Checking both sides, he was relieved there were none. "In just a couple more days, we'll take that bandage off. Your scar should be healing well now."

The horse butted his head.

"Hey, you want to be fed don't you?" Kentucky tried again, but missed. "Meds haven't quite got your nerves working right yet, huh boy. Okay, you deserve a song just for that." He could use one too to recapture his excitement at having a new purpose in life. "How about, 'Here Comes the Sun'?"

He started singing as he moved to the feed bins and followed the routine Riley used. He had ideas for how they could be more efficient, but he'd wait until he was officially on board. As he worked, he sang. He added "Good Day Sunshine" to keep his upbeat mood.

By time he'd stepped outside again to feed Meeko, his heartache had subsided back into its assigned corner. He made notes in his head of what he would suggest for changes as he walked.

He approached the corral with the shaded cover on one side. His theory was that the horse was just strung too tight. It was part Thoroughbred, part Quarter Horse, and part Wild Mustang. That combination could make for a behavior problem, but he'd read the paperwork when Meeko came in and according to his last owner, he'd been a well-behaved horse until the young woman had passed away.

He could understand that. He'd only started saying the wrong things after Gramps died. Was it the pain of losing Gramps or how he acted because Gramps wasn't in his life to hold the structure together?

He had no idea, which is why he was anxious to get settled. He needed something else to keep him on the straight and narrow. He didn't want to find out how he might be if left to his own devices. It was a pretty sad situation for a man to be in and he hated it. *It's the hand you were dealt, so play with it.*

His grandfather's words seem to come to him just when he needed them. The old man might be gone, but he was still in his head…like brainwashing. He grinned at the thought. "Okay, Meeko. How about some breakfast?"

The horse stood on the far side of the corral, but Wyatt knew better than to trust him. While he thought they had an understanding about feeding time, since Riley was happy to let him do that, he knew better than to count on it. He held up the bucket and shook it.

Meeko stared at him, not a muscle moving.

He took the last two steps to the corral fence and lifted the bucket over it, hanging it on a hook on the post for just such a purpose. Not taking time to see if the gelding was closing in, he quickly stepped back.

Meeko chuffed as he raced to the fence, stopping just before it and letting out a loud whinny.

Now that he'd made the correlation between his and Meeko's situation, the animal's whinny sounded like pain more than aggression. He looked forward to finding out what Whisper would say. For all he knew, Meeko had a girlfriend back at the ranch he came from and he missed her.

He returned to the barn to bring out the horses who could congregate in the south corral while Meeko solely occupied the north one. Enjoying his work, he had everyone taken care of and two stalls cleaned out before his stomach started to rumble.

It was earlier than usual, but he'd been up earlier than usual, so he headed inside to wash up and see what leftovers he could find. Jogging upstairs, he washed his hands in the bathroom on the other side of the stairs from his bedroom. That it was truly his bedroom now and for the foreseeable future had his mood improving even more.

Once downstairs again, he headed into the kitchen where he found Annette making a list. She was dressed in a pair of pale blue slacks and a white blouse with blue bells on it. Her white hair, which was usually in a ponytail was wound up into a neat bun and if he didn't mistake his guess, she had some blush on. This was definitely not her usual jeans and button-down collared shirt.

He whistled at her and she looked up, her cheeks flushing. She waved her hand as if she could brush off the compliment. "Oh please, Wyatt. Just because I'm not in a pair of jeans, it isn't cause for celebration."

He grinned as he grabbed the chair opposite her, spun it around, straddled it, and laid his forearms on the back of it. "You are looking might pretty today, Mrs. Benson. Something special going on or are you just dressing up for me?"

"Young man, you're a smooth talker and that's going to get you into trouble one of these days."

He shook his head. "I save it only for you."

She rolled her eyes. "Lucky me."

He laughed, pleased that he could make her feel good.

"As a matter of fact, I'm going to our monthly ladies' lunch. Me and the girls get together and support one of our local establishments. This month we're going to Ollie's. Remember a couple of weeks ago you brought that message back from Connie?"

He frowned. "Connie?"

"Ms. Richards."

He barely held back a grimace. "I remember."

"I spoke to her yesterday. She hadn't heard that Ms. Parker was back at work yet." Annette's keen gaze studied him.

That didn't surprise him based on how stiffly Alyssa was moving the last time he saw her. Even as he pictured her sitting in her dad's recliner, he wanted to go over there and see how she was. "I imagine she may be out all week. She was hit pretty hard. It totaled her car."

"Oh, the poor woman. Maybe you should check in on her and see how she's doing."

"Me?" He sat back, bracing his hand against the chair back. They didn't really know each other very well. She probably had half the town visiting her. "I'm sure her father is taking very good care of her." The fact that he wanted to go, didn't keep him from denying it.

He didn't want to make things difficult for Alyssa if Connie

Richards heard he'd been there and started spreading gossip about them. For all he knew, she had someone in her life already.

Annette leaned forward. "That Roy wouldn't let a fly bother her if he had a choice. But last I knew, he was still working. He isn't leaving Gila Bend Construction until the end of the year. When I get back from lunch, I'll make up a pot of my homemade chicken soup for Ms. Parker."

He smirked. "Chicken soup? Isn't that for people who are sick?"

Her brows rose. "Good point." She paused, obviously thinking of alternatives. "I could make my chocolate chunk brownies."

He shook his head. The last thing she needed to be doing was cooking brownies in the heat of the day. The house may be air-conditioned, but with the temperatures over one hundred, the oven would negate any successful cooling. "Ms. Parker already has a cake from the grocery store, and I'm sure others have sent food." From the way it sounded, the whole town not only knew Alyssa but loved her.

He could understand why. She wasn't just pretty but kind with a strong sense of right and wrong. She also had a backbone. The way she'd stood up to the man who hit her despite her shaking had been admirable. *You can tell good breeding when you see it, boy.* Gramps' comment on one of the ranch hand's wives came to mind.

"You're right, of course. I'll pick up a nice card and drop it off before I come home from lunch." Annette gave him the side eye. "Unless of course, you'd like to drop it off."

He widened his eyes. "And deny her the pleasure of your company? She would never forgive me."

Annette laughed. "Wyatt Ford, you are a charmer."

He stiffened. Anger, harsh and heady surged through him.

His mother described his father as a charmer. He was nothing like his father. He refused to be, even if he almost followed in his footsteps. "I'm not a charmer. A charmer's words are calculated. My words come from the heart."

Her eyes rounded at his tone. "I never thought about it that way."

"My father was a charmer."

Annette's gaze turned curious. "You never talk about your father."

He shrugged and rose. "There's really nothing to say." As far as he was concerned, his father didn't exist. Too bad the man had a tendency to show up out of the blue. Moving to the refrigerator, he opened it to find last night's leftovers in plastic containers. "Is anyone saving the meatloaf, mashed potatoes, and string bean casserole for anything?"

When she didn't answer, he looked behind him.

"You're a puzzle, young man."

"Because I like your homemade meatloaf?"

She smirked. "No. Never mind." She waved her hand. "Go ahead and eat whatever you can find. No one else will. I've got a lunch to get to." She rose slowly. "I probably won't be able to walk by time those old biddies finish talking. I'll be stiffer than overdone beef jerky."

He grinned as he pulled out the food. "If you want, you can always leave early. Tell them I need your help here at the ranch."

"You mean lie?" She placed her hand on her chest. "And allow them to talk about me the rest of the afternoon. No damn way."

He laughed as she walked out of the room, a jaunt in her step that wasn't there the other day. He never noticed the aging changes in his grandfather, but he noticed them in Annette when they were present. Why hadn't he? If he had, could he have saved Gramps a heart attack? The thought caused his gut to tighten. Had he neglected his own blood relative?

Or was it that Gramps hadn't shown any signs?

As his food heated, he went through the last days of his grandfather's life. Nothing stood out as unusual. Slowly, his stomach relaxed, then growled at him again. Taking his food out, he ate standing at the counter.

Abel Ford had been a tough man who rarely smiled, but he'd been a good man through and through. All his ranch hands, customers, and neighbors had respected him. That much was clear at the funeral. That his own children were surprised by the turnout probably had more to do with them than the old man.

Wyatt paused in mid-chew. He hadn't thought about it before, but Cole's relationship to his grandparents was better than to his own parents as well. He continued eating. Maybe that's why he felt so comfortable at Last Chance.

The sound of the front door opening had him thinking Annette had forgot something.

"Wyatt! I heard I'm supposed to check on a horse?"

As Whisper's steps came down the hallway, he opened the fridge and placed his plate inside to get back to later.

She came around the corner dressed in a t-shirt, jeans, and cowboy boots. Her long straight black hair was loose beneath her beat-up cowboy hat. Her grey gaze took in everything at once. "Sorry to disturb your lunch, but this is the only time I could get over here. What's the problem?"

From the way everyone talked about her, she could work miracles, but all he'd seen was the down to earth, blunt woman before him. "He's out in the corral. His name is Meeko."

She spun on her heel and headed back down the hall without him.

He strode out to catch up, but before he could open the door for her, she was already outside.

"Must be that one." She pointed to Meeko as they strode toward the north corral.

"Yes. He's part Thoroughbred, part American Quarter horse, and part Wild Mustang."

That caught her attention. "Wild mustang?"

He nodded. "Yeah."

Meeko, as if knowing he was the subject of their conversation turned toward them but remained on the far side of the corral as usual.

Whisper made to open the gate.

He jumped around her and grasped it. "Wait. He'll bite you or run you over if you go in there."

She stepped back and placed her hands on her hips. "Well, how the hell do you expect me to help him standing out here? It's not like I'm—well freakin' A."

"What?"

She didn't answer. Instead, she moved past him to lean on the top rail of the corral.

He didn't trust her to not jump over and get herself killed, so he stepped up next to her in case he had to grab her. "What is it?"

"I can feel it from here. He's in so much pain."

Great. It looked like they would have to get a tranquilizer gun to put the horse to sleep so Dr. Jenna could treat him.

"Meeko, I know it sucks." She spoke to the horse from where she was. That she hadn't climbed over the rail meant she could tell how dangerous the horse was.

He wanted to know what the problem was but wasn't sure how Whisper worked.

"Listen, I get it. I lost my mother and father when I was

younger than you. I was probably lucky because after a while the memories faded and all I knew was Uncle Joey."

The horse stood stock still, his gaze riveted to Whisper.

Wyatt hadn't met Uncle Joey, but he knew the man lived with Whisper and wasn't well.

"I know. It's not fair and it hurts, bad. Hurting someone isn't going to make it feel any better, but you do what you need to do."

Was she giving the horse permission to trample them? He lowered his voice to a whisper. "You know we need to be able to feed him, right?"

She gave him a quick scowl before returning her attention to the horse. "I promise, you'll have an Uncle Joey too, someone to love you. That's why you're here." Whisper stepped away from the rails and started to walk the perimeter of the fence toward Meeko. Wyatt followed, prepared to protect her if Meeko decided to get nasty again. The horse didn't move but he watched their progress.

"What happened to his owner?"

A chill raced up his back. "Why do you think something happened to his owner?"

Whisper sent him a glare over her shoulder, but she kept walking. "Meeko was very attached to his owner. What happened to her?"

Now he was definitely uncomfortable. How did she know the owner was a woman? "It was a car accident. The paperwork said it was a hit and run. The parents couldn't bear to have Meeko around as a reminder of their daughter."

"She must have been young."

He had no idea how old the owner had actually been, just that it was a young woman, so he didn't comment. Instead, he stayed alert as they came face to face with the horse.

Whisper leaned on the railing, only feet from Meeko.

The animal focused solely on her.

Wyatt watched her, his protective instincts warring with the glock she had tucked behind her in her waistband. On one hand, he didn't want her getting hurt, and he'd seen what Meeko could do, but on the other hand, he didn't want to get shot for his trouble.

"Meeko, I feel you. So much heartache. It's not going to be easy, but it will get better. You have to work with us to help you. See this guy?" She pointed to him.

The horse actually moved his gaze to him for a second.

Hell, the woman was scary.

"He's going to be feeding you and giving you water and cleaning up after you. If you let him, he'd even brush you."

Wyatt tensed at that. It was hard to imagine the horse allowing that.

"Your Uncle Joey is coming. I want you to be happy and healthy when that happens because he'll love you like you used to be. But you have to be alive for that to happen."

The horse finally moved, but it was toward Whisper.

She reached her hand out, and Wyatt clamped down on her arm. "He'll bite you."

Without taking her eyes off the approaching horse, she responded as if she were saying good day. "If you don't remove your hand from my arm, I will do it for you."

She was one of the few he hadn't pissed off while at the ranch. He didn't want to do so now, but he also wanted her to be safe.

"Be careful." He removed his hand with that warning, his body ready to jump the fence if he had to.

The horse stopped inches from Whisper's hand.

She growled. "Stop thinking he's going to bite me. He can feel your tension. Either step back or relax."

Both were impossible, so he took a few deep breaths to loosen his muscles while he stayed alert.

Whisper raised her hand.

Afterwards, if someone made him swear to what he witnessed, he'd refuse. The damn horse looked him in the eye before moving his head against Whisper's hand.

She stroked Meeko while Wyatt just stared. There were no soothing sounds coming from Whisper and no movement from the horse except the closing of his eyes.

Whisper suddenly chuckled, and the horse opened his eyes. "No worry, Meeko. He's just here to take care of you. He has his own horse."

Meeko lifted his head away and stepped back. Then after a good ten seconds, he walked away from them.

Whisper turned away and headed back around the corral. "Don't let anyone near him unless they are interested in adopting him. Not Logan, not Cole, not even Trace. Got that?"

"Yes, but why is he so nasty."

Whisper stopped suddenly and spun around to face him. "I can't believe you needed me for this. How did you feel after your grandfather died?"

His gut tightened. "Like shit."

"And how many people did you piss off around here?"

"Everyone but you." That wasn't exactly true, but close.

She pointed to the horse. "Well, what you felt, what you feel, is what he's going through."

Full understanding dawned and he looked at the horse, sympathy for the animal filling him. "I didn't realize."

Whisper turned away, continuing around the fence. "Both the owner and Meeko were young, so the bond was made early and the ending of it unexpected." She stopped again, but this time looked at the horse. "It may not be an Uncle Joey after all."

"What?" Her references to her uncle confused him completely.

"Nothing. I have to get back to the trailer. Trace said he wanted to have sex this afternoon, and I still have to check on Viola's babies. The littlest one isn't eating enough."

That was far too much information for him, so he ignored the comment. "If I keep everyone away from Meeko, will he behave if I want to bring him into a stall?"

"No. He'll behave if you care for him in the corral. He needs more time before he'll be willing to have you move him." She opened the door of her truck and hopped in. "But if someone new comes by, keep them away unless Meeko puts his head over the fence. Right now, he's dealing with his pain in his territory, but if he reaches beyond that, it means he wants to connect. Got it?"

He nodded. "Got it."

Whisper didn't bother saying goodbye, have a nice day, or see you soon. She just closed the door and started the truck. He'd known her long enough to know she wasn't being rude. She was just…Whisper.

As the woman backed out of the yard then headed down the dirt road to the highway, it made him think of another woman with backbone he knew just enough to want to know more.

He strode back into the house to rewarm his lunch. He'd like to call Alyssa, but that would mean asking Annette for her phone number, and he preferred not to do that. She already insinuated there was something there, and right now that was just a hope. He did want to know how she was doing, but he also just wanted to see her.

Not thinking twice about why, he mentally rearranged his chores, so he could leave right after the horses were settled in for the evening. He returned his plate to the microwave and started it. He was pretty sure he could find his way back to Alyssa's father's house…if she was still there. And if she wasn't? "Damn."

He pulled his plate out and remained at the counter eating. Maybe Annette would say something at dinner. And if Alyssa was at her place, he had no way of knowing where that was without asking.

Frustrated, he finished his food and rinsed the plate, adding it to the dishwasher. *Sometimes the boulder in your path was meant to warn you off.* His grandfather's words to him, those times when hurdles had stopped or delayed his goals, echoed unwanted in his head.

Maybe the old man was right, as usual. He needed to settle in at the ranch first and stop the nightmares. Then he could get himself a life again.

Chapter Seven

Alyssa drove down the dirt road toward Last Chance Ranch in her dad's truck. She'd been carpooling with Marty all week, but today she'd stayed late to help a student and didn't want to inconvenience her friend, so she'd dropped dad off at work. He wouldn't be done for another couple of hours because of a meeting.

She had a big decision to make—buy a new car and delay buying a house for at least another year, or move in with her father, give up her apartment to save the money faster so she can buy a house sooner. She didn't like either option, so she did what she always did when faced with a major life decision, she focused on something else and put it off.

This time that something else was Wyatt Ford. She'd been upset that he hadn't visited again or called her, but her father had made a good point. How was Wyatt supposed to contact her if he didn't have her phone number or address? She'd only been able to stay with her dad one night, his constant care becoming stifling, so Wyatt wouldn't have known where she lived.

So here she was, driving to a ranch she'd never been to in order to see if he had any interest in her. She'd never done this before, pursued a man, but she couldn't deny the feelings she had when he was around. Even in the aftermath of her accident, while still a nervous wreck, those tummy butterflies were flitting everywhere as he helped her.

The main concern she had was the fact that he could have asked Mrs. Benson where she lived. The woman had, after all, stopped by with a lovely get-well card. Or he could have visited her dad who would have gladly given Wyatt directions to her apartment. Fudge. Her father probably would have escorted the man there. For some reason, he'd had taken a real liking to Wyatt.

But what if Wyatt didn't really like her? That thought nagged at her and had her lifting her foot off the gas pedal. Now that she was so close, the doubt returned. Maybe he was just being polite when he'd helped her after her accident.

LAST CHANCE RANCH. The sign hanging between two tall posts told her she had found the right place as the truck coasted into the dirt front yard. A white double cab truck was parked next to a darker truck in front of a large porch.

The two-story house reminded her of something she'd seen in an old western movie once. Despite its age, it was well kept. She wasn't surprised as Mrs. Benson was known for being both a force to be reckoned with and very neat.

She didn't see anyone about, so she turned off the truck and exited before she lost her nerve. Heading for the front steps, she stopped at the sound coming from out back. Hoping she could avoid Mrs. Benson and just see Wyatt, she started around the house. There were two corrals. One on the north side had a shelter and a single horse standing at the back. The one to the south had a number of horses and the very man she was looking for.

She halted and stared.

Wyatt, bare chested, worked a post hole digger into the ground then squeezed it and lifted dirt out of the hole. His abdominals rippled, his biceps flexed, and his skin glistened in the heat. No butterflies flitted about in her stomach now. What she felt was the pure sting of bumble bees deep in her core.

As if he sensed he was being watched, he looked up after sinking the tool deep into the ground again. His lips split into a wide smile. "Alyssa."

Her body temperature must have jumped ten degrees suddenly, and she swallowed hard against the closing of her throat.

He started toward her, his bright smile threatening to buckle her knees.

She returned his smile but couldn't seem to get her legs to move.

He reached her in less time than she needed. "How are you?" His gaze swept over her quickly, but he could have taken an hour for how off-balance she felt.

"I'm fine." This close she could smell hay, leather, a slight soap scent, and male sweat.

"You look a little over heated. Why don't we go on the porch?"

She stared blankly at him for a moment before mentally shaking herself out of her stupor. "That's sounds great."

"This way." He held his hand out for her to turn around and precede him.

Maybe it was just the sun. It was after three in the afternoon and the desert was fairly baking. Forcing herself to move, she turned about and retraced her steps. Once on the porch, she stood motionless until he joined her.

"Have a seat. I'll grab us some fresh cold lemonade. I was about to take a break anyway."

She nodded, still not willing to trust her voice beyond a few words. She moved to a comfortable looking rattan chair set next to a small round table at the far end. The banging of the screen door made her jump as she turned around and took a seat.

Taking a few deep breaths, she tried to regain her composure. She was not only flustered but heated, and she took off the shrug she wore to cover her bare shoulders at school. Her pale pink dress with tiny red roses was one of her favorites, but with the spaghetti straps, she rarely wore it to school.

It wasn't as if she hadn't seen a man without his shirt on before. No, it was that Wyatt was the best-looking specimen of a man she'd ever seen in real life as opposed to the movies. What was she thinking that he might be interested in her?

Despite the extra care she'd taken getting ready this morning, she still felt like an ugly duckling, no, an ugly ostrich next to him. She'd just say her thank you, her excuse for coming to the ranch, and then be on her way.

Since she faced the whole porch, when Wyatt reappeared, she had an unimpeded view of him. He'd donned a light blue t-shirt, which helped her keep her concentration, and he held a tall glass of lemonade in each hand.

"Here you go." He handed her the glass, already dripping with condensation. "You still look a bit warm. "Do you want to go inside where it's cooler?"

She shook her head, preferring not to have to chat with anyone else.

He sat down and lifted his glass. "Welcome to Last Chance Ranch."

She smiled. "Thank you." She took a sip, feeling the cool liquid go all the way down to her stomach. Already, she felt more like herself. "This is exactly what I needed."

"Annette makes excellent lemonade." He took another gulp, his glass already half empty.

"I didn't mean to interrupt your work. I just came by to thank you for all the help after the accident last week."

"It was my pleasure. Has all the stiffness gone away?" His clear green gaze revealed honest concern.

"Almost. My neck is still a little stiff, but I'm back at work. Though that's been a little tricky without a car."

He set his glass down on the table between them. "Will you be buying a new one?"

She sighed. "I haven't decided." She didn't want to go into that.

"I'm glad you came. I was going to call, but I didn't have your phone number and decided not to ask Annette."

She lowered her brows, very curious about that in particular. "Why not? Don't you get along with her?"

He grinned. "I do." His smile turned into a grimace. "But she's a friend of Connie Richards, and I got the distinct impression she may be the town gossip."

Relief flowed through her at his admission. That he had wanted to contact her made her feel a whole lot better about her visit. "You're correct to a point." She chuckled. "Connie has been in everyone's business since she moved here a few years ago."

He nodded.

"But…" She held her hand up. "She keeps the information to herself unless she's helping someone. She's a very unusual town gossip."

Wyatt's brows rose slightly. "I'll take your word for it."

He was obviously not convinced, but she didn't mind. He'd learn soon enough. "What about you? It looks like Last Chance hired you." She pointed toward the back of the house where he'd been working.

"They did." His smile was beautiful to look at. It was clear he was happy now.

"I'm sure they need another hand. I imagine there are a lot of horses that have to be rescued, unfortunately."

"More than there should be." His face turned serious. "Many have health problems when they first come here. We rehabilitate them and adopt them out to better homes. It's a lengthy process. I think it could be streamlined through a more automated website. I'd also like to have the entire valley fenced in for those horses who are comfortable together."

For a man who had just been hired, he already had a lot of ideas to improve the operation. She found that very attractive. "Do you think you'll stay here for a while then?"

He looked startled by her question. "I plan to stay here as long as they'll have me. I have nowhere else to go." He quickly looked away as he took the last gulp of his lemonade.

The look she'd seen in his eyes the day she met him was back. There was something beyond sorrow in it, but she couldn't quite place it. Besides, she didn't want to have him thinking about sad events. "How many horses do you have here right now? Will all of them be adopted eventually?" Her distraction worked.

Wyatt set down his glass. "That's right, you've never been here. Would you like me to show you around?"

"I'd love that." She took another sip of the lemonade and stood. "Just so you know, if my phone rings, it means I have to go. My father has a meeting this afternoon, but when he's done, I need to drive him home since I have his truck."

He had risen when she did, so he gave her a short bow. "Then let's get started. There's lots to see."

She walked beside him as he showed her the barn, explained the new wagon, and pointed out his beautiful horse, Tundra. The horse was a giant but so beautiful. It looked like it was white but had run through ash with its spray of gray. Then they started for the corral where he'd been working. She pointed to the lone horse in the other one. "Did he do something wrong?"

He chuckled. "More like he's never done something right. Actually, that isn't fair. This week, he hasn't tried to bite me or trample me when I feed him."

"What's his name?"

"Meeko. We think it's due to the death of his owner that he's being mean, but it's hard to tell."

She looked him squarely in the eyes. "You know what that's like, right?"

His eyes widened. He looked at her then back at Meeko. "I'll be damned." The words were barely a whisper, but he quickly turned toward her. "Pardon my language. I just didn't realize the connection was so easy to see. I had missed it until a few days ago."

She waved his comment off. "No harm done. I'm a big girl."

As he gazed at her, she'd swear she could see appreciation in his eyes. It had to be a trick of the light. Not used to being looked at in quite that way, she glanced beyond him at Meeko. "Will he have to be alone forever?"

"I hope not."

Something in his tone of voice had her snapping her gaze back to him, but he was no longer looking at her.

"Over here, I'm working on a shelter like the north corral has." They leaned against the corral fence as he talked.

She found his ideas made a lot of sense, and the stories he told about the horses in the south corral had her laughing so hard that she cried. She wiped happy tears from her eyes. "It sounds like Cyclone needs a job of his own. What a fun place to work."

He scanned the area. "I've only been here a short time, but I feel as if I've found a new home."

And there it was. The underlying truth to the man before her. It was as if he'd lost his way for a while and finally found his place. "I can see that. This place is very special. I wish my students could see it."

"Why can't they?"

His question surprised her. "Well, we would need permission forms, a bus, parent chaperones, and a reason for the field trip."

Wyatt shrugged. "That all sounds doable to me."

Once again, he surprised her. She was so used to teachers complaining that it was too hard to organize a field trip that she'd boarded that impossible-train without thinking about it. It was definitely doable. "Can you provide proof of insurance?"

He nodded. "I'm sure I can. If Cole doesn't have it, Lacey or Annette will. I'll just make sure it's okay with them then we can set a date if you can handle all those forms."

Excited by the prospect of her students seeing a ranch for horse rescues instead of the typical ranch they might live at, she nodded. "I can. Thank you." She rose up on her toes and gave him a kiss on the cheek.

Wyatt grasped her shoulders, gazed into her eyes, then with no warning, lowered his lips to hers.

Tingles of excitement ran up her spine as his tongue breeched her lips and leisurely explored her mouth, causing her to close her eyes and enjoy. He tasted of lemonade and man all at once, causing her insides to melt. She couldn't have pulled away if she wanted to, and she definitely didn't want to.

He reached around and pulled her closer, even as he angled her face with his other hand, deepening the kiss.

She was thankful for his arm about her because her knees felt like melting ice cream, and a swirling need started in her abdomen. Tangling her tongue with his, she did her own exploring, learning the taste of him and loving it. Her heart raced and excitement grew.

His tongue retreated as he kissed the edges of her lips, almost as if he didn't want to stop, but had to.

She didn't want it to stop either, but as he pulled away, she let him, her left side still flush against his hard build. Opening her eyes, she looked into his bright green gaze and straightened her head. "Ouch." It must be stiffer than she'd thought.

Concern crossed his face immediately. "Did I hurt you?"

She started to shake her head but caught herself. "No." Massaging the muscles in her neck, she assuaged his worry. "I guess I'm not as fine as I thought. I probably just need a few more days to be back to normal."

A nudge of her arm surprised her, so she looked at what caused it. The horse called Lady nudged her arm again.

Wyatt's chuckle reverberated through her. "It seems we have a jealous horse here."

She raised her brows. "You mean Lady is jealous that you're kissing me?"

He shook his head. "No, she could care less about me. She's jealous that you're paying attention to me and not her."

"She's a female. Surely she can see that I find you more interesting."

His gaze turned soft. "I find you more interesting as well."

Her heart sighed as she lost herself in his eyes. She could almost see forever in their green depths. "I—" The push she received this time had her holding onto Wyatt to stay upright. "Okay, okay." She squinted at Lady. "It looks like we need to have a heart-to-heart girl talk."

Wyatt released her, which wasn't what she wanted at all, and stepped back. "You better give her a pet or two. She's a true diva."

"That reminds me of a certain ostrich I know." She stroked the pretty Quarter Horse on the side of her neck. "Is that better?" The horse simply pressed closer against the fence. She was definitely all about the attention.

"Do you ride?"

Wyatt's question caught her off guard, though she shouldn't have been. "I don't."

He stroked Lady on her nose. "You're obviously not afraid of horses. Did you have them when you were young? I saw you had a barn."

She had this question asked all her life, and normally she didn't mind answering it, but it was different with Wyatt. His life was lived around horses as far as she could tell. "We did have horses, and I did ride, at least until I was nine."

She kept her attention on Lady. Though her mom had been gone over twenty years now, she still remembered how beautiful she was. "My mom died when she fell off her horse. It was a freak accident thanks to a rattlesnake, but ever since then, I've stayed off them out of respect for my father."

When he didn't say anything, she faced him. She thought she'd see sympathy, compassion, or understanding in his face, but instead, she'd swear it was admiration. "What?" She couldn't help responding to such a look.

He leaned against the fence again. "I think it admirable that you put your father's feelings above your own. It must have been hard growing up around here with all your friends riding."

It was if he'd read her own heart. While she was young, it had been a very hard sacrifice, but she didn't want to ever worry her dad. There was a reason they no longer had horses after finding good homes for the three they had had. "It was, but my friends preferred to come to my house when I was younger."

His eyebrows lifted. "Why? Because they preferred geese and ostriches?"

She laughed. "Oh, yes. Though to be fair, the ostriches are new. My father was always adding a new animal to our menagerie. We had pet racoons, burrows, tortoise, bats, deer, prairie dogs, llamas, peacocks, camels, h—"

"Camels?" His crooked smile made it clear he thought that was the weirdest.

If he only knew. "Yes, though we only had one camel to be completely honest. They are a desert animal after all. We just had him until he grew up, then he went to the zoo."

She stepped away from Lady. "My dad is in construction and has built a lot of buildings for a lot of people, so his connections, though strange, are wide ranging." She leaned closer to him and lowered her voice. "You'd be amazed at how many rich eccentric people live around here."

Instead of responding, he took the opportunity to snake his hand around her waist and pull her toward him.

He was the first man she'd been interested in who made her feel feminine and small. At about six feet tall, though she refused after eighteen to let the doctor measure her anymore, she was usually the same height as the men she dated, and sometimes, she felt bigger in stature. That was definitely not the case with the cowboy who held her standing between his legs. She tilted her head carefully. "Are you sure it's safe to take our attention away from Lady?" She glanced at the horse standing very close, watching them.

He clicked his tongue. "Go."

She watched, amazed, as Lady turned away and walked toward the paint with her colt. "How did you do that?"

He grinned. "We go way back. But you are new to me and far prettier to look at."

It was such a simple compliment, but the way he said it, as if it was simply a fact, had her cheeks flushing. "I'm glad you're staying in town."

His smile faded as he stared into her eyes. "So am I."

Her heartrate picked up speed as anticipation uncurled in her belly. This time when he lowered his head to kiss her, she was ready. Grasping his biceps, which fairly bulged out of his t-shirt, she leaned in.

Excitement zinged through her as his tongue swept into her mouth and he pulled her against his hard body. She wrapped her arms around his neck as their tongues entwined.

Heat built in her abdomen and traveled between her thighs, her attraction to Wyatt causing all her senses to go into overdrive. The heat on her back seemed to feed the fire inside her. The scent of horses and sweat excited her to the core, and the taste of him reminded her of a dessert she couldn't stop eating.

Something in the back of her mind was telling her to slow down, but she didn't want to. She wanted to know everything about this man right now, including every inch of his body.

He cupped her head with his hand even as his other arm remained an iron band around her waist. His tongue played with hers, seeking then retreating then surrounding, but not leaving.

All feeling was centered in her mouth and at her core. She wanted, no needed, to be closer. To have him—the ring of her phone startled her. Pulling her head away, she found her breaths were short and fast.

Dang-it, her father! "I have to answer. It's my dad."

Wyatt dropped his arms, and she reached into her dress pocket to pull out her phone. For the hundredth time, she wished her father would just text her. "Hi, Dad." She forced herself to step away from Wyatt.

"I'm done. You ready to come pick me up?"

"Of course. I'll be there shortly." It felt weird talking to her dad with an audience. She turned away.

"Good. I'll be outside. Been in that blasted refrigerator cube for too many hours."

To her dad, any four walls that were airconditioned except his house, were considered refrigerator cubes. "Okay, see you soon. Love you."

She hung up and faced Wyatt. "I have to go."

"I understand." He gave a quick nod. "I'll walk you out."

They started back toward the house. It seemed like she should say something. She definitely wanted to spend more time with him. Maybe she could suggest—

He interrupted her thoughts. "If you would be interested, you could come over Saturday afternoon and we could plan out your class visit."

Her heart skipped a beat, and she looked up at him. "I'd love that."

He gave her a genuine smile. "Good. Annette and Ed are heading out for the weekend so it will just be me."

He was all she wanted. "What about everyone else? Surely, it's not just you here?"

"I'm the only one living here at the main house besides Annette and Ed."

She looked around but didn't see any other buildings except the barn.

He didn't wait for her to ask the obvious. "Cole and Lacey have a new home further back in the valley. Trace and Whisper live up on the mountain near the conservation land but still on the property. Logan lives with his daughter Charlotte at Dr. Jenn's family home, and Riley lives with Garret in Wickenburg."

It relieved her to know he didn't work the ranch alone. "I would be happy to come on Saturday."

They stopped at her dad's truck, and she leaned against the driver side door. Remembering her excuse for coming in the first place, she placed her hand on his arm. "Thank you again for your help last week."

"I'm glad I was there, and I'm glad you came today." He cupped her head once again and kissed her gently. "See you Saturday."

She nodded as she stepped away from the vehicle and he opened the door for her. Once inside, he closed it and stepped away, tipping his hat up.

She backed up and pulled out. Looking in the rearview mirror, she could see him watching her leave. "Yes!" She grinned. Checking in front of her again, she straightened the wheel to avoid hitting the signpost and left Last Chance Ranch.

But she would be back and she couldn't wait.

Chapter Eight

Wyatt turned the steaks on the grill and leaned into Garrett. "Did Cole give you any indication why the family dinner was changed to tonight instead of Sunday?" He was thankful he hadn't had to change his date with Alyssa.

Garrett, who was a former Hot Shot, current horse transporter, and the first person Wyatt had met from Last Chance, shook his head. "No. I even asked him outright, and all he would say was that there would be some big changes on the ranch."

His gut tightened. He had yet to unpack his box trailer that sat out in front under the large mesquite tree. The last thing he wanted was more change. "Well, it can't be about me working here fulltime. I think everyone already knows that." Cole wouldn't hire him then sell the place, would he? Despite the pleasant smell of the almost done steaks, his appetite disappeared.

Garrett squeezed his shoulder. "And glad we are of that. Just the other day Riley was telling me Cole needed to hire you. I guess he finally noticed the need."

Wyatt didn't explain the situation. He hadn't asked for a job since he'd become a grocery store bagger when he was fifteen. He'd been desperate to get a break from raising his two sisters, and it forced his mom to stay home a few more nights…mostly.

Though asking to work at Last Chance had come when he was in a far more desperate situation, he hadn't felt like a beggar like he had at the grocery store. "Hand me that platter?"

Garrett walked to the picnic table not far from where they stood in the backyard. It was the heat of the day, but he had stepped out to help. He brought the platter and held it as Wyatt pulled the steaks off the grill and piled them on.

When Wyatt had all but the last two steaks on the pile, he pointed to the house with the tongs. "You can bring those in if you want."

Garrett shook his head. "They won't get cold in this heat. I'll wait until you're done."

Wyatt grinned. "Is it Dr. Jenna's wedding plans that sent you out here or Logan's latest story about Charlotte's amazing intelligence?"

"Both." Garrett laughed. "It's nice that the Benson's consider us part of the family, but weddings and babies aren't what Riley and I are about, at least not yet."

"Really? Then where's Riley?"

"She bailed on me." He took a sip of his beer. "She and Whisper went out to the barn to check on Kentucky, though I'm pretty sure they were escaping as well."

Wyatt laughed. He couldn't help but wonder where Alyssa would be if she were with him. Would she escape to the barn or stay inside to listen to wedding plans and babies? He'd like to think she'd hang outside with him, but he couldn't be sure. He definitely wanted to find out.

Everyone at Last Chance had a significant other or wife. He found himself thinking about that kind of future for the first time in his life. At High Mountain, he'd never thought beyond the next weekend, perfectly happy in his present. He didn't plan on making that mistake again. *No mistake is a waste of time as long as you learn from it.* He grinned. Gramps had a lesson for everything.

He stabbed one of the last two steaks. "Well, there's no delaying things now. These are done."

Garrett picked up the plate again and brought it over. "Good thing. If these didn't smell so good, I'd stay outside."

"No, you wouldn't." He dropped the steak on the pile and speared the last one. "Riley would have your head if you didn't come in."

"True that." Garrett motioned with his head toward the picnic table. "Can you grab my beer. I'll carry these in."

"Sure." He grabbed the beer bottle and followed Garrett inside.

As they entered the large kitchen, they found everyone gathered there. The noise increased tenfold when clapping ensued. Garrett set the platter on the counter which served as a buffet during family dinners. Despite the kitchen's size, some of them would move to the living room to eat.

"Finally, I'm starving." Trace picked up a plate from the counter.

His wife Whisper followed suit. "So am I."

As everyone else helped themselves to the food, Wyatt stood back. This tradition of once-a-week dinners reminded him of the monthly cookouts they had at High Mountain Ranch. The hands would bring their families, and it would be a celebration of sorts or as his Gramps called it, *a celebration for no reason.*

"I thought you don't drink." The soft voice at his side had him turning to look down at Annette.

"I don't. Garrett asked me to bring it in for him."

"Why don't you drink?"

He shrugged. "Just don't." He wasn't willing to go into it.

She gave him the side eye. "For such a simple man, I think your convictions run deep."

Before he could reply, she strode to her vacant seat at the table where a full plate awaited her as if she were queen of her castle, which she was. Her husband, Ed, smiled warmly at her.

Wyatt liked to think his convictions were set in stone even if he hadn't obtained many of them until his grandfather took him in. *Idle hands run amok* was one that had been driven into him the first year he arrived. Though he'd fought it, every step of the way, he'd learned to work hard, study hard, and take pride in what he'd accomplished. He firmly believed Gramps saved his life.

The pain of loss rose in his chest, and he forced himself to move to the counter to fill a plate now that everyone else had taken their fill, or rather their first helpings. He moved into the living room to find Uncle Joey seated next to Whisper and Trace. He'd met Uncle Joey when they had arrived. The older man had suffered a serious stroke or two and was wheelchair bound, barely able to communicate, but he still heard and understood everything.

Uncle Joey gave him a lopsided smile as he sat across from him.

He smiled back with a quick nod before digging into his steak. The knife fairly floated through the meat, but as his dish was nudged, a piece flew to the floor, only to be gobbled down within the same second by Butterball, Dr. Jenna's bulldog.

The laughter from Uncle Joey erased his irritation.

"Butterball, go back to your mama. Now." Whisper pointed to the other room and damn if that roly-poly canine didn't give her a smug look before waddling back to the kitchen. She turned to Uncle Joey. "You could have warned Wyatt."

Uncle Joey shook his head and grinned, obviously having enjoyed the dog's ingenuity.

"I think I can spare one piece of meat." He looked Uncle Joey in the eye. "Only one, mind you." Then he winked to let the man know he appreciated the dog's cunning.

Whisper stabbed a piece of steak and plopped it in her uncle's mouth, to keep him occupied.

Her husband, Trace, looked expectantly at Wyatt. "I heard you are full-time now. Is that why I didn't get a frantic call from Cole this week?"

He finished chewing. "Probably. After helping Riley, I have a pretty good idea of how things are run, but I'm sure there will be more to learn. If you have any suggestions or advice, I'm open to it."

Trace gave him an odd look. "You are? I thought you were the ultra-organized one who wanted horses taken care of in an exact way? Don't get me wrong, this place could definitely use some of that. I'm just surprised by your question."

He felt heat rise in his face. "I did get overly specific about Guinness, Blaze, and Lady, but to be honest, I knew very little about this place and as the last of my grandfather's horses, I wanted to be sure they would be well cared for."

Trace opened his mouth, but Whisper elbowed him. "He lost his grandfather. What do you expect?"

As if that made all the sense in the world, Trace nodded. "Then I suggest you involve Cole as little as possible. He loves this place more than anyone, but he has too much on his plate. If you have an idea, just go with it, unless it costs a lot of money, then go to Lacey and get approval."

He raised an eyebrow at that. It definitely wasn't the advice he'd expected. "So, if I want to fence in the valley to give some of the horses more space, I should just go to Lacey?"

"Yes."

He stared at Trace. "What about Annette?"

"What about her? She doesn't get involved in the rescue ranch. To be honest, her focus has been on Ed and Charlotte."

Charlotte was Logan and Dr. Jenna's little girl and Annette's great-granddaughter. He knew Charlotte before he ever met her because of all Annette had told him. Still, he'd feel more comfortable telling her at least his plans before he implemented them.

He went back to his meal as the ideas that had been buzzing around in his head for the ranch began to find fertile ground. He was anxious to get up to his room and his computer to put together a plan.

Just as he was finishing, everyone started to pile into the living room. Cole stood in front of the large window that looked out onto the porch and down the road. Lacey sat in a large recliner next to him.

Though they barely all fit, it still felt comfortable, even to him. They were all part of Last Chance in some way, and he was counted among them. Some of the tightness around his chest eased. He hadn't been looking for a home. He hadn't been looking for anything. He'd been stuck in time after his grandfather's death, but sitting here, he could start to think about tomorrow and the day after that.

Cole cleared his throat, but the family continued to talk amongst themselves. He cleared his throat, again. "Attention!"

Everyone went silent immediately.

"I'm glad to see my Captain skills work here as well."

People smiled, until little Charlotte held up a rather ragged teddy bear with a cowboy hat on it and yelled "Attension!"

Logan beamed and pulled his three-year-old daughter onto his lap then put his finger to his lips. "Shh." When he set his hand aside, she put her finger on his lips. "Shhhhh."

Quiet chuckles filled the room.

"I'm sorry for the early family dinner this week, but

since Grandma and Grandpa are leaving tomorrow for a long weekend, I had to gather you today."

Riley spoke up. "We already know you hired Wyatt, and we all approve."

"Whole heartedly." Trace lifted his beer in salute.

Cole grinned. "I know. I think I speak for everyone when I say that he is a welcome addition to the Last Chance family."

Everyone lifted their drinks. "Here. Here."

Wyatt swallowed hard, the feelings in his chest new for him. This definitely wasn't the kind of welcome he had to his grandfather's when he'd arrived, or rather been dumped on him. Yet, here he'd technically been dumped on Last Chance, too. As everyone looked at him, he forced himself to speak. "I promise I will do my best."

Annette, who sat next to him on the couch patted his leg. "We know you will."

This time when Cole cleared his throat, everyone looked at him expectantly. "Well, I have spoken at length with Riley, and I would like to put Wyatt in charge."

"What?" He was so surprised, he couldn't keep his reaction to himself. "I've barely worked here a week."

Riley spoke. "But you've been here longer and know horses. Cole doesn't have time and with me here only three days a week, it makes sense that you take charge." She lowered her brows. "But if you start slacking, I promise you, I'll kick your butt back into gear."

Still in shock, he nodded. "Yes, Ma'am."

That caused more chuckles.

"Our next bit of news comes from Grandma." Cole held his hand out to indicate Annette. "Grandma?"

"Well, actually, it's our news." She reached over and took Ed's hand. "We're moving out."

Immediately everyone spoke at once. Questions about when, where, and why flew around Wyatt, but all he could feel was a now familiar sense of loss.

Annette held up her free hand. "Be quiet and let me speak."

Everyone clamped their mouths shut. "First, we aren't going far." She looked at Ed and smiled before facing everyone. "We've decided to build a small one floor casita on the property. As to when, we have just decided on our design, so we'll start looking for contractors when we get back from our trip to Vegas."

Wyatt took a deep breath as the feeling of impending loss dissipated.

"But why?" It was the first time Dr. Jenna had spoken since the meeting started.

Annette smiled at her before moving her gaze to Charlotte then to everyone. "If you haven't noticed, we're getting older, and this house is too big to take care of. We want a smaller place where our great granddaughter can visit us, but a place we can still leave to enjoy the activities of our golden years."

The relief in the room was palpable as people commented on the idea. But what would they do with the current house? Since no one seemed concerned about it, he'd ask Annette in private.

Cole finally interrupted the conversation. "If you can bear with me for one more announcement, we can end this meeting before midnight."

Laughter followed and Trace yelled out. "Party pooper."

Cole's smile grew large. "I don't think so, because I'm pretty sure the party is about to start."

That got everyone's attention.

"Lacey, will you do the honors?"

Lacey stood, her pale lavender blouse loose over a deep

purple long skirt that came to the ankle of her white cowboy boots. "Everyone, we're pregnant."

The room broke into cheers and conversation erupted except from the woman sitting next to him. Wyatt looked at Annette. "You knew."

She nodded. "I did. There are some advantages to being the matriarch of the family."

"Congratulations on being a great-grandmother again."

"Thank you. It was about time they started a family. Maybe the others will follow suit as well."

He scanned the room. The happiness and togetherness felt comforting. What would it be like to have a family of his own on this ranch? He had no idea how to be a father and his mother had barely had time to be a parent. His role models were sorely lacking. Just as doubt started to wheedle its way through his thought process, his grandfather's voice floated through. *You gotta trust your instincts, boy.*

His doubt evaporated. He had a great role model. If he could be half as good of a parent as his grandfather was to him, he'd be happy.

"I think that's the first time I've seen you smile all evening." Annette bumped her shoulder to his.

"I guess when I heard there would be announcements, I didn't expect so many good ones. Are you sure about moving out?"

She placed her hand on his arm. "I am. But if you ever want to visit, you know you are always welcome." She leaned in and kissed him on the cheek.

That action did not go unnoticed, and he soon found himself the object of Uncle Joey's wit. By the time the family broke up to leave for their respective homes, his mind was a whirlwind of thoughts, and for the first time in over a month, his heart was at peace.

Chapter Nine

Alyssa couldn't help feeling like a five-year-old. How long had it been since her father had had to drive her somewhere and make arrangements for someone else to bring her home?

She'd hoped by now she would have heard something, but Wyatt had been right. The jerk that hit her was denying he was at fault despite the police report. She really had to buy a car.

As the two-story house at Last Chance came into view, her stomach tightened. She was excited and nervous, excited to be spending the afternoon with Wyatt, but also nervous about her growing feelings for the man.

"Nice spread." Her father drove the truck under the wooden sign that hung across the entrance to the dirt parking area in front of the house.

She scanned the area looking for Wyatt then checked the time. They were early. What if he was cleaning stalls or out for a ride?

Before she realized what he was about, her father had turned off the truck and opened the door to get out. She grabbed his arm. "Where are you going?"

He shrugged. "We're early. I thought I'd take the time to see the place."

She dropped her hand and kept her groan to herself. That's why he insisted on leaving so early. He wanted to do what he called reconnaissance. He did the same thing to her in high school with her first date.

Jumping out, she closed the truck door and headed for the front steps. The sooner she found Wyatt, the less trouble her father would cause. Opening the screen door, she knocked. Listening, she didn't hear any footsteps. Wyatt might be out back.

Turning, she noticed only one truck besides her dad's. That made sense. He'd said no one else would be home. Looking beyond the vehicles, she was in time to catch her father walking into the barn. "Dad." He was too far to hear, so she didn't bother keeping the whine out of her voice.

Jogging down the steps in her cowboy boots, she strode toward the large structure. She was half way there when she heard a horse chuff. Slowing her stride, she looked over at Meeko. He looked so alone. Her heart melted, but she knew enough from her friends who owned horses that despite his looks, it was best she keep her distance. It didn't keep her from feeling sorry for him though.

Voices inside the barn had her picking up her pace.

"How many do you think you'll hire?" Her dad's voice floated out to her.

"I'm not sure yet. I still need to get a handle on how many horses come in a month and determine which long-term projects I want to put into place for down times." The deeper voice was definitely Wyatt.

She walked past a horse in an outside stall and stepped into the barn then stopped to let her eyes adjust.

"What problem does this one have?" Her father pointed to Cyclone, who she'd met earlier in the week.

She couldn't help answering. "He breaks fences and stall walls if he's not put to work."

Wyatt, who wore a blue checked long sleeve cotton button

down shirt, blue jeans, and his white cowboy hat turned at the sound of her voice and smiled. "That's right. Cyclone is a work horse through and through."

To her surprise, her father reached out and stroked the Clydesdale's neck. "My kind of horse."

Since when had her father stopped hating horses? Puzzled, she walked closer. "He's the one Wyatt uses to pull an old-fashion buckboard type wagon."

Her father stopped touching the horse and pointed to another across the way. "You got a Percheron Cross here?"

Wyatt gave her a quick wink before responding to her father. "Yes. This is Tundra. He's been with me since a foal."

Her father whistled as he looked into the stall. "He's a beauty."

"Thank you. He doesn't break things if he's not worked, but he does get cranky if he isn't ridden regularly."

Her father nodded. "Typical horse."

Having never seen her father around any horse since her mom's death, she felt incredibly uncomfortable, though she wasn't sure why. "Um, dad, aren't you going to be late?"

He looked at his watch. "Yeah, probably will. I guess I'll just have to come back and get the full tour another time."

Wyatt held out his hand. "You're welcome anytime."

Her father shook, then started toward her. "You behave."

"Dad! I'm not a child."

He chuckled. "Take good care of her, Wyatt." And with that, he stepped out of the barn.

Her hands fisted as her cheeks flushed. Her father hadn't embarrassed her like that since, since… she sighed. Since the last man she dated.

Wyatt moved toward her. "He's just looking out for you, which I believe is what a father is supposed to do."

134

Though his words were said to relieve her, she understood the underlying message. He'd had no father to look out for him. His simple statement erased any embarrassment she'd felt. "I know. I just think sometimes he forgets that not only am I a grown woman, but I'm taller than he is." She grimaced.

Wyatt stopped within a foot of her. "I think you're the perfect height."

She didn't have to ask for what because his hand cupped her cheek and his lips brushed hers. The tightness in her stomach broke into tiny sparks of happiness. As he lifted away, she had to keep herself from drawing him back. "Hi."

"Hi." He brushed back a loose strand of hair that had escaped her ponytail. "We need to get you a hat."

She grinned at the odd statement. "Is that a requirement for walking the ranch?"

He shook his head. "No, but I think my girlfriend needs to own a cowboy hat to protect her face from the sun."

Her breath stopped at his words. When she could get her lungs to cooperate, the word came out in a huff. "Girlfriend?"

"Or whatever they call it today. I'd like to see a lot more of you. I'm hoping that you feel the same way about me."

"I do. I mean I'd like that."

His smile grew wide. "Good." He took her hand in his. "Then I'd like to show you my new home, and we can talk about how we can make your students' experience a good one."

She strode out of the barn with him, barely able to focus on his words because she was too busy enjoying his hand in hers.

His first stop was the wagon she'd told her dad about. "I thought with a bunch of hay filling up the bed, we can offer a hay ride. How many students do you have?"

She forced herself to concentrate. "I have twenty-one, but I also invited another class. Will that be okay?"

"Yes. I'll call in Trace, Riley, and Logan to help. We can have different activities and groups of ten can rotate." He paused, deep in thought. "I better invite Whisper, or she'll show up anyway. At least if I invite her and she tells me she won't come, I'll know she's not coming."

"She's the horse whisperer, right?"

He leaned his back against the wagon and pulled her between his legs. "Animal Whisperer. She talks to every animal you can think of, even mountain lions."

She found that a bit difficult to believe, but she wasn't about to argue with him since he'd pulled her against him and kissed her.

Her whole body lit up with excitement from her fingers to her toes to the deepness of her woman's core. The only heat she felt was the fire burning inside her as his hand cupped her butt and pulled her against him.

Then as quickly as it started, he broke the kiss. His hands came up to cup her face. "You make me forget what I'm about."

She quirked her lip. "Were we about something?"

His deep chuckle reverberated through her where they remained touching. "Yes, and if we are to do this right, meaning both your class visit and our relationship, we need to prioritize."

She was all for that, and exploring their relationship was at the top of her list. Unfortunately, he must have decided that her class took priority because he stepped away and took her hand again.

"We can set up Logan with giving rides on one of the horses. Black Jack, the horse by the barn, or Blaze or both." As they approached the corral, he pointed at what looked like an American Quarter horse with a white blaze on his nose. "Logan has a three-year old, so he's good with kids. Do you think the students would like to feed a horse? Or we could put them to work stacking hay or cleaning stalls."

Despite her disappointment, she caught his enthusiasm. "Some of them live on ranches while others have never been to one. I think we should stay away from the mundane chores and focus on what's unique about Last Chance."

He leaned on the fence rail, one foot on the bottom. "What's most unique about this place is the story of the horses. Trace knows them all and would make a great storyteller. I could station him in the barn with a select group of horses and let him tell the stories of the most interesting ones. That would make three activities."

"Then we'll need a fourth one. Is there a history to Last Chance? We've been discussing the beginnings of Arizona in class lately."

"There is an old copper mine on the property, but it caved in and isn't safe to go near. Riley and Garrett were actually in it at the time. They were trapped in there for a couple of days."

"What?" The thought of being buried alive had her shivering despite the heat.

He looked away. "I had just arrived here and there was no one about. I was spent from the funeral and the last-minute details of transporting Tundra and myself, so after feeding the horses that were here, I fell asleep on the couch. It wasn't until the next morning that I decided something was wrong and that someone should have been here to care for the horses by then. I should have called Cole sooner."

She touched his arm. "It sounds like you were exhausted. If you had just arrived, you had no idea how the ranch was run. I assume they are still alive, right?" She dreaded his answer but tended to be an optimist.

"Yeah, they're fine. Garrett tells me he was happy for the

extra time to get to know Riley. She's a veteran and pretty tough, but I guess Garrett got through to her."

She breathed a sigh of relief. "Then it sounds like there's nothing to beat yourself up about."

His gaze snapped to hers. "Gramps used to say that."

"Then your grandfather was a wise man."

"He was." Wyatt's gaze drifted to some time in the past.

She kept her voice low. "He was the father you never had."

He looked at her then. "He was the only person on this Earth that gave two shits about me. His words not mine."

"It appears he gave more than that because you turned out pretty dang good."

He lost his smile. "We still need to figure out another activity for your students."

She wasn't unaware that he had suddenly changed the subject. That was curious. Why would he not want to take credit for the man he'd become? "Well, let's see. Their favorite time of the school day is lunch and recess."

"Lunch? I didn't think about lunch." Wyatt frowned as he started to walk toward the north corral.

Obviously, the man expected to think of everything. He did seem to like organizing and details now that she reflected on it. Falling into step next to him, she waved off his concern. "That's no problem. We can have the students brown bag it, and for those on the meal program, the cafeteria will prepare theirs to pick up that morning."

He nodded but didn't say anything as he came to a stop about ten feet from the corral with Meeko, who stood under the covered shelter today. Wyatt scanned the area as if he looked for something.

"Did you forget something?" She looked around, too, though she wouldn't know what he searched for.

He stopped facing the corral, but his gaze was in the distance.

She followed his line of sight and saw a house to the south in the distance. It really was a big, though somewhat narrow, valley. And he wanted to fence it in?

He turned toward her and smiled. "I know what can be the fourth activity."

Jiminy Cricket, when he graced her with that full-on smile her heart leapt, making it difficult to breathe. "What? Don't leave me hanging."

"You said to highlight what makes Last Chance unique, right?"

"Yes." She could seriously stare into his excited green eyes all day.

He flung his arms wide. "Last Chance is owned by a firefighter."

She wanted to celebrate with him, but she didn't see what that had to do with a student activity. "So that means my students could…"

If anything, his smile widened. "I'll have Cole bring one of the fire trucks and have a couple of firefighters talk to the kids about fire on a ranch. Cyclone has the scars from a fire to prove the point. They could climb on the apparatus, with supervision, of course."

"That's a great idea, but can you get the fire station to agree? And what about all the people you'll need to run the other activities. I don't want you to owe everyone you know here a favor. That wouldn't be fair."

He tipped his hat to her. "Actually, Ma'am. You're looking at the new manager of Last Chance Ranch, so I see no problem arranging everything as long as we have enough lead time."

Her happiness for him exploded. "That's fantastic!

Congratulations!" She gave him a hug, excited for herself too, since he wouldn't want to leave anytime soon with such a good position.

His arms came around her as he hugged her back.

When she lifted her face, he was staring into her eyes. "You are a very caring woman."

She'd always thought so, but no one had ever actually told her that to her face. To be appreciated for that meant a lot. "Thank you. I find it especially easy to care about you."

The vestiges of his smile disappeared as he stroked her cheek with his finger. "I care about you, too."

The imp in her couldn't resist. "I care about you more." She felt him stiffen and wished she hadn't said it. But then his mouth took hers in such a searing, you're-mine kind of kiss that she lost her thoughts all together.

When she was completely out of breath, he broke away.

She swayed at the loss of his support, and he quickly grabbed her arm. "I shouldn't have kept you out here in this heat. We can go inside and discuss the rest of the details."

Details? What details? As her world righted, she found herself trying to remember what they'd been talking about. "I'm fine. I grew up here, remember?" Movement behind him caught her attention. "Look at Meeko. Is he okay?" She couldn't quite keep the worry from her voice, for the gelding had his head over the corral fence and lowered almost to the ground. It made her think of a child crying.

Wyatt looked over his shoulder. "I'll be damned."

"Is he okay?" She tried to walk around him, but he still had her arm.

"Whoa, slow down there." Wyatt kept her from running over, but he did allow her to get a little closer.

It was hard to reconcile this sad looking animal with the mean one that Wyatt claimed he was. "Hey, Meeko. It's okay."

The horse lifted its head and looked at her.

She moved a little closer, careful to stay out of his personal space. "Let me try to pet him. It may be just what he needs, a little human connection?"

Wyatt's face tensed, his jaw line hard, but he finally gave a slight nod. "Move slowly to his side."

She took another step closer and paused, watching for a reaction, but also keeping her eyes mostly lowered to let him know she was no threat. Then she took a step that would bring them within touching distance of each other.

Meeko remained where he was but he chewed as if he'd just eaten something when she knew he hadn't.

Keeping her voice soft, she addressed Wyatt. "I can feel your tension. I'm sure he can, too. Do you think you could relax a little?"

Though he didn't reply, she heard him take a long slow breath and let it out.

She smiled. The man was pretty savvy. Lifting her hand, she held it out for Meeko to accept or reject. "You're a beautiful boy, Meeko. A horse as handsome as you makes people want to pet you. Will you let me?"

Meeko's nose lifted. He sniffed at her, catching her scent.

She remained absolutely still. It was up to him. He was the cranky one. She could wait all day. Though she'd rather spend it getting to know Wyatt better, Meeko's story pulled at her heart. Was that what attracted her to Wyatt?

Finally, Meeko nudged her hand and carefully, she rubbed his nose. He let out a heartfelt sigh and she grinned. "Feels good, doesn't it?"

Not willing to relax her guard too much, she moved to petting his neck in long smooth strokes. When he leaned against her hand, she wanted to jump for joy, but she forced herself to keep her strokes steady.

Wyatt touched her on the shoulder from behind. "It's time to stop. His left rear leg is lifted. He does that when he's about to charge."

Slowly, she pulled her hand away and stepped out of Meeko's space. His left rear leg came down. She looked over her shoulder at Wyatt. "Thank you. You must have watched this horse quite a bit to notice that."

"It doesn't take long to recognize a horse's behavior when you are trying to feed him and he charges at you every time."

At that she turned and faced him. "Every time?"

"Yes." He paused to spare a glance back at Meeko, who walked away from them as if they were uninteresting. "At least until Whisper spoke to him. Now, he allows me about twenty minutes before he decides I need to get out of his territory."

She raised her brows. "I think I have to meet this Whisper."

"I'm sure you will eventually." He took her arm. "Why don't we go inside where it's cooler to finish our planning."

Actually, that sounded perfect, so she let him escort her. "How do you know so much about what third graders would like?" She immediately felt his arm tense beneath her hand. She was already learning his cues.

"It's not third graders in particular, just kids. I had a single mom who worked, and I had two younger sisters."

"Ah, so you ended up watching them when they came home from school until your mom got home from work."

"And after dinner." He opened the door to the house and let her precede him.

She waited in the entry before a staircase with open doorways to her right and left and a long hall in front of her.

"This way." He led her down the hall then took a left into a country kitchen.

"Your mom worked two jobs?" She took a seat at the large table.

He pulled a pad of paper and a pen from a drawer and sat down at the head of the table catty-corner to her. "Not exactly. My mother was always on the hunt for her next man. She seemed uneasy unless she had a man in her life. Usually, after she made dinner, she'd go out. Not every night, but four or five nights, so I put my sisters to bed. If mom didn't come home that night, I'd make sure they had breakfast, packed them a lunch, and got them to the bus stop before I walked to school."

She wasn't oblivious that he avoided looking at her, instead drawing on the pad of paper. "That was a lot of responsibility for you to take on as a young boy."

He shrugged. "I'm not unique." He pointed to a spot on the pad. "I think we should have the firetruck parked here. That way if they have to leave on a call, it's easy access to the exit."

Forced to leave her thoughts about him, she focused on the plan.

Chapter Ten

Wyatt set the pen down on the table and leaned back. "I think we've thought of everything. Anything that comes up unexpectedly, we should be able to handle, even injuries." It was another reason he liked the idea of a fire truck on site with trained people.

Alyssa widened her eyes. "I don't think anything could come up that you haven't already thought of. You are very thorough."

That was his Gramps. He never left anything to chance. "I like everything accounted for. It keeps things running smoothly."

She relaxed back into her chair. "I'm very excited for this field trip now. I just hope none of my parent chaperones are afraid of horses."

That didn't make sense. "Why would they volunteer to go on a field trip to a ranch if they're afraid of horses?"

Alyssa groaned. "You'd think they wouldn't, but I have some overly protective parents who can't bear to have their child go on a field trip without them. One year, we went to the Desert Botanical Gardens, and I had a parent who was allergic to just about every plant there. She had to be taken away in an ambulance because her airway closed up."

He shook his head at the stupidity of the woman.

"But that was nothing compared to the father who just had

to come with his son to the Old West Living History Museum. He was in the carpenter shop with some of the boys and decided he knew how to use one of the old tools. He took it off the display and ended up with it through his foot."

"It sounds like you need chaperones for your chaperones."

She blew out her cheeks and rolled her eyes before releasing her air to speak. "I know."

He sat forward and picked up the pen again. "I'll be sure to let my staff know to pay attention to both the kids and the parents." He wrote a note on the line next to staff meeting, then put down the pen. At the thought of watching parents, it reminded him that her father had come out to the barn when they arrived. "I was surprised to see your dad pat the horses."

"I was too. As far as I know, he hasn't been around one in years."

Though they spoke about her father, his interest was on her. The only way he'd been able to get anything written down was to not look at her. She was beautiful when she wore a dress, but it made him feel like there was a wall around her that he shouldn't cross. But today, in her jeans and purple tank top, she seemed more than approachable. She was downright touchable, and it had taken a lot of restraint on his part not to touch her more than he had.

Her brows knit and she folded her arms. "Losing mom so unexpectedly had devastated him." She lifted her gaze to him. "He had to make the decision to let her go. He only let me see her once after the accident. She was hooked up to machines. It scared me back then. I didn't really understand what he had to do until I was a teenager." Her voice lowered. "But even as a child, I could feel his anguish. A couple days later, I overheard him tell one of his friends that if it wasn't for me, he'd just give up on life."

His heart constricted at the vision of a little girl seeing her mom in a hospital bed and hiding behind the doorway listening to such an adult conversation. "That must have scared you."

"Oh, it did. I determined right then and there that I would be grateful that I still had my dad in my life every day." She smirked. "I was even on my best behavior for a good eleven days."

"You did a lot better than I've done, and I'm an adult."

She dropped her arms and reached across the table to grasp his hand. "Your reactions were as legitimate as mine. There's no one way to deal with grief. We all have to come to terms with our loss in our own way." She squeezed. "How many days has it been since you pissed someone off?"

He chuckled. "I'm sure it's been at least five."

She grinned. "See, you're coping."

No, she was wrong. "Actually, I'm better than coping." He removed his hand from hers and rubbed the back of his neck. "When Gramps died, it was much like your mom, sudden and unexpected. He had always talked about me taking over the ranch when he passed. I was prepared to do so, but he never got around to changing his will."

"No wonder you've been biting everyone's head off. You're like a Gila Monster whose burrow with her eggs has just been crushed by a bulldozer."

She'd just nailed exactly how he'd been feeling. "Been" being the operative word. He took her hand where it lay on the table. "But things have changed in the last couple of weeks. For the better."

"I'm glad." Her light brown eyes darkened.

He pulled her hand toward him as he leaned in to kiss her. Without words, he needed her to know that she was the reason.

As he set his lips to hers, her mouth opened, allowing his

tongue entrance. His heart filled at her acceptance of him even as his body reacted to their kiss.

Letting go of her hand, he cradled her cheek, enjoying the taste of her, wanting so much more from her. When her hand grasped his hair, he felt his jeans grow tighter. Damn, he wanted this woman, heart, body, and soul.

But even as she moaned into his mouth, doubt crept in. He was no more than a cowboy with a tainted past. And she was everything good, real, successful, and happy. Despite the need growing inside him, he gently broke their connection.

She blinked a few times as her eyes opened, her mouth still slightly open, tempting him to take her upstairs to his room and make love to her. But that wouldn't be enough. It may have been with the other women he'd dated, but they were different. Alyssa was…more.

Color rose in her cheeks. "I guess you can tell I like you."

His heart stuttered at her words, his hope and fear colliding. He had to remember she didn't know everything about him yet. "I like you, too." Hell, he sounded like a nine-year-old. "You are the most special woman I've ever met. I want to know all about you."

She chuckled uneasily. "There's not much to tell. I'm afraid if I let you know everything, you'll soon grow bored."

He shook his head. "Never."

Looking away, her eyes suddenly widened. "Well, fudge. It's past four. I still have a ton of stuff to do before Marty picks me up."

Fudge? He couldn't help smiling at the word. It made sense since she taught elementary school. "If you like, I can bring you home now."

She sighed. "I wish I could stay longer, but Marty insists on going to the Black Mustang whenever the karaoke man is there.

Her husband despises karaoke, so I get to fill in." Her eyes lit with sudden interest. "Do you sing?"

"Only to horses." He rose. He didn't want to delay her. *Punctuality keeps everyone on the straight and narrow.* He smirked as his grandfather's voice floated through his head.

She stood. "Horses? Oh, you are going to have to tell me that story. No, let me guess, you sing off key, and they are the only ones who will put up with you."

He motioned for her to precede him, opening the door before answering. "It's more like a cowboy's gotta do what a cowboy's gotta do."

She jogged down the front steps and turned to face him. "You do know that makes no sense in the context of our conversation, right?"

He laughed, the fun of keeping her guessing too great to hold inside. "Maybe and maybe not."

She shook her head but smiled as she grabbed his arm and they walked to his truck. "I'm going to find out eventually, you know. Just like I tell my students, you can't hide anything from me forever."

He almost missed a step at her words but managed to open the passenger door and help her inside.

Walking around the front of the truck to his door, he tamped down the panic she'd conjured with her chiding. If he really did want a relationship with this woman, he was going to have to let her know everything eventually.

Steeling his resolve to be honest with her always, he hopped in and started the vehicle. "You'll have to tell me where we're headed."

"To Canterbury, of course."

Her smile was contagious and he returned it, relaxing back into the comfortableness of their conversation as he drove down the road.

148

"I'm sorry you have to drive me. I've started looking for a new car. You were right. It was totaled. I'm trying to find a reasonably priced used car since I'll have no insurance money to help with it yet."

He didn't like the sound of that. "You should get some for your injuries."

She waved her hand. "Yes, but who knows how long that will take. Like you said, the jerk is fighting the process every step of the way. In the meantime, I need a car. Unfortunately, paying for it is going to come out of my savings, which was for a house."

He remembered her crying about that. It was very important to her. "But you are alone."

He glanced at her to find her giving him a hard stare. "So? I'm perfectly capable of affording a house on my income. The monthly mortgage payment will be cheaper than my rent. It's just the down payment that's hard to come up with."

"I didn't mean any offense. I just never thought about buying a house unless I married, and since Gramps was giving me the ranch, it hadn't occurred to me."

She patted his thigh. "Considering your life expectations, I can forgive you."

He glanced at her to see if she was sarcastic, but her smile was genuine. "I'm guessing you planned to buy a house soon then."

"Next month. I have the down payment, or should I say, I *had* the down payment."

He stopped at a red light. Her shoulders were slumped forward, and she stared at her hands clasped in her lap now.

He covered her hands with his hand. "It's not forever. If you had the willpower to save enough money for a down payment, I have no doubt you can replace what you need to buy a car."

149

She looked at him. "I can, but it would take less time if I moved in with my dad and saved the money I spend on rent." She pointed. "It's green."

He put his focus back on the road. "Where do I go from here?"

"Go past the school two miles then take a left on Ridge Road. We'll come to a tan apartment complex on the right."

"Got it. Does that mean you're going to move in with your dad?"

She sighed. "I don't know. He wants me to. Actually, he never wanted me to move out in the first place. But…"

"But what?" He didn't understand her dilemma. Roy seemed like a great guy and a very caring father. He also appeared to be a lot less strict than Gramps had been.

"It's just that since mom died, my dad focused his life on me. I had to move out for both of us. He needed his own life, and I needed to be able to make my own decisions without his input. Living in my apartment enables that. This way when I want his opinion on something I can bring it up when I see him on Sunday mornings. And if I don't, I keep it to myself."

He was starting to understand. "Then you're afraid if you move back in with him that it will change the way he treats you?"

"Oh, I know it will change the way he treats me. I don't know if you've noticed, but I'm a woman. It would be different if I were his son. Fathers treat sons differently."

Or not at all. He shoved the thought away. He didn't care that his father only popped into his life every few years. The man was worse than not having a father around. "I think I see what you mean. But if it's only for a short time, do you really think it will hurt your relationship?"

"I don't know. He's being forced to retire in the next four months, and he doesn't know what he wants to do. I'm afraid

I might become his next big project. And how long I stay with him is all about how much I pay for a new car."

The apartment complex loomed large on the right, and he turned in. "Where to?"

She pointed to the left. "That building over there. I live on the second floor, in apartment 2106. You can park in any of the open spaces."

He parked in front, then walked around to open her door.

"Thank you." She climbed out.

He looked up at the building. "It looks like a cube."

"Not you, too?"

"What? You think so, too?" He fell into step beside her. He needed to be sure she was safely home before he'd feel comfortable leaving.

"No, my dad calls my apartment a cube. Though to be fair, he calls any building besides his house, a cube." She smirked. "Though I do admit, that was my first impression when I saw it."

He liked that she was so comfortable with herself. He liked a lot about her. In fact, he hadn't found anything he didn't like about her and that was unusual for him.

They climbed the outside stairs together. At the top, she turned right and unlocked the only door on that side. Opening it, she stepped inside then faced him. "Thank you for dropping me off and for an exciting afternoon."

He leaned his hand on the doorframe, not wanting to leave her, yet knowing it was time. "You're the one that made it exciting."

Though color rose in her cheeks, she didn't look away. "I think we make a great team."

He wanted them to be more than a team. "If there is anything else you think of, you can give me a call."

She patted her phone. "I've got your number right here and now you have mine, so there's no excuse not to call me." Leaning in, she placed her hand on his chest and raised up to kiss him.

He lowered his head to meet her halfway. Her soft lips pressed to his in a chaste kiss, but chaste wasn't what he wanted her to remember. Wrapping his hand around her neck, he pulled her closer.

She didn't pull away. Instead, she wrapped both arms around his back and opened her mouth to push her tongue between his lips.

The ignition was instant. Letting go of the doorframe, he used his arm to pull her against him. She tasted so good, felt so good, fitting him like she was made for him.

Her hand moved lower, and she grasped his ass, spiking his excitement. That her passion for him matched his own, made staying in control that much harder, but he didn't want to take her to bed until she was fully aware of everything he was.

Barely able to keep from grinding his growing erection against her, he spun them around and pinned her against the inside wall of her apartment. He realized his mistake as his shirt was pulled from the back of his jeans and her hand slipped inside to cup his ass directly.

Alyssa let out a half groan, half moan and pressed her hips hard against his cock.

Shit. *Don't start something you can't finish, boy.* His grandfather's words floated through the blood pounding in his ears. They had to stop, but her floral scent filled his nostrils, her soft body pressed against him with need, and he wasn't made of steel.

He ran his hand up her side, lifting his chest away to give himself access to her breast. He cupped the full globe and gently squeezed. *Keep the end in mind. Rushing in without forethought spells disaster. Rashness begets remorse.* His grandfather's phrases beat against his growing lust.

He should stop.

Alyssa's mouth left his lips as she tilted her head to the side, drawing in quick breaths. She arched into his hand as much as her position would allow.

Planning saves having to clean-up a mess. Only move forward when you've determined the risks. The call of Alyssa's soft skin was far stronger than the words in his head, and he unbuttoned two buttons to slip his hand inside her shirt. With nothing but his need guiding him, he hooked the cup of her bra with his finger and pulled it down to expose the beauty that was her.

Pulling his hips back, he forced her to let go of him, but his chest filled with warmth as he lowered his head to lick the tight peak surrounded by the puckered pink areola before him. *When you have a goal, boy, don't let anything stop you from achieving it. No hurdle is too high if you want something bad enough.*

"Yesss." Alyssa's whisper validated the words in his head.

With his mind and craving in sync, he took the rigid nipple in his mouth and sucked.

"Oooh." Alyssa's sounds of pleasure made his heart swell.

He wanted to give her everything she desired. He bit lightly before rolling her sweet nub between his teeth.

"Oh, Wyatt." Her hand left his waist and came up between them.

He lifted his head to find her unbuttoning more of her shirt.

The open doorway cooled his ardor like an air-conditioner. How could he have let her be exposed to anyone out there? Quickly, he moved around her to shut it.

When he turned back, her shirt was off and she reached

behind her to unclasp her bra. He couldn't move, couldn't breathe as he waited to see all of her.

Movement on the couch behind her startled him. Glancing to the large piece of furniture, he froze.

Every nightmare he'd ever had flashed through his mind in seconds, and he stepped back, his only thought to get away. Spinning around, he grabbed the door and raced out, closing it hard behind him.

He leaned against the outside wall, closed his eyes, and tried to breathe but the panic, fear, and past seemed to tornado through his chest like a stampede of cattle.

He heard the door open. "Wyatt?"

At the concern in her voice, he tried to open his eyes, but it was no use.

The door closed again, causing his panic to rise.

He'd lost her.

She didn't want a broken man.

He pressed his fist against his chest as if that could help him breathe, but it didn't. A whoosh sounded in his ears as dizziness filled his head and bright sparks of light floated beneath his eyelids.

"Breathe slowly." Alyssa's voice next to him refocused his attention. Her hand covered his on his chest, and he grasped it like a life line.

"In…and out. In…and out."

To his surprise, his breathing started to match her words.

"Good. You're doing good. Keep going. In…and out. That's it."

He wasn't sure if it was her words or just the fact she came back outside, but eventually he felt his chest expanding and his lungs filling fully. Tentatively, he opened his eyes.

Concern radiated from her face. "Do you have these often?"

"What?" Happy that the single word didn't steal his breath, his body relaxed even more.

She'd put her shirt back on but she still looked well kissed. "Panic attacks?"

He frowned. "I don't have panic attacks."

She cocked her head to the side. "Okay, then have you had this happen to you before?"

"No. I've never..." Or had he? Memories returned of waking up in the holding cell as a teenager, waking up the night his grandfather locked him in the shed, and the night after finding out Gramps hadn't changed his will. It never occurred to him it could be a panic attack. That had to be a regular thing, didn't it? "I think this has happened three times before. Twice while a teenager and once about a month ago, but always when I was asleep."

She peeled his fingers back from her hand, the imprints leaving a mark. "Do you know what triggers them? That was pretty violent. I thought you were going to pass out on me."

He took her hand in both of his and lightly rubbed it. "I'm sorry." Here she was, trying to help him, and he'd practically cut off her circulation.

He tried to think of what his last three instances had in common. All he remembered were the stupid rabbit nightmares. He didn't want to admit that to her. "I've never had one while awake. This was a hallucination. I thought I saw a rabbit in your apartment."

She grinned at that. "You did. That's Snowdrop, my pet."

He dropped her hand and scowled. "You have a white rabbit for a pet?" Irrationally, he felt as if she'd betrayed him.

Her grin disappeared. "I do. Why? Is that a problem? Rabbits are prey not predator. Are you afraid of rabbits?"

"No." He turned away. Only giant white male rabbits from

"Alice in Wonderland" that put him through hell. Fuck. He rubbed the back of his neck. How could he explain that? How could she have a pet rabbit? "Is your rabbit a female?" Maybe he could get beyond this thing with that tiny detail.

"No, he's a male." She touched his arm, but he didn't look at her. "Wyatt, talk to me."

If the door of opportunity is open, you walk in, boy, not slam it shut. He closed his eyes at his grandfather's voice. It had been one of the few times the old man had been disappointed in him as an adult. As a teenager, he'd always disappointed him, but not as an adult.

Every nerve was geared for flight mode, but his grandfather shaking his head at him when he'd turned down an opportunity to spend two weeks on a ranch in Hawaii had him standing his ground. "It's a nightmare."

When she didn't say anything, he finally looked at her. It was all there in her face, her concern, her caring, her wanting to help. He wanted all that from her and more, but she had to know. *Partial truths will come back to kick you in the ass.* Damn, the old man was getting aggravating…just like when he was alive.

Taking a deep breath, he leaned his back against the wall again. "I've never told anyone." He hadn't even told his grandfather what his nightmares were about, just that he had them. Gramps said his nightmares were his conscience getting back at him. But he needed to tell her. She needed to know how important she was. "I'm not afraid of rabbits." Fuck, this was harder than being locked in his grandfather's shed for twenty-four hours after running away the first and only time.

"Is it white male rabbits?"

He widened his eyes at her guess. "It's one particular white rabbit."

~~*~~

Alyssa's heart still hammered in her chest, but she forced herself to remain calm. She'd never seen a grown man have a panic attack. Her training at the school in helping students navigate anxiety had worked, but she was still shaken to see such a strong man fight to breathe.

She really thought he'd leave and she'd never see him again. Male egos were so fragile that for her to have witnessed him in that state, she wouldn't be surprised if he didn't want to talk to her again.

But he hadn't left. He'd stayed. Hope filled her. She recognized how hard it was for him. And now he would tell her something he'd never told anyone else. That had to mean his feelings were as strong for her as hers were for him. "From childhood?"

He shook his head. "No, I was almost sixteen." His gaze left hers as he remembered. "My mother's favorite book was 'Alice in Wonderland.' I always thought it had to do with her name being Alice. She read it to my sisters, and it soon became their favorite." His gaze returned to her. "I didn't get it. It made no sense and was just weird."

She vaguely remembered reading the story. "From what I remember, I agree. Ah, it's *that* white rabbit?"

He looked away again but nodded. He didn't say anything for a long time. It made her nervous, but she kept her mouth shut. If he was doing her the honor of telling her about some teenage trauma, she needed to listen.

"Of course, the more I said I thought it was stupid, the more my sisters wanted it read to them at bedtime. It had gotten to the point where I could practically recite it verbatim." He paused, working his jaw as if he didn't know how to continue.

Maybe she could help. "That had to be frustrating."

"It was just one more frustration on top of another. I was a teenager, and I started to want my own life, not one saddled with taking care of my mother's children. I got a job bagging groceries to earn some cash. My mother wasn't happy, but I refused to quit, so she told me I had to pay rent. It seemed unfair." He snorted. "What did I know?"

She wanted to say she understood because she knew what being a teenager was like, but she didn't have nearly as much to deal with as he had.

"One afternoon, I was hanging with some friends who were equally discontent with their homelife. One of them knew a guy who knew a guy who could make all our troubles go away." Wyatt swallowed hard.

There was such self-loathing in his face, she wanted to hold him and tell him it would never be like that again, but he wasn't a third grader. He was an adult and his anger was directed inward.

He looked her in the eye. "It was oxycodone."

She opened her mouth, but didn't know what to say. That was the last thing she'd expected. "Did you become addicted?" Well, that was really blunt.

"I was arrested."

Her mind spun. Something was missing here. "And the rabbit? You said you always woke not being able to breathe. Did your mind process the story differently in your dreams?"

"Nightmares." He pushed away from the wall and walked to the top of the stairs as if he was ready to leave.

Her heart rose into her throat. She didn't want him to go. She wanted to know everything. "If you want, we can talk about this inside."

He faced her then, but her relief was short lived. "Inside? With your rabbit?"

158

Fudge. "I can put him in my bedroom. Then if you feel up to it, maybe you could meet him."

His lip curled up. "Like face my fear and all that."

She tried not to be offended. Instead, she shrugged. "I'm just guessing here."

He looked toward her door then shook his head. "No, I better go. You said you have things to do, and your friend will be arriving."

"Nothing is more important than what is obviously something very disturbing for you."

He finally moved his gaze back to her.

For a moment, she thought he might stay, but then he shook his head.

"No, it's not important. I'm fine now." Then he tipped his hat and turned, jogging down the stairs.

She walked to the railing to watch him leave, but he never looked back. What the hell had happened to him? More importantly, what scared him so much he couldn't breathe? She didn't believe for one moment it was the white rabbit from a children's story. Whatever that rabbit morphed into in his nightmares had to be his fear.

Walking back to her apartment, she wished she could talk to someone about it, but there was no way she'd tell Marty. This was too important.

"Dad." Letting herself in, she closed the door and locked it. Her dad would keep it between them, and he may have some insight into how to get Wyatt to talk about it. Luckily, her father would be picking her up for Sunday breakfast in the morning. Unluckily, she would be facing more pressure to move back home.

Snowdrop hopped from the top of her couch onto the seat and looked at her. She sat down and scooped him up onto her lap. "Snowdrop, you males are so complicated."

He buried his nose against her stomach, and she smiled. "Well, the human versions are, anyway."

Chapter Eleven

"Dad, you sit. Let me do the dishes." Alyssa rose to take the dishes to the sink.

Her father held onto his dish, not letting her take it. "Sit? I don't want to sit. I need to do things."

The tone clued her in that he was alluding to his impending retirement again. He always went back to that when he was irritated. And he was definitely irritated with her for refusing to make a decision yet about whether to move in again or not. "Then why don't you take a look at those used car specs I printed out. I have five different cars I'm thinking about."

He shook his head even as he brought his plate to the sink and stubbornly started to rinse it. "What do I know about cars. I'm not a mechanic."

She closed her eyes and counted to ten. What was with the males in her life? Was there a full moon on the rise? She opened her eyes again and brought her dish to the sink. Her father grabbed it and started rinsing.

Was she missing something? His movements were far jerkier than normal. "Dad, what's wrong?"

"Nothing." The word came out on a growl.

Ah, she was right. Something else was going on. She leaned against the counter next to the fridge and waited.

He finished loading the dishwasher then washed out the sink. After washing his hands, he dried them and turned. His gaze met hers. "What?"

She shrugged. "You tell me."

He threw his hands up. "There's nothing to tell." He strode into the living room.

She followed, close on his heels. "Obviously, something is up."

He continued out of the living room and down the hall to his room. "What are you, my shadow."

"Yup."

He looked over his shoulder and scowled at her before ducking into his room and closing the door in her face.

She grinned. This was something big. He only closed her out of his room when something was seriously bugging him. She leaned one shoulder against the door. "So what is it? Work? The guys? The gals?" It was her go-to question whenever he wouldn't talk. He knew it was coming.

Grumbling came through the door.

Listening, she heard his closet door shut. Was he getting dressed? He hadn't said anything about going out. Her curiosity was starting to get the best of her. She was about to ask another question when the closet door opened again…and shut again. "Dad, do you need help?"

The door opened so fast, she barely kept herself from falling into his room and into him.

"What the hell do you wear to a charity dinner?"

Charity dinner? Her father was going to a charity dinner? "Um, that depends on where it's being held. If it's at the Old West Town, I'd suggest western, but if it's at The Grande in Scottsdale, you'll definitely want to wear a suit."

"It's the Biltmore."

If she could whistle, it would have come out instantly, but she'd never learned how. Not that he hadn't tried to teach her. "If it's a dinner at the Biltmore, it's probably a tux."

"I don't own no damn tux."

Her heart went out to him. "I'm sure a nice suit will be fine. Who invited you to a charity dinner at the Biltmore?"

He turned away, mumbling.

"What?"

"I said, Ms. Davis." It wasn't much above a grumble, but she heard it clearly.

Stunned, she didn't know what to say. "You mean you're going on a date?" Her father hadn't dated a single woman since she was nine years old, or rather none that she knew of.

At that, he finally faced her. "Not a real date. It's just the company buying a few tables at this charity thing, and she was in charge of filling them. I'm only doing her a favor." He looked at her hopefully. "But if you don't want me to go, I can cancel."

At the thought that he would cancel a night out because of her, she quickly responded. "No, not at all. I want you to go."

"You do?"

Did she? Fudge, she'd never thought about her father dating. All these years, twenty-one to be exact, and he'd put her first, always, even now. More confident, she nodded. "I do. Now let's see what fits."

His eyes widened. "Fits?"

She barely kept herself from rolling her eyes. "Yes, fits. If I'm not mistaken, it's been years since you wore a suit. Do you remember the last time?"

His brows knit together then he shrugged. "What's that got to do with my suit?"

She moved to his closet, on a mission now. They may need to go shopping. "Let's just see what you have." He had a nice size walk-in closet but still only used half of it. It saddened her to know her dad had kept to the course for her all these years. No wonder he wanted her to move in. The house was far too large for just him.

Feeling unflatteringly selfish, she moved to the far end of the closet where he kept his nicer clothes. He followed her in.

Three suits hung in the last section. Pulling one out, she held it up. "First, let's see if this is even in style." Turning it around, she determined it to be nondescript enough to not be considered outdated. "Here, hold this."

He did, and she pulled out the next one, which also got handed to him. Then she pulled out the last one.

"No."

She looked at her father. "I haven't even checked it out yet."

"I don't care. I'm not wearing that suit ever again."

She peered at it under the closet light. "Why?" She looked back but he had walked out of the closet. She didn't remember him wearing the black suit before, but he had a number of business engagements that she had not been privy to over the decades. Hanging it back up, she heard a crinkle in the pocket.

Shaking her head, she reached her hand in. It was so like her father to leave a few dollars in a pocket. She grasped what felt like a business card and pulled out the prayer card from her mother's funeral.

She swallowed hard against the emotion that rose in her chest as she looked toward the bedroom. As a child, she'd been consumed by the loss of her mother, and only after hearing she was the only reason her father was still with her, had she pushed that aside for him. But she'd never considered what he'd gone through those days after he'd agreed to let the doctors stop all life support.

It made sense that he didn't want to wear the suit, but why did he keep it?

Taking a deep breath, she took control of her emotions and walked into the bedroom to see her father wearing one of the suit coats with his t-shirt.

"What do you think? I don't have to button it. If I leave it open, no one will know it's too small, right?"

She bit her lip to keep from smiling. "Did you try the other one?"

He shook his head. "I like this brown color better than the blue."

She wasn't going to tell him that no one would care what color his suit was if he wore that one because it was clearly far too small. He'd always been in shape until a few years ago and then suddenly he'd begun to develop a belly. He wore his jeans under that belly, holding them up with a belt. "I think you should try the other one first. The fit is really what makes the man."

"You think?"

She nodded as he shucked off the suit coat and pulled the other from the hanger. She moved closer and helped him on with it.

"See, I can't close this one either." He tried to pull the sides together while arching his back.

"Dad, stand up straight and stop that."

He grumbled like a little boy as she checked to see if the two sides would meet. Buttoning it, she stepped back. The button held, but it pulled on the sides. "From what I see, you have two options. Wear this suit, but don't button it." She stepped forward and unbuttoned it then stepped back again. "Or go shopping. When is the dinner?"

"Tonight."

"And you didn't say anything?" Her voice rose of its own accord. She was very surprised and just a little bit hurt.

He strolled into the walk-in closet to look at himself in the full-length mirror. "There was nothing to say. It's just a charity thing for work. Besides..." He stopped looking at himself and turned his head toward her. "Your date is so much more interesting."

She slumped against the closet door jam. "*Was* interesting. I'm not sure anymore."

He immediately walked to her. "What do you mean? He didn't dump you, did he? I'll set him straight if he did."

She backed away and sat on his bed. "No. At least I don't think so."

Her father shrugged out of the suit coat and hung it on his door on top of the pants. "Then what's wrong?"

She clasped her hands and looked down at them, still having trouble reconciling her strong feelings for the man with their last encounter. "Maybe you can tell me. I'm pretty sure it's a male ego thing."

"Wyatt? That man doesn't seem to have an ego. He's all polite and attentive. A real cowboy."

She nodded. "All that's true, but he's a male nonetheless."

Her dad sat next to her and put his hand over both of hers. "Tell me what happened. You know I'm always good at the male point of view."

He said it with so much pride that she found her lips lifting into a half smile. "That's true. You do have a very keen insight on the male psyche."

"Why, thank you." He pulled out his t-shirt collar with his index finger and lifted his chin as if he were some great scientist.

She gave him a full smile, feeling lucky she had such an amazing dad. "We have to keep it between us for—"

"Let me guess, his ego. I'm not the town gossip. What's up?"

She went ahead and related the whole episode with Wyatt, leaving out what they were doing before he saw Snowdrop. Her dad was wonderful, but he was still a dad.

He'd remained silent through her whole retelling. Finally, he nodded. "You're right. Something is missing and that something is what has him scared beyond rationality. Honestly, Allie, I can't believe he told you as much as he did. I wouldn't have."

That worried her and thrilled her at the same time. "That means I mean something to him, right?"

"Yes, but…"

Her stomach tightened. "But now that he's told me so much, he might push me away?"

Her father nodded again.

"So what do I do?"

He put his arm around her shoulders. "That depends. How much does this cowboy mean to you?"

She didn't even hesitate. "I'm falling in love with him."

His eyes widened in shock. "You've never said that before."

"Because I've never felt this way before."

He studied her as if to determine if she really meant it. "Even though his past isn't as clean as we first thought?"

"Dad, you can't blame people for their past, especially if they've learned from it."

"Do you think he has?" He frowned, obviously still skeptical. "He obviously has some unresolved issues. Do you really want to take that on?"

It wasn't a matter of wanting to. "The way I feel, I have no choice." She looked askance at him. "You were the one who was all gung-ho about Wyatt. Are *you* having second thoughts?"

He shook his head. "I trust your judgment. If he makes you happy, and he better make you happy, then I'm behind you."

"Thanks." She kissed him on the cheek. "Then what do I do now?"

Her father gave her shoulders a small squeeze. "Don't let him push you away. Make him face you, talk to you, or that texting stuff. Keep yourself in his head."

"I can do that, but what do I say?"

Her father looked her in the eye. "Anything you want, just don't bring up what happened or what he said."

She pulled away and stood. "What? That makes no sense."

Her father rose. "Trust me. If he wants you to know more, he'll tell you, but badgering him about it will just put him on the defensive. He has to come to you."

She put her hands on her hips. "Why do I feel like I'm coaxing out a feral cat?"

"Because you are, or rather a feral rabbit." Her father chuckled at his own wit. "Now, tell me what shirt I should wear."

"I can do that." She walked back into the closet to search collared shirts that would still fit.

"By the way, you had a big package delivered here on Friday. I put it in the garage next to that dresser you're making. It had fragile written all over it."

She stilled. "You didn't open it, did you?"

When he didn't answer, she pulled three shirts on hangers from the rack and strode out of the closet, only to find he wasn't in the room. Somewhat relieved, she hung the shirts on the doorknob and went in search of her dad.

It was so hard trying to build him a retirement gift when she had to use his garage and his tools, but it would be frowned upon in her apartment complex if she started using a skill saw in her living room.

"Dad?" She stopped in the middle of the house and listened. Had he left the house? Glancing outside, she grinned.

Diva, Nina, and Pinta, the three female ostriches were following her dad across the yard in single file. It must be feeding time.

Quickly, she took a picture and texted it to Wyatt. *I think my dad has a harem.*

She waited, hoping he'd respond. For all she knew he was out for a ride, or unloading hay, or working on that fence he talked about. When a few minutes passed, she slipped her phone back in her jean's pocket and took the opportunity to check on her package.

Slipping into the garage from the side door, she flicked on the light. She walked around her dad's truck to the far corner where her project sat beneath a blanket. On the floor next to it was her box. Lifting it, she shook it lightly. No rattle. Breathing a sigh of relief, she set it down and headed back inside.

Building what she called a memory cabinet was a labor of love. Her dad had taught her everything there was to know about building, and she had put just about every lesson to use in the cabinet as a testament to him. Once she added the glass doors that had been specially made to her specifications, all she needed to do is stain it then fill it.

She had just entered her father's room when her phone buzzed. Her heart leapt. It could be anybody. Still, she whipped her phone out to read the message.

Wyatt: *Lucky man.*

There was no smiley face or anything, but she'd take it that way. Nervously, she typed. *Are you jealous?*

When it took a while, much longer that it took to type a simple "No" or "Yes," her hands started to sweat. Obviously, he meant a lot if she was waiting breathlessly for a return text. What was wrong with her?

Wyatt: *No. I have everything I need.*

Her throat closed. Did that mean he didn't need her? *You do?*

Wyatt: *I have you.*

She sat down hard on her dad's bed, relief sweeping over her. She needed to say something back. Jiminy Cricket, what should she say? "Oh." Smiling now, she texted back. *Yes, you do.* About to continue with *For better or worse*, she stopped herself. He wasn't ready for that. Heck, she wasn't ready for that, was she?

She waited, but no further text came. She was fine with that. At least he hadn't pushed her away. Could she see herself married to him? Alyssa Ford. Mrs. Ford. It actually sounded quite presidential. Where would they live?

They could buy a home together. That thought sent a spike of excitement through her chest. She quickly tamped it down. First he needed to feel comfortable enough to share his fear with her. She'd let it go for now, but before any future permanent plans were laid down, he would have to share.

And if he couldn't? She didn't like the answer to that, so she stopped getting ahead of herself, something her dad often called her out on.

Rising, she looked around the room. Right now, she needed to get dad ready for his very first date. The idea was so foreign to her, she couldn't quite grasp the significance, but she would help.

She'd met Ms. Davis before and had seen her around town. She seemed nice, polite, but a little lost. She was always involved in raising money for a different organization. The woman was attractive for her age and seemed to take care of herself, but beyond that, Alyssa didn't know much. No, she did know what her dad said. He always seemed to complain about Ms. Davis being too nice, yet he always bought whatever she was selling.

Hmm, did he really like the woman and didn't want his daughter to know?

If her dad was dating someone, as his daughter, should she

vet them like he'd checked out her boyfriends over the years? This was so new to her, she wasn't sure what she was supposed to do.

All she knew for sure was that dad was going on a date. A date! Shaking her head in befuddlement, she walked to the door where the shirts hung. Checking the sizes, she kept the largest out and headed back into the closet to see if any others were that size or larger.

And here she'd thought getting herself ready for a date was tough.

Chapter Twelve

Wyatt set one foot on the bottom rail of the fence at the south corral and rested one hand on the top. Inside the corral were a number of the horses, who milled about watching all the activity. He scanned the area. Everything seemed to be going smoothly. The busses had rolled in promptly at nine-thirty, and it was almost lunch time.

Whisper had joined them and stood guard over Meeko, which was the perfect place for her. The last thing he needed was for her to tell a third-grader that she had to leave early to go have sex with her husband.

Trace had a passel of students in the barn regaling them with slightly enhanced tales of the most interesting horses, including Phoenix which Dillon, Cole's brother, had brought over just for the kids at Cole's request. Outside the south corral where he stood, both Logan and Annette were giving "pony rides" around the main house. Meanwhile, he could see the wagon making its way back up the road from Cole's house, Riley at the reins, but Cyclone putting on quite the show as he lifted his hooves high.

And out front, which he couldn't see from where he stood, Cole had not only brought a ladder truck but had stationed himself there, while his firefighters gave instructions on how the equipment was used.

Garrett had joined them and showed the kids his scars to enforce how dangerous fire could be. Wyatt knew that was difficult for him, but the kids' fascination and questions had seemed to put him at ease.

Even Lacey had chipped in, taking the day off work to oversee the setting up of the tables and chairs in the tents beneath the mesquite tree, after she insisted he move his box trailer and have it emptied by the end of the month. She said she didn't like the thought that he could hook it up to his truck and leave them. He'd moved it that very day.

She then commandeered the spot for its shade during the heat at lunch time. She'd even created a first aid station on the porch which had a paramedic who, so far, had only to clean two cuts and add band aids. At the moment, a teenage boy sat on the porch steps. Either he was supposed to be helping to chaperone, or seriously behind in school.

They all had lucked out. The weather had dipped under triple digits for the first time since May, so everyone seemed to be in a good mood. His gaze returned to the other side of the south corral, where Alyssa was encouraging a young girl to take a ride. Though they had talked on the phone, he hadn't seen her since he'd left her apartment so abruptly last Saturday.

Yet here it was Friday, and she walked off the bus smiling, giving him a wink before corralling the ten children she'd taken as her group like a mother duck gathering her ducklings. Dressed in a tan short sleeve dress that came in at the waist and flared out at her knees with little brown horse silhouettes on it, plus brown cowboy boots and straw cowboy hat, she looked ready for a cowboy's picnic.

Movement to his left had him turning as a young girl with blonde pigtails, a pink blouse, white jeans, and pink cowboy boots came and stood next to him. He'd noticed her before. Her name was Lydia, and she was one of two children Alyssa had told him about who had physical issues and may not be able to participate in everything. He smiled at her. "Hello."

She looked up at him. "Hello. Thank you for letting us come to Last Chance, Mr. Ford."

"You're welcome."

"Ms. Parker said you bought us our hamsters. Is that true?"

Hamsters. He didn't, oh the gift certificate. "Are hamsters what your class chose for your pet then?"

She nodded, the pink ribbons at the end of her pig tails bouncing. "Yes. I wanted ferret, but I changed my vote because Jimmy said if I went with hamster he'd get Ms. Parker to buy two."

Jimmy sounded pretty savvy. "How did he get Ms. Parker to get you two hamsters?"

She leaned against the wooden fence. "He refused to move his vote to hamster unless we all convinced Ms. Parker to let us have two. She was teaching us about building con...con... consensus." She smiled as she remembered the word.

It sounded more like Jimmy has mastered the art of blackmail. "Are you going to ride the horse?"

She shook her head. "I want to, but mom told me I can't until Dr. Santos says I can take off my brace. I have a curvy spine."

Alyssa had said it was scoliosis. From his height, he could clearly see the white plastic coming up from beneath her blouse behind her neck. "Did Dr. Santos say when that would be?"

She sighed. "He said I might have to wear this until I'm sixteen. By then I'll be too old to ride horses."

Wyatt swallowed his chuckle at the girl's perspective on age, but he couldn't stifle his smile. Squatting down, he pointed to Annette who had just come around the corner of the house leading Lady, a young boy on her back smiling from ear to ear. "See that woman over there."

The girl bent awkwardly to look under the top rail. "Yes."

"Do you know that she goes riding at least twice a week?"

Lydia's eyes grew wide. "But she's a great-grandma. She told us that when Ms. Parker introduced her to us."

He nodded solemnly. "That's right, but she still rides like the wind. Her horse is named Sadie." He pointed to the horse. "That's her, the sorrel Quarter Horse with four white socks."

Just then, Kentucky dropped to his knees. The poor horse looked startled as if he had no idea what happened.

"Oh! Mr. Ford. That horse. Is he hurt?" Lydia's voice sounded like she was about to cry.

"Watch, then you tell me."

The little girl's gaze stayed glued to Kentucky as he realized he didn't want to be on the ground. Starting with his front legs he then heaved himself back up. "He did it!"

"Yes, he did. Kentucky's had a lot of practice." He pointed. "See, we even got him knee pads."

Her little brow furrowed. "That happens a lot?"

"Yes, but we're helping him."

"Will Kentucky get better?" The hope in her eyes, made him want to lie.

His first meeting with Alyssa reminded him that the truth could be told in many ways. "Yes, we can make him better to a point, but he will never be able to carry a person on his back."

Lydia looked back at Kentucky, who had moved to a chunk of hay and started eating as if nothing had happened. Finally, she turned back to him. "Then he's the lucky one."

Her conclusion stymied him. "Why do you say that?"

"Because he'll never have to obey anyone's commands, just walk and run how he pleases."

He hadn't thought of it like that. With horses like Tundra who insisted on being ridden, he had never thought about a horse not wanting a person on its back, but that made a lot of sense, since they originally had been wild animals.

"Mr. Ford? Why does that happen to Kentucky?"

The glint of the sun off a metal buckle on her brace as she cocked her head, had him choosing his words carefully. "Unlike you, Kentucky doesn't have a curve. His problem is in the back of his neck which stops some of his brain's signals to his body, causing him to stumble."

"How long will it take before he doesn't stumble anymore?"

Now she'd gone farther than his own knowledge, since he was still learning about wobbler syndrome. "I'm not sure, but it will be quite a while."

She looked back at Kentucky, who was now standing with Blaze, who had been passed over for pony rides since Lady loved the attention. Then Lydia turned back to him and smiled. "If Kentucky can get better than so can I. And if I can't do everything that the others can do, then I'll be like Kentucky and enjoy what I like to do best."

He grinned at her. "And what is that?"

"Sing. Do you want to hear?"

"Of course, I would —"

"There you are Lydia." Alyssa approached smiling as usual. "I was looking for you. It's time for lunch. You don't want to miss lunch, do you?"

"Oh, no." Turning back to him she held out her hand. "It was nice talking with you Mr. Ford. I learned a lot."

He carefully shook her little hand then watched her run off toward the tents, her back brace not impeding her at all.

"You two looked like you were having a very important conversation."

He returned his attention to Alyssa, suddenly wondering what her children would look like. Would they have her beautiful eyes and height? "I think she appreciated learning about Kentucky."

"He's the wobbler, right? I saw him drop but he seemed alright afterward."

He couldn't take his eyes off her. "He's fine. We'll check him for scrapes and cuts at the end of the day as we usually do. He also tends to misjudge distance sometimes and walks into things."

She lowered her voice. "It's really good to see you. Thank you so much for all this." She swung her arm out to indicate the activities they'd set up. "Even the children who live on ranches are having a wonderful time."

"I was happy to arrange it. It has given me more ideas on what this ranch can do."

She chuckled. "You mean like field trips?"

He nodded. The realization that he'd missed her, struck him suddenly. *You never know how good you've got it, boy. Always looking for greener pastures, you are.* His stomach tightened as his grandfather's words hit him hard. The old man was right. He needed to do whatever was necessary to keep Alyssa with him. Part of that was telling her how he felt.

"Well, I need to get over there to my tent or I may well have a food fight on my hands." She started to turn away.

Not daring to touch her in case anyone was watching, he barely kept from grabbing her hand. "Would you like to stay after the kids leave so we can analyze what worked and what didn't?"

She stopped, her smile disappearing, which made his gut clench tighter. "I can't. School policy." Her lips lifted again. "But I can come back once all the students have left the school."

"That works."

She looked around then back at him. "There's going to be some clean up to do as well."

He shrugged, really not caring what they did as long as she was with him. "We can assess the damages when you get here."

"Great. It's a date then." She whirled away and strode for the tent.

He watched until she'd disappeared beneath the white canopy, his body relaxing now that he knew she'd be back. Turning around, he headed in the opposite direction to speak with Whisper.

The woman stood with her butt against a corral post. Luckily, Trace had convinced her to leave her gun, Sal, at home. Wyatt wasn't sure how Trace had done that since he'd never seen her without it until today. Her arms were crossed and as he came closer, he could see her brows were lowered beneath her beat-up cowboy hat.

"Too many kids." The words were followed by her spitting on the ground.

The sentiment surprised him. He'd equated someone who felt so much for animals with someone being great with kids. It seemed she'd had more than one motivation for volunteering to keep kids away from Meeko. "There's only thirty-eight. Two didn't come."

"Too many." She turned away from him and looked at Meeko.

He walked up next to her. "How's he doing?"

"Not good. He doesn't like all the activity. Too much noise. Look." She pointed at Meeko who started to walk to the other end of the corral away from them.

"Walking probably helps him get rid of his nervous energy."

She threw him a scowl. "Not the walking. Look at the ground."

178

When he did, he understood what she meant. Meeko had been pacing. He'd thought Whisper was projecting her own feelings about the kids onto Meeko, but the horse was obviously very anxious. Even he could see that. The question is, what to do about it. The classes still had one more hour after lunch.

Frustration mounted. He should have thought of this. He'd been so concerned about the students' safety, he'd forgotten about how Meeko felt. All these new horse conditions were more than a challenge, but he could learn. "What do you suggest?"

"Make the kids go away."

He swallowed a growl. He should have seen that coming. "They are here for one more hour after lunch, then they'll leave. Is there anything we can do for Meeko to help him cope?"

Whisper shrugged. "He needs something to calm him."

"You mean a tranq? I'd rather not."

Whisper turned and without warning, threw a punch.

He caught her hand inches from his face. "Whoa, what's that for?"

"Don't you ever tranq one of these horses unless I tell you to or Sal will deal with you. Understood?" Her grey eyes had turned to hard silver.

She meant every word, and he believed her, but he was the boss now. However, he also needed Whisper's help. It was invaluable. "I promise if I have the time to let you know a horse needs to be tranquilized, I will let you know. But I'm not going to put my staff in danger if a horse is uncontrollable. Do you understand?"

The woman pulled her hand out of his grasp. "You will not tranq Meeko."

"No, I'm not going to tranq Meeko. He's got enough issues, but we need to—" The image of Alyssa calming him when he couldn't breathe at her apartment had him pausing. "I have an idea."

Striding away from Whisper, who he was sure was burning holes in his back with her gaze, he headed straight for the tent where Alyssa had gone. It was a long shot, but if her tentative connection with the horse could help Meeko, he was willing to give it a try if she was.

Stepping up to the tent, he scanned the occupants. The kids were excitedly talking while the adults were walking around. He caught sight of her at the same time she saw him. He motioned with his head toward the outside. She nodded.

He stepped outside and waited.

She hurried out and seeing him, approached. "What is it? Is something wrong?"

He nodded. "Yes, it's Meeko."

Immediately, she frowned. "What's wrong? Did he get out?"

"Can you come with me while I explain?"

She looked back and nodded.

As they walked, he explained the situation and his idea.

"You want me to help calm the horse by having him breathe slower? You know this is a long shot, right? I mean, I'm willing to do what I can, but I hope you aren't expecting success."

"I know. I'm not expecting Meeko's breathing to change, but I think your attention and voice might at least calm him a bit." They halted as they reached Whisper. "Whisper, this is Alyssa. She's built a connection with Meeko and might be able to help."

Whisper pushed up her hat and looked up, studying Alyssa. "You don't know horses." The words were clearly meant as an insult.

Alyssa stood a bit straighter and smiled. "Not as well as

you, but from what I hear, no one knows them as well as you. However, I did ride when I was younger. Then my father started bringing home different types of animals, like peacocks, llamas, and a camel."

The feeling of pride in his chest at how Alyssa handled Whisper was completely unwarranted, but it felt good just the same.

The switch in Whisper's demeanor just about knocked him off his feet. The woman's face changed from closed and protective to brimming with curiosity. "A llama? Can I meet him?"

Luckily, Alyssa didn't seem phased at all. "I'm afraid we don't have her anymore. But we do have three female ostriches at the moment, some goats, and a gaggle of geese."

As if she'd been caught being nice, Whisper immediately rolled her eyes. "I don't do birds."

Wyatt was losing patience with Whisper. She may have grown up off the grid, but she was an adult and didn't need to act like a child. "What about the Bald Eaglet you saved this past spring?"

Whisper shrugged. "That's different." She waved toward Meeko, who had stopped pacing when Alyssa arrived, but addressed Alyssa. "Go see if you can help. I doubt it will make it any worse." She glared at him. "It's already as bad as it can be."

Though he had already turned his back on Whisper, Alyssa remained a few seconds longer. "Thank you. I hope I can help." She then caught up to him as they walked around the outside of the corral.

He stopped about fifty feet from Meeko and took a few deep breaths to calm down. Whisper being rude to Alyssa had him too wound up. Her hand on his arm had him turning his head to look at her.

"It's okay. I deal with childish behavior all the time in school. It doesn't bother me."

He almost burst out laughing, but held it back for Meeko's sake. "Are you ready?"

She nodded, looking a lot more confident than he felt.

Wyatt had them meander closer, letting Meeko get used to their presence. His nostrils flared and he sniffed the air. Did he enjoy the fresh daffodil scent that Alyssa wore as much as he did?

"Hello, Meeko. Do you remember me?"

The horse walked toward them, moving his head past the corral rail.

Alyssa raised her hand slowly, close enough that he could sniff it if he wanted.

He did, then after a short chuff, he lowered his head.

She moved her hand to his side and began stroking his neck. The poor horse shivered, but not from the cold.

Wyatt's conscience got the better of him. He should have figured out a way to keep the activity out of sight of Meeko.

"That's a good boy. It's all going to be okay."

As Alyssa spoke in soothing tones, Wyatt watched for any signs that the horse had had enough, but he stood stock still.

"Meeko, you're going to be okay. I'm going to have to leave you for a little while, but I'll be back later. Is that all right with you?"

Though the horse's ears turned to listen to her whenever she spoke, it still didn't move.

She moved her hand away and looked at Wyatt. "I feel so bad that having the kids here caused him so much distress."

"So do I." He looked past her at the horse, whose gaze remained on her. "It's something I'll make sure to consider in the future for whatever horses we have here. It's no different than deciding which horses are best for pony rides and which are best for pulling the wagon. I should have considered Meeko."

"I'm just as guilty. Too bad we didn't have a manual on handling horse mental health issues."

He shook his head. "I'm sure we can find something."

"Better yet, I'll ask our librarian at school. And speaking of school, I think the students are about to exit en masse. Are you ready to give the final farewell after their last activity?"

He rolled his eyes. "If you insist."

"I do." Her smile of admiration had him wishing he could take her in his arms and kiss her, but movement beyond the corrals told him lunch was over.

"We best get you back to your group of students." Knowing that she would return later made it easier to let her go.

She turned to look at Meeko. "Hang in there. Just a little longer and then all will be quiet and calm again. I'll be back to check on you." With that, they started to walk slowly around the corral.

Wyatt wasn't unaware that Meeko walked parallel to them. When they were close to where Whisper waited, Alyssa stopped. "Time to stop being the horse whisperer and back to being the teacher."

Just as she took one step away, Meeko snatched off her hat.

"Hey." She spun around and the horse backed up, waving the hat in his mouth like a prize.

Whisper's laughter floated over to them.

Ready to save her hat, Wyatt jumped up on the rail.

"No." Alyssa grabbed his arm. "Let him have it. It was a cheap one I bought for a hoedown a few years back. If it helps him, it's worth it."

Appreciation for how big her heart really was had him jumping back down. "Are you sure?"

She grinned. "Yes. And I can tell the students the truth, that I got too close to the corral and Meeko took it. They've been far too interested in coming over here."

"Okay, I'll walk you back." At her nod, they strode back around to the front of the house and past the porch. The teenager who had been there was gone, reminding him he'd wanted to ask about the boy. "I noticed we've had a teenage boy hanging around, but not participating. Is he supposed to be a chaperone?"

Alyssa, sighed. "No, he's with Jimmy's mom, Ms. Harkin. He was suspended from school, so she made him come with her today since she refused to let him stay home alone."

Suspended wasn't great. It sure beat being arrested though. "What did he do?"

"He hacked into his teacher's computer and changed his grade."

"So he's a smart kid that's not being challenged."

"Exactly. But she's a single mom of two boys." Alyssa nodded to a small boy, who was small even for his age, standing in line to go into the barn to hear about the horses. "Jimmy is in my class. Landon is a junior in high school."

She looked around. "I don't see Landon. He must have wandered out back. I hope he's not getting into trouble. His mom is beyond herself. All he does is sit in his room on his computer, except when he's taking care of Jimmy. Then he sits in the living room with his computer."

There wasn't much the teenager could do with Whisper guarding Meeko and the house locked. Just from what little he knew already though, he had a feeling that trouble was right around the corner for Landon. "I'll look for him. You go ahead with your last activity. I can see that Jimmy is getting anxious." He grinned at the boy who was peeking around the corner of the barn door while two of his classmates held onto his shirt to keep him from going in.

"Yes, that's Jimmy. All the impatience and none of the sense. Thanks." She strode off toward the front of the line, little Jimmy immediately behaving when he saw her coming.

As Alyssa lead her group into the barn to the waiting Trace, who had dressed in full cowboy gear, including chaps, Wyatt strode off in search of the lost teen. Now where would he go if he wanted nothing to do with a bunch of third graders and his mom?

Wyatt went back to the steps of the porch. This had been a perfect spot when the kids had gone into lunch. Where would Landon go now that they all had returned to their activities?

Looking around, he grinned. There were only two places he would have gone, and Landon sounded a bit like himself at that age. His guess was either to the lunch tents or the mesquite tree. His bet was on the tree, since that would give a good view of everything that was happening.

Striding in that direction, he searched the branches for the teenager in black...and found him. Maneuvering between the tents, he grabbed a hold of the bottom branch and hoisted himself up.

"You don't have to come up. If my mom wants me down, I'll come down."

Wyatt paused in his climb. "I don't know which one is your mom, so I have no idea if she wants you to come down." Grabbing onto another branch, he stepped on one more before taking a seat on a hefty branch near Landon.

"If not her, then who sent you up here?"

Wyatt ignored him and looked out over the ranch. He'd climbed all the way to the top of the tree the third day after he arrived to get a sense of the property. From the top, the whole valley could be seen, but from this height, the view only reached to Cole's house. Even now, the wagon with Riley at the reins and the back full of kids and two adults was making the trek that would take them around the hill where Cole's house sat before it made its return trip.

"You deaf?"

He turned around to look at the young man. It was like looking at himself fourteen years ago, just with a few modern accessories like an earring and leather necklace. "Not at all. Just checking out the view."

"I've seen better." He had a twig he'd pulled off the tree and was in the process of breaking it.

Wyatt barely kept himself from smiling. "Did you check out the horses?"

The kid shrugged. "What's to see? They're just horses. It's not like I haven't seen a horse before. I'm not some third grader."

"No, third graders are better behaved."

Without missing a beat, or looking Wyatt in the face, he responded. "That's because they don't know any better. They don't realize that they are being molded into mini-me's by their parents and teachers so they can perpetuate someone else's values and mores."

He widened his eyes at that. It sounded very smart, but it also sounded like Landon had read it on the internet. "You mean they teach you stuff like cheating isn't right and working hard is how to succeed? Yeah, definitely stupid ideas."

Landon's head snapped up at that. "What do you know, cowboy?" He gestured with his hand to the ranch. "This isn't real life. You just take care of your stupid animals and muck out the shit. Leave the rest of the world to the IT generation."

IT generation? That was a new one. "Let me guess. Your mom took your phone, so you're taking your anger out on a twig. Hmm, yeah, that makes sense."

"Fuck off." Landon threw the twig to the side and leaned his back against the trunk, folding his arms across his chest.

Wyatt smirked. Yup, Landon sounded just like himself, just with a few different words. "Running a ranch is a lot more than horses. It's about ordering the right supplies, scheduling staff, profit and loss statements, FDA regulations, lobbying against unjust laws, creating a website, taking orders, maintaining a social media presence, vetting clients, purchasing equipment, getting bids, in addition to waking up at the crack of dawn and caring for the animals that bring in the money."

The silence that followed was deafening. The kid was processing the information. That's what he had done when Gramps had given him a similar spiel. But he'd had a lot of anger built up after a night in custody and his mom dumping him off.

Landon finally spoke. "Yeah, well one day all that will be automated, and you'll be out of a job."

He grinned. "Now that's a day I can't wait for. Maybe I could retire early."

Landon frowned at him. "As soon as I graduate, I'm out of here. I know there's more to life than school and taking care of a skinny little brat."

"You mean the little guy with all the energy?"

"Yeah. That's Jimmy. Never sits still. I'm trying to play Magic Throne to relax after school, and he keeps getting into things. Then I have to get after him, and I'm the one who gets in trouble because 'I'm supposed to be watching him'." The last was said mimicking his mom's voice.

"I know what you mean."

"No, you don't."

"Yeah, I do. I went to school in South Phoenix. I had not one but two younger siblings, and they were girls."

Landon's eyes widened.

"My mother worked too. I had to walk them to the bus stop in the morning and put them to bed at night and even read them stories."

Landon frowned, obviously taking that all in. "But you're a cowboy?"

Wyatt chuckled. "Yeah, now I am. I got into trouble, and my mom dumped me on my grandfather's ranch and told him to raise me."

"My mom wouldn't do that." Landon unconsciously pulled off another twig and began to worry it. He didn't sound entirely sure of himself.

The kid wasn't dumb, he was just in a tough situation, one too many kids his age were in, but they always felt like they were the only one. "Did you give yourself an A on that test? Is that how you got caught?"

"Hell, no. I gave myself a B. I had an A, but the last thing I want is for my mom to think I'm good at writing. If she thinks that, she'll be having me write her press releases. I helped her with a blog post for work and it went over really well, but when I asked to be paid, she said having a roof over my head was payment enough."

Wyatt suppressed his grin. Things hadn't really changed much after all. An idea was starting to form. "Is it true you are really good with computers?"

"I'm good enough."

"What about websites?" If Landon could create a more automated website for Last Chance, that could help them find good homes for the horses faster.

Landon thought for a moment. "I've done blogs, online articles, a database, and social media for a school event, but I've never done a website."

"You want to create one for me? I'll pay you."

Landon changed his position on the branch to face him. "For what?"

Wyatt spread out his arm toward the house. "For this place. The old one is out of date, not user friendly, and needs more automation."

"In addition to my hours, it will also cost for hosting and the program I'd want to use."

"That's not a problem. But I'm not paying for you to watch internet videos on how to build a website. That's on your time."

"Are you paying me hourly?"

That was his plan, but he could see Landon getting too excited about the site and making money and not getting schoolwork done. "Yes, but only twenty hours a week, and you have to keep your grades up."

"Up as in where they are now?" He looked far too hopeful.

Obviously, he'd been slacking. "No, up as in A's and B's."

A shrewd look came into the youth's brown eyes. "How much an hour? I'm not cheap."

"I'll pay you minimum wage."

"Minimum wage? For my expertise?"

For the all the boy's intelligence, he hadn't learned street smarts yet. "You admitted you've never built a website, so where's the expertise?"

He thought about that a moment. "Yes, but you said your website sucks, so you *need* me."

Obviously, he was a fast learner. "No, I need *someone*. I can hire an expert and get it done in half the time, but I'm giving you this opportunity."

For the first time, Landon grinned. "I'll take it."

Wyatt held out his hand and the kid shook. "Now, you might want to spend the last half hour you are here to learn about the place. It's a little more complicated than it looks. Cole Hatcher, the fire captain over there by the ladder truck is the owner, and the one with the least amount of work to do at the moment. You probably should start with him."

The smile disappeared. "Shit." Within seconds, Landon was clambering down the tree and hightailing it off toward Cole.

Wyatt chuckled, pleased with the teenager's excitement. Maybe Landon would even tap into his little brother to find out what else he needed to know.

He'd be sure Landon had his personal number as well as the house phone number in case he had more questions. Not that Landon would make the same mistakes he did, but it didn't hurt to put an intelligent mind to good use.

Wyatt watched until Landon cornered Cole then his gaze wandered toward the barn. Alyssa's students were still inside. He wanted to tell her about his idea for Landon. He wanted to share with her the triumph of the day. The bottom line was he wanted her in his life, if she'd take him, faults and all.

Climbing down from the tree, he headed toward the barn to get Tundra ready for the farewell. Though he wasn't one for dramatics, Alyssa wanted it, so he was happy to oblige. He just hoped Tundra decided to cooperate, which wasn't always a given.

Chapter Thirteen

Despite Trace Williams' very intriguing story about his horse Lightyear, Alyssa sensed the second Wyatt stepped into the barn and slipped into Tundra's stall. She'd insisted Tundra not be out in the corral because she wanted the horse's true size to be a surprise.

When Trace asked for questions, every hand went up. She quickly interrupted. "We only have time for three on this story as it's almost time to board the bus."

A chorus of disappointment followed that statement, so when Trace actually answered five, but very quickly, she didn't stop him. As soon as he finished, she herded the children back outside into the sunlight and over to the front of the bus where one group was already standing and another was getting down from the wagon to join them.

When Marty saw her group emerge, the other teacher corralled her own students and herded them from the fire truck to the bus area.

Alyssa strode to the front of the growing group. "Okay, everyone, stand still so your chaperones can count and make sure we have everyone." She counted her ten then looked to the other adults, waiting for a nod from each of them. "Wait, where's Landon?"

Marty hooked her thumb over her shoulder. "I think he's still talking to the captain."

Landon's mother pursed her lips then started off to retrieve her son.

Alyssa felt bad for the woman. Little Jimmy was a ball of energy and Landon was constantly in trouble. "Attention everyone. Mr. Ford is going to say a few words before we leave."

Everyone quieted down and looked around. She glanced toward the barn to see Wyatt emerge on Tundra. Her heart almost stopped. If ever someone needed a picture of a cowboy hero, now was the time. And if ever she knew she was in love, it was gazing at the man on horseback, easily controlling his beautiful beast.

Moving to the side of the group, so she could watch their faces, she stood next to Marty.

Wyatt rode the big horse over at a walk to face the entire group. The students' eyes were large. The white horse with the gray pattern had to be at least 17 hands tall. With Wyatt at six foot four inches, it made for an impressive sight.

Marty whispered in her ear. "If you haven't yet, you should make a move on that man."

She frowned at Marty like she frowned at her students who disappointed her, and put a finger to her lips.

Marty just smiled and then took in the view.

Despite the fact that Marty was happily married, Alyssa felt jealousy creeping up her back just because Marty was appreciating the tableau that she herself had orchestrated. She needed to get her head examined.

Wyatt cleared his throat. "Thank you for visiting us at Last Chance Ranch. I hope that you learned a few things and will go home today with good memories of us."

The students nodded, their surprise having turned to beaming smiles.

Wyatt continued. "If there is one thing I want you to take away from today, it's that—"

"We should be kind to animals." A girl in the back row yelled.

Lydia, standing nearby, spoke up. "No, it's that animals, like people, may have problems with their bodies."

"Oh, I know. I know." Jimmy was practically vibrating with his excitement. "We should be safe around fire and horses."

"No, dummy. It's that everybody, including horses, has a past." Emanuel added that to the impromptu conversation.

A little girl from Marty's class who stood in the front row was waving her hand crazily.

The boy next to her scowled at her. "He didn't ask a question, silly." Immediately, her hand came down and tears filled her eyes.

Wyatt leaned over the neck of Tundra and looked right at the little girl. "What do you think is the most important lesson from today?"

She sniffed and wiped her eyes with her hand. Her voice was so quiet, Alyssa had to strain to hear it. "I think." She took a deep breath. "I think, Mr. Cowboy, that the lesson is that everyone deserves to have a home and people who care for them. Even horses and other animals."

Alyssa felt tears gather in her own eyes as Wyatt nodded. "You're one hundred percent correct."

The little girl's smile caught Alyssa off guard, and she moved her gaze to Wyatt who had straightened in the saddle.

He should be a dad.

The thought struck her hard in the chest. Was that something he wanted? Or had taking care of his sisters ruined that idea for him? Her stomach tied in knots at where her mind was headed, and she forced herself to focus on what was playing out in front of her.

"In case you all didn't hear that." Wyatt addressed the group with a strong voice. "The most important lesson is that everyone deserves a home and people who care for them, including horses and other animals." Wyatt gave the little girl a wink. "So be sure to tell everyone about Last Chance. Now, I have to get back to my chores, but Tundra and I want to wish you safe travels, right boy?"

He patted the horse on his neck and Tundra neighed, much to the delight of the children, some of which neighed back. Then Wyatt let out a truncated whistle and took off his hat as Tundra bent one leg beneath him and they both bowed.

When they had talked about what Tundra could do, she had thought that rearing up would be exciting, but Wyatt had nixed that as too dangerous around the children. She was glad he refused because the bow the two made had the children giving out soft oohs.

When they straightened in perfect unison, Wyatt pulled his reins to the right and Tundra went around in a complete circle before the two bounded off down the road toward Cole's distant house.

Conversations erupted and she had to force herself to leave off watching Wyatt and gather the children onto the bus. Once all were on board, she counted all the heads to make sure she had the right number of children and the right number of adults. "Landon?"

"Here." Landon raised his hand then went back to excitingly talking to his mom. Maybe the trip had been good for him too. Nodding to the bus driver, she sat in the front seat next to Marty and the bus pulled out, the children waving to the firefighters who were packing up their gear and first aid station.

"Please tell me you two are an item."

"Really Marty? We're on a field trip."

The woman lowered her voice. "Okay, then just give me a nod or a shake of the head. I'm dying over here. Remember, I'm an old married lady, and I have to live vicariously through you."

She rolled her eyes. Marty had a hunk of a husband that she absolutely adored, and except for her karaoke nights when he took the opportunity to play poker with some friends, the two did everything together.

"Come on, Lys. Are you two a thing?"

The hope in her friend's eyes was too much, so she gave a single nod.

"Whoop!"

One of the children behind them stood up, holding onto the back of their seat. "What is it, Mrs. Langley?"

Marty didn't miss a beat. "Ms. Parker said that we can come back next year with our new classes."

A boy across from them jumped on that idea. "My sister will be in third grade next year. Maybe I can come as a chaperone."

"You can't be a chaperone. You have to be eighteen."

"Uh-uh, Jimmy's brother came and he's not eighteen. That means I can come."

"Cannot."

"Can to."

"Cannot."

As the children's conversation devolved, Alyssa gave Marty a scowl. "We can talk about this after school lets out."

"Of course, teacher." She laughed before her attention was taken again by the boys across the aisle who had started to get physical in their argument.

The fact was, she did want Wyatt to be hers. And she wanted to enjoy the success of the day with him, not with Marty.

It didn't seem fair because she shared most of the successes and failures with her fellow teacher, but this had been a team effort with Wyatt.

He hadn't simply gone out of his way to make the day memorable for their students. He'd interacted with them and even finished the day the way she wanted him to. Now she wanted to share their success together, alone.

It seemed like forever to get the kids off the bus, to their classrooms, and then onto the buses to go home. Avoiding Marty, she had quickly jumped in her dad's truck and headed out.

Luckily, dad had taken the day off to work on some projects at the house. He said he was trying to figure out what it would feel like to be retired. He had so much time coming to him, he could probably take off the next four months and still have vacation time.

She lowered her brows as she turned onto the dirt road that led to the ranch. He could have worked on his projects on the weekend. What was one more day? Unless he had a date this weekend. A spark of happiness hit her at that idea. No matter what she thought of Ms. Davis, she was happy her dad had something to look forward to…if that was it.

At the sight of the Last Chance sign, all thoughts of her dad evaporated. She pulled in past where the fire truck had been. Jumping out of the vehicle, she looked around. The tents were still up but she could see the chairs and tables were gone. There had been so much to set up and take down for Wyatt and his crew. Maybe she could pitch in a little.

Not seeing anyone about, she strode toward the barn. She gave Black Jack a pat on her way in since he'd greeted her in his outside stall. She'd learned from Trace today why the horse was never put inside. Stepping in, she let her eyes adjust then walked down the center.

Tundra was back in his stall, so that must mean Wyatt was around somewhere.

She looked into an open stall to see if he was there, when she heard a step directly behind her. Suddenly, an arm came about her waist from behind.

She yelled.

"Whoa, it's just me."

Wyatt's deep voice floated over her as the scent of soap filled her nostrils. She turned in his arms to find him hatless and his hair wet. "You smell clean."

He chuckled. "I hope so. I just took a shower."

"In the middle of the day?"

He grimaced. "Tundra decided he deserved a ride and a roll for behaving today. My clothes were so full of dirt even I couldn't stand myself, and believe me, I've been pretty caked in mud and dirt in the past."

She wrapped her arms around his neck. "Don't get me wrong. I'm not complaining."

He grinned. "Good." Then he lowered his mouth to hers.

She sighed into the kiss. Being around him all day and not being able to touch him had been like holding a puppy before a child and not letting her pet it. She moved her fingers through his wet hair as she tangled her tongue with his.

Happiness filled her chest and an odd peace she didn't remember feeling since she was a child descended upon her.

Wyatt broke the kiss, having much more will power than she had. "Would you like to come inside where it's cooler. I want to share everything with you."

Everything? A surge of excitement ran through her. Would he finish telling her what he'd started to last week? "I'd like that."

Releasing her, he took her hand and strolled to the house.

As they climbed the steps, she realized all the trucks that had been parked there earlier were gone. "Where'd everyone go?"

He opened the door for her. "They helped me clean up and then I sent them home. Annette and Ed headed up to Sedona for the weekend. It's become a new pattern for them. They decided the weekends were made for getaways. But they'll be back for Sunday dinner."

He stopped her from going farther down the hall. "I have something for you. I cleaned it up."

She turned back and he plopped her hat on her head. "Thank you. I liked being a cowgirl today."

"It looks good on you. I'm going to have to get you a real one."

That simple thought had her insides fluttering.

He took her hand again and led her into the living room. She sat on a couch, expecting him to sit with her, but he pulled over a comfortable looking chair and faced her.

Again, that feeling of excitement fluttered in her stomach at the thought of him revealing what bothered him the most.

He took both her hands. "What did you think about today?"

It wasn't what she was expecting, but she was more than happy to start there. "Today was amazing. The children loved everything about the ranch. On the ride back to the school, they couldn't stop talking about it. And the chaperones volunteered to come again next year."

"I thought it went well, too. I talked to everyone else and they actually enjoyed themselves. I think some of them thought our idea wasn't going to fly, but once put into action, it soared." He let go of her and moved one hand upward like a plane taking off, the smile on his face revealing how much he enjoyed the success of the day.

She laughed, happy to share the joy with him. "You were

so wonderful with the children. I guess after you talked about your childhood, I didn't think you would be excited to interact with them."

His smile lessened, but it didn't disappear. "I think that was my favorite part of the day. I used to avoid kids, but after living with my grandfather for a few years, the chip on my shoulder fell off." He snorted. "It was more like Gramps knocked it off."

"I can tell you admired him. It must have been so hard to lose such a mainstay in your life."

"Admired him? I've never thought about that. I did respect him and love him." Wyatt sat back. "He was a tough old coot, who didn't accept anything but perfection. Everything had to be in the correct place to avoid chaos, or so he said."

Wyatt shook his head. "I wasn't a very fast learner in the beginning."

She laid her hand on his knee, not wanting him to pull away completely. "I find that hard to believe."

This time he laughed. "You wouldn't have known me then. After I got arrested, I spent the night in juvey. Mom refused to come to the police station and take me home. Then when she did pick me up, she drove me straight to Gramps. She'd thrown everything in my room in a garbage bag and dumped me on the old man."

"Oh, Wyatt. You must have felt so abandoned."

"I'm pretty sure that might have been it deep down, but all I recognized at the time was anger. I was angry at her. I was angry at Gramps. The first few days only made me angrier. The old man expected me to get up and do chores then go to school and come home and do chores then homework then to bed. If I did something wrong, he slapped me."

"He what?" Her heart was breaking for the teenager Wyatt was.

"Oh, don't think I didn't try to give as good as I got, but the old man was strong and wiry from working the ranch, and I was a teenage kid who sat in an apartment or at school. That just frustrated me more. Finally, I'd had enough."

Relief washed through her. "I'm glad. What did you do?"

He smirked. "Something stupid. I told Gramps not to expect me home after school because I was never coming back."

She didn't see the humor in that. "What happened?"

"He told me if I didn't come home, he'd find me and lock me in the shed for twenty-four hours."

Her breath caught in her throat. She couldn't even ask what she wanted to know.

"When I didn't get off the bus at the ranch, he went out looking for me. I was brand new to Cave Creek, but Gramps knew everyone."

Angry at his grandfather, she wanted to rail, but could only get out two words. "He didn't."

Wyatt took her hand in his. "Yes, he did. He found me and was true to his word."

She pulled away. "That's child abuse. Did you report it? They should have taken you way from him."

"And sent me where?"

That caught her up short. His mother didn't want him and his grandfather abused him? She felt near to tears. "They could have put you in foster care." But even as she said it, she knew that wouldn't have worked either for an angry teenager.

He took her hand again. "Don't you see. Gramps may not have been the nicest of men, but he kept me from going down the wrong path. I never tried to run away again. At first, I did what I had to keep from getting slapped, biding my time until I graduated."

She studied him as he got lost in his memories. How could

such a good man come from so much abuse and abandonment? "But you stayed with him." Just like abused spouses did, brainwashed into thinking they didn't deserve any better.

He nodded. "I did. Because by the time I was eighteen, he wasn't slapping me anymore. In fact, he was pretty proud of me. His parenting skills were just old fashioned, not abusive. He didn't find things to pick on just so he could smack me. He really wanted me to get my act together." Wyatt smiled. "And I did."

She wasn't sure what to say to that. It was so opposite of how she was brought up. "Is that how he raised your mother?"

Wyatt's brows drew together. "I don't know. Grandma was alive then." He thought for a moment. "That could explain why she and her brothers were surprised by how many people showed up at Gramps' funeral though."

"They did?" She was surprised herself.

"They did, by the hundreds." He squeezed her hand, pride coming through in his voice. "Gramps was well respected. He knew his stuff, he was fair, and he didn't hesitate to help a neighbor. I think that's why he took me in, teenage-know-it-all that I was."

He shrugged. "For me, it was probably like going through bootcamp in the military. Once I understood the rules and the reasons, I rose to the challenge. I'm guessing my mom and uncles didn't see it that way."

That he could see it that way had her heart melting. "Then I guess you liked working the ranch in the end?" There must have been something to make Wyatt miss his home so much.

"I loved it. I still miss it." He looked away, clearly recalling his early years. "Yes, it was hard work with the cattle. We raised a select herd for local butchers, a couple of restaurants and dozens of families."

She didn't understand the appeal, but most people wouldn't understand why she enjoyed teaching third graders.

"We had a lot of good times." He looked at her again. "Every month Gramps threw a cook out for all the hands and their families. We even had music and dancing and a few times a year there were even fireworks. That was after all the cattle had been sold or butchered. The Christmas gathering was especially fun because Gramps bought the presents and I handed them out. He even made me go to church on Christmas Eve and Easter Sunday." Wyatt shook his head. "He was definitely set in his ways."

He took her other hand and stared into her eyes, his own full of excitement. "I want to bring some of those traditions here. I plan to bring on a few hands, possibly even ones from High Mountain."

She recognized a kindred spirit in his passion for his work. "Do you think they would move here. That's a long commute on top of long days."

"No, they can stay here. There are three bedrooms upstairs. I'll invite the single men unless you think there is housing for families close enough."

She shook her head. "Not really. At least nothing I would live in." That he'd asked for her input made her feel a part of his life.

Abruptly, he stood. "I want to show you upstairs. Maybe you could tell me if one of the rooms would be okay for a small family?"

"I'd be happy to give you my opinion, but I'm not an expert on a family's needs." She rose, their hands still clasped.

He pulled her closer and cupped her face with his hand. "Not yet, but you have a sensitivity to what children and parents need."

Looking into his eyes, she found herself wanting to see him with his own children someday. Before her mind could explore that idea, he'd started pulling her toward the hallway.

She laughed, his excitement contagious. "If you have one of the rooms, that only leaves two for ranch hands."

He let go of her and let her precede him up the stairs. Halfway up, she looked over her shoulder to find him staring at her butt. She snapped her head forward, her ego soaring.

That he found her attractive fed a need in her that she'd fought since high school when she'd sprouted up above everyone in her class, even taller than some of her teachers. At the time, she didn't realize that boys grew taller later than girls.

When she reached the top, Wyatt's hand on her lower back guided her to the left. They stepped into a long room with two twin beds.

"This is the room I thought a husband, wife, and possibly a child could use. Can you see it?"

She walked further into the room, her heart rate rapidly increasing at his question. It was as if he was asking if she could see them living in the room. She tried to focus on the question. "This would just be their bedroom?"

He nodded. "Everyone will have the run of the house."

She widened her eyes. "And Annette and her husband are okay with that?"

"Yes. They are going to have a small house built on the northside of the property. Annette doesn't want to have to spend time caring for such a big house."

Her interest shifted. "Who's building it?"

"They haven't looked for anyone yet. Annette is still tweaking her drawing of what she wants."

She walked back to him. "I wonder if my father could help with that. He retires the end of the year."

"Of course." Wyatt threw one hand up. "I should have thought of that."

"No, you shouldn't." She smiled at him. "He's *my* dad. I can't help thinking he'd be interested in building their house." She stood next to him and reviewed the room. "This could work for a bedroom if the child isn't older than maybe two."

Wyatt pondered that a moment. "Or I could use it for two grown men and that would make it possible to have four hands living up here."

"Then where would you sleep?"

"Annette and Ed have a room with its own bathroom downstairs. I could move into there when they move out. My room now is across the hall." He strode out and she followed, curious if he kept his room as neat as he kept himself, the stables, and his truck.

She walked into a smaller room than the last one with a queen size bed, a dresser, a closet, and a chest in it. The bed was made and there were no clothes in sight. She grinned. Just as she would have expected. "Do you always keep your room neat?"

"Yes. Structure is what keeps me on the straight and narrow."

Though he said it with a smirk, she could see he wasn't completely comfortable with her observation about his neatness. It was kind of cute. "I don't know if you noticed, but my place isn't quite as neat as yours."

He shrugged. "I don't expect other people to have the same habits I have. When Annette has little Charlotte visit, I find toys everywhere. Even found a rubber ducky in the downstairs bathroom sink."

She laughed, imaging him going to wash his hands and finding the toy there. "That's good to know."

He stepped closer. "There are times when leaving things about is appropriate."

She raised her eyebrows. "Oh, really? Like when?"

Lifting her hat off her head, he tossed it on the dresser. "Like when there are more important things to do."

Her heart jumped at what those things might be considering they were alone in the house and standing next to his bed. She placed her hands on his chest and moved them up to unbutton his top button. "Like when taking off your shirt, perhaps?"

She continued down the row until the red-checkered shirt gaped enticingly. Not able to resist, she slipped her hands inside, feeling his pectorals move beneath her palms.

"Yes."

She let her hands travel lower over his abdomen. The taut ripples there made her anxious to see them again. Pulling her hands out, she tugged his shirt out of his jeans then smoothed it over his broad shoulders and down his arms. It got stuck at his wrists where it was still buttoned.

He lifted his hands up as far they would go. "I might need some help."

She was far too busy enjoying the view. Unable to resist, she ran her hands over his chest and abdomen again. The muscles moved beneath her fingers. "You obviously work hard."

He took a breath, his chest expanding. "Running a ranch will toughen anybody."

She nodded. "Definitely." Since his hands were still stuck in his shirt, she decided to make the most of her advantage. She let her fingers trail even lower and unbuckled the sturdy belt.

"Alyssa, what are you doing?" His low voice had grown lower.

It sent a thrill from her heart to her toes. Feeling

adventurous, she unbuttoned his jeans. Did she dare unzip them and see what had caused the hard bulge in the fabric?

One second, she was contemplating her choices and the next she found herself with her back to Wyatt and her hands held behind her back.

"I think it's my turn now."

His deep voice in her ear sent thrills to her very core, but the imp in her couldn't resist. "I wasn't done."

A kiss landed on her neck just before his tongue darted out and licked up to her ear.

She brought her shoulder to her ear. "Wyatt, that tickles."

"Good to know."

As one hand held her wrists behind her, the other came around and started unbuttoning what she referred to as her western dress. Because she lived alone, all her dresses buttoned down the front or were pull-on. Why they made dresses with zippers in the back was beyond her. But she never realized how tantalizing it would feel to have the man she had fallen for unbutton it for her.

As he reached the third button, his hand brushed the bare skin on the insides of her breasts. The light touch had her catching her breath, her skin growing more sensitive by the minute. As his hand worked the buttons down to her waist, her mind caught up with her. "How did you get out of your shirt?"

A soft chuckle in her ear sent shivers racing along her skin. "I reached behind me and unbuttoned my sleeves. It's on the floor where it should be right now."

Reactively, she looked down. Her dress would be there as well soon, if she let it be. She couldn't imagine where else she would want it.

But he stopped undressing her and his hand moved up, touching her bare belly before moving over her bra-covered breast, mimicking her movements on him. He continued to her shoulder, pushing her dress over it before he took a detour and lowered his hand to pass over her other breast before pushing the material off her other shoulder. He let the dress fall, where it stuck on her hips and forearms.

"Your skin is so soft I could touch it all day." His lips found her shoulder and kissed it then continued up her neck.

She let her head fall to the side, enjoying his light touch, her whole focus on where his lips touched her flesh. Her bra tightened around her for a second and then went loose.

That simple act caused her insides to jump. Whoever said anticipation was everything must have told Wyatt. His hand smoothed down her back, then around her waist to slowly, ever so slowly, rise over her rib cage to finally cup her bare breast beneath the loosened bra.

She leaned her head against his neck as he enveloped her breast in his large palm and lifted it before moving his thumb lightly over her nipple.

"So soft." His voice made her feel as if she floated on a cloud of desire. Her taut peak was hard and her body wanting.

When his hand left her breast, she moaned.

His chuckle reverberated through her. "I want to know every inch of you. I must be thorough."

Knowledge of what that meant for him had her sheath contracting. If he said every inch, he meant it.

As his hand found her other breast and lifted then stroked it, her heart sang. Everything about this was right, perfect, meant to be. Her nipple grew so hard, she arched her back, her need escalating.

"Shhh, not yet."

Something in his voice made her wonder if he used that voice to calm an over excited horse, but before she could contemplate that further, his hand moved over her stomach and dipped beneath the elastic of her slip and panties.

With adept fingers, he pulled them down, one side then the other. She wiggled her fingers in his other hand to see if he was ready to let her go, but nothing changed. She had to ask. "How did you get so good at using only one hand?"

"I broke my arm once when I fell from a horse." She could hear the smile in his voice. "Never realized how helpful that would be."

Just as she started to wonder if that meant she was the first he'd held captive with one hand, his other moved over her mons.

Her breath caught as two of his fingers played with the small patch of curls there. Then as she had hoped, expected, and wanted, those fingers moved between her legs and she exhaled, closing her eyes. He took his time exploring her damp folds then her clit. The lightness of his touch was a tease in itself.

She'd never orgasmed during foreplay before, but this could well be the first time.

His fingers stroked her clit before testing her moist entrance and then back again. She spread her legs, thankful that she wore cowboy boots instead of heels as her balance was shaky at best.

With no warning, his fingers slowly slid inside, holding her to him, her hands pinned between them though he'd released them. His free hand now making lazy circles over one nipple.

He was behind her, in front of her, around her. He surrounded her with his touch and his clean scent of soap, but overriding that was his strength and maleness.

"You make me feel so good." Her words came out as barely a whisper because his fingers inside her began to move in and out slowly. Everything about his love making was slow, building her need with each minute that passed.

Her breathing grew shallow as her body tingled with

craving. His hand left off its slow circles, and his fingers held her nipple, rolling it back and forth in rhythm to the fingers inside her.

"Come for me, Alyssa. Let me feel you shatter in my arms." The words whispered through her, sending another shiver over her and bringing her to the edge.

She tried to say yes, but her body was too busy feeling every sensation, reaching for satisfaction.

Wyatt pulled her tight against him, without changing a beat.

Her excitement rose, her breath shortened as every muscle tightened and she flew into the abyss of pleasure. Her heart pounded as wave after wave of ecstasy rolled through her like a stampede of wild horses, shaking her to her core.

As the feelings subsided into a low rumbling, she blinked her eyes open. Wyatt's arms were wrapped around her, keeping her safe against him.

As her senses came back to her, she could feel the hard ridge against her lower back. She wanted him to know the same feelings. She wiggled her hands.

Wyatt released them by moving his hips back, but he kept her wrapped in his arms.

She turned within them and lifted her arms around his neck. "You make me feel so good."

For an answer, he lowered his mouth to hers.

It was no gentle kiss. Her body leapt at the sheer sexual need in him as his tongue swept through her mouth, eagerly tasting her satisfaction. But all she tasted was his need for her. Pulling her mouth away for a change, she broke the kiss.

He blinked at her as if he didn't understand.

Without hesitation, she pulled her arms down between them and unzipped his jeans.

The motion had him stepping back.

"It's your turn." She pointed. "Off."

As if he couldn't think beyond her command, he started toeing off his boots.

She quickly unbuttoned the rest of her dress and threw it on the dresser as well. Pulling her own boots off, she finally took off her slip and panties. As she laid them on top of her dress, she grinned and grabbed up her hat. She was going to ride her cowboy.

Chapter Fourteen

Wyatt dropped his jeans and stepped out of them. The cool air-conditioning coming from the vent above him helped to gain back some of his control. He'd known having Alyssa in his arms as she came would be beautiful, but it had seeped into his very soul. He didn't think he could ever be whole again without her.

As much as he wanted to wait to make love to her until she knew everything, he couldn't resist her. He tried to be an honorable man, but he was a man first and she was his weakness.

She turned around to face him in all her naked glory, long legs, flared hips, full breasts, and a sultry smile that made his balls ache. She'd donned her cowboy hat and looked sexy as hell.

He stifled a growl of need, and held out his hand.

She ignored it and placed her hands on his chest pushing him back so the bed hit the back of his knees. "It's your turn." Her hands left him, and she tipped her hat down then looked up at him from under the brim. "I'm ready to ride my cowboy."

All thoughts of making sweet love to her vanished at the sultry look in her eyes. He gave her a smirk. "Are you sure you can handle me?" He meant it as a challenge, but as her gaze swept downward to look at his erection, he realized how she'd taken the comment.

She touched his chest again, this time with a single index finger. "Absolutely." She pressed her finger harder making it clear she expected him to get on the bed.

He grasped her hand with his and wrapped his other arm around her. "Then show me." Pulling her tight to him, he fell back on the bed.

She laughed, a sound so light, he could listen to it for the rest of his life.

Damn. He really could.

Feeling her move her leg as if she planned to rise, he lifted his head and kissed her. This time he had some control, but he wasn't above showing her with his tongue how much he wanted her.

She broke away and shimmied back into a sitting position on his thighs. She held her hand up and shook her finger at him. "Nice try, cowboy."

He widened his eyes pretending all innocence, and her laugh filled the room again. He needed her in his life. She was all that was missing, even while at High Mountain Ranch. She was the someone he wanted to share the joy with, and even the grief.

Her fingers on his cock had all thoughts of the future disappearing as his body focused on the here and now.

"I like this." Her gaze was on her fingers and his cock between them. "It's like you, strong, tall, but kind and caring."

He tried to focus on what she meant, but logical thought wasn't coming to his aid.

"I need this inside me."

"Yes." The word came out of its own accord. He wanted her to be a part of him and he a part of her.

She lifted her soft ass off his thighs and moved over him.

When she didn't move directly onto him but hovered just beyond touching, he looked away from where they were about to join and met her gaze.

A slow smile spread her lips. "You like it slow, right?"

He groaned. He couldn't help it. If she was planning to torture him with pleasure like he had done to her, he was in trouble.

"You're lucky I'm not good at slow, but I'm going to give it the old college try." With those words, she lowered herself gradually onto him.

As he sunk deeper and deeper into her warm sheath, he let out a long breath and closed his eyes, every fiber of his being feeling a peace he'd never known. He grasped her hips to keep her there, afraid the feeling would dissipate if she moved an inch.

Opening his eyes, he gazed at her. She had also closed her eyes, but as they fluttered open, he thought he could lose himself in their golden depths forever. Or just maybe, he'd find himself there, in her heart.

"Wow." Her word came out on a breath.

He agreed but couldn't muster the words. As she sat there, impaled on him, her sexy sweetness called to him. She must have pulled her hair from her ponytail because half of it fell over her shoulder to lay on her breast, ending at her nipple. Her face was flushed, and the cowboy hat added an erotic aura to her wholesome goodness.

"I suppose I should move, right?" She gave him a lopsided grin.

He squeezed her hips. "Not yet. Too good."

A wicked gleam game into her eyes before her hands moved over his stomach muscles, making them contract of their own free will.

"Alyssa?" He put a warning tone on his question.

"Yes." She smiled innocently as her hands moved further up him to brush over his hard nipples.

His balls tightened. He had a feeling slow sex may not be in her vocabulary even if she had just orgasmed. Then again, in the state his body was in, she may have it right. Slow may not be the best choice at the moment.

He released her hips and moved his hands to her breasts, purposefully squeezing them lightly. "Beautiful."

She grasped his wrists and held on as she lifted her hips upward and glided down again.

His breath came out in a whoosh as electric sparks seemed to shoot through his body. No, there would be no slowing down for their first time together. With her hands on his wrists, he brought them forward and lifted his head to taste one hardened nipple with his tongue.

She gasped, letting go of him and bracing herself on the bed, her hips having risen as he brought her forward.

Then without warning, he sucked the nipple into his mouth.

Her hips came down on him hard. The feeling was impossible to ignore for either of them.

Releasing that nipple, he moved his head to the other and took it between his teeth to roll it.

Again, her hips went up and down. This time she rocked them forward. She sucked in a breath before speaking. "You're supposed to lay back and let me ride, cowboy."

He released her breast and let his head fall back. "Is that what you really want?"

She nodded. "I do. Let me make you feel what you make me feel. Put your hands behind your head."

Shit. He wanted to give her whatever she wanted, but to not touch her and simply watch her? All he could do was try.

Folding his hands behind his head, he looked her in the eye. "Are you sure?"

Her smile took his breath away. "I am."

He gripped his fingers together as she let her hands rove over his chest again. Even as she tweaked his nipples, he managed to remain where she wanted him.

Then she sat straight up, burying him deep inside her.

He stifled a moan, not wanting to curtail any of her movements. But when she reached behind her, arching back slightly and cupped his balls in her hand, he doubted his hands would make it through the encounter. The zing of pleasure that shot through his cock had him cutting off the circulation in his fingers.

"Hmm, so nice." She practically purred the words before releasing him.

His control had never been tested like this before. Then again, he'd never felt like he felt for Alyssa with anyone, either.

When her hands came forward again, he tensed, but she simply braced herself on his chest and lifted her hips. As she came down, she rocked forward, every movement controlled and deliberate to bring him and her the most pleasure.

And it was going to kill him.

He was barely holding back. As much as she wanted him to lie back and enjoy, he wanted to actively pleasure her.

This time when she lifted up again, he pressed his hips up.

"Oh, that's good."

It was, too good, but he couldn't muster the energy to answer since every ounce was focused on holding back the building pleasure each of her plunges sent throughout his body.

She moved up and down with a bit more speed, her rocking motion at the end making him grit his teeth. Small noises escaped her, and her lips parted as her rhythm increased.

Each wet slide of her body up and then down made his balls tighter and tighter. Just as he thought he couldn't hold back another second, a small squeak issued from her mouth and her whole body convulsed around him.

He let go, pressing his hips higher, lifting her from the bed as he moaned with pleasure. Unclasping his hands, he held her as they reached the peak together, releasing himself into her pulsing sheath.

Alyssa fell forward onto him, her hat rolling away as he clasped her to him, their bodies joined and tight against each other. Having her in his arms was like catching a piece of heaven and holding tight lest someone try to take it back.

As their breathing slowed, she straightened her legs to lay completely on top of him without separating them.

The feeling of her covering him almost completely was both comforting and satisfying.

She lifted her head. Her gaze was soft and filled with so much emotion, he was afraid to hope.

He brushed her hair back and gently pulled it to one side of her neck, the feel of it as it fell against him beyond silky. He loved everything about her. Without thinking of what his grandfather might say, he made his decision. "I love you."

Her eyes widened then started to water. "Oh gosh, I'm so relieved. I fell in love with you days ago."

"You did?" His heart thundered in his chest as joy burst inside him like a firework.

She nodded and sniffed. "I did. I was so afraid to say anything because we've known each other for a short time, but it just feels like I know who you are as a person, and I love that person."

Don't pretend to be something you're not, boy. It will get you into trouble every time. He forced his grandfather's words away. He wasn't pretending with Alyssa. With her, he was more open than with anyone he'd been with in his life, including his grandfather. "I'm not perfect, you know."

She smiled, her eyes no longer watering. "Neither am I.

Far from it. But I think it's your imperfections that I like most about you."

He couldn't hold her gaze. He would have to tell her everything if they were to have a real future together.

Alyssa started to bring her knees up as if she'd break away.

He grasped her to him and rolled them over, never breaking their connection. "Where are you going?"

She laughed again.

Shit, he loved that sound.

"Nowhere, obviously."

"Good." He liked the feel of her beneath him. Hell, he liked the feel of her on top of him, in front of him, anywhere with him. "I still need to learn every inch of you."

Her breath caught before it came out almost on a whistle but not quite. "I'm not going anywhere now. Your words just turned every muscle to jelly. I guess I'm all yours."

A rush of love and the need to protect caught him by surprise. She was *his*. No one had been his before, and if he had to prove it every day for the rest of his life, he would show her that her trust in him wasn't misplaced.

With no words left, he began by kissing her forehead, on a path with many detours and possibly some orgasms, that would lead to her toes.

~~*~~

The room had darkened with the deep purples of a setting sun in Arizona.

Alyssa turned on the light as she dressed.

He wanted her to stay the night, but that was impossible. She had to return her father's truck to him.

What would it be like waking up in the morning with her?

He'd never lived with a woman. Never had the inclination, but now he wanted to. He wanted to live with her and wake up beside her every morning. He would kiss her as she slept then start her coffee before going outside to tend to the morning chores.

The vision struck him so hard, he opened his mouth to ask her to move in, but he clamped it shut quickly. Just like at High Mountain Ranch, he still needed to check with others. He didn't own the house he lived in now or with Gramps. It was frustrating. Maybe he was never meant to own his own place and he should just accept that.

"What are you thinking about. I can feel your tension."

"You aren't even touching me."

She stepped closer and put her hand on his shoulder. "Yup, stressed."

He wrapped his arm around her and pulled her back down on the bed, her little shriek was followed by a laugh. "Maybe I'm stressed because I want to make love to you again and we've run out of time."

"Oh, I like that. Just think, now you have something to look forward to." She lifted her head off the bed and gave him a light kiss. "But if I don't go now, my father is going to be asking more questions than I'm comfortable answering."

He reluctantly let her up when she pushed against his chest. She grabbed her two cowboy boots which somehow got separated and bent over to put the first one on.

Her neckline gaped and he enjoyed the view, still wishing she could stay. "If you'd like me to go with you to look at possible cars, I'd be happy to help."

Her head snapped up at his offer. "Really? I'd love that. Buying a car as a woman is a pretty rotten experience."

He rose from the bed. "If you want, I can intimidate the hell out of the salesman for you."

She chuckled. "I'd like that, especially if I don't know who it is." She pushed her second foot into her boot and stood.

He raised his brows. "I thought you knew everyone in town."

She snatched up her hat from the floor. "Not everyone, but close." She scanned the room obviously checking to make sure she hadn't left anything.

He wished she could leave something. If not now, maybe soon. "Did you want a water for the ride?"

She moved toward the door. "No, I'm fine." She started down the stairs.

He followed in his bare feet, determined to keep her in his life. "Do you have plans for tomorrow?"

She'd reached the entryway and turned to look up at him. "Actually, I do. My dad is supposed to be gone all day, so I'm working on his memory cabinet. I can only do it when he's not home and I can be there. It's getting harder and harder to hide it."

"Do you need any help?"

She shook her head. "I appreciate the offer, but I really want to do this on my own." She opened the front door and stepped out onto the porch.

He followed, swallowing hard to keep from asking her to stay.

She turned and faced him. "But if you'd like to drop by my dad's house Sunday morning, I'm sure he wouldn't mind making extra pancakes for you."

Somehow her offer eased his anxiousness about her leaving. "Have I mentioned I love pancakes?"

She wrapped her arms around his waist. "Hmm, no, I don't think so, but that's definitely a good thing to know."

He held her to him, enjoying her physical and emotional warmth. "You should also know that I love you."

She gave a short nod. "I love you, too."

He lowered his lips to hers and let her feel how much he cared. That her feelings matched his had his tension melting away. This time, she broke the kiss and winked. "Dream of me."

He grinned. "Yes, Ma'am."

She stepped away and jogged down the steps to her dad's truck. Once inside, she waved before backing out and heading down the dirt road.

He watched her until he couldn't see her anymore. Then still, he stood there. There were sounds of movement in the barn as the horses settled in. The valley had quieted from the activity of the day. Even he felt a new peace in his heart. "I'm going to marry that woman, Gramps."

He half expected his grandfather's voice to come out of the growing darkness, but all remained silent. It was time to move on. Time for a new chapter in his life. This one he would be in control of and no one else. Or rather he and Alyssa.

~~*~~

Wyatt lifted his hat and wiped his brow. Marking the new perimeter was taking far longer than he expected. The sky was already turning red and the shadows of the valley's mountains were making it hard to see. It had to be almost seven in the evening, but the heat, which had gone back into triple digits, hadn't lowered much.

Though he wanted to continue, he knew better. His grandfather always said, *pushing the time meant mistakes would happen*. Gathering up his tools, he straddled the ATV and started it up. As he drove back to the house, he surveyed his progress. It wasn't half bad for one man in one day. But at this rate, it would take a year before a full fence was complete. He wasn't afraid of hard work, but if measuring and marking took this long, getting the poles in the ground and the rails connected would take a lifetime.

He drove the ATV into the barn then exited. He gave Black Jack a pat and some encouragement. Logan still hadn't built an outside stall for his horse at Dr. Jenna's place, so the horse didn't get ridden much. He'd ask Riley on Monday to take the animal out.

Letting the screen door slam behind him as he entered the house, he closed the front door and strode into the kitchen. The ideas for the ranch kept coming to him, and he now had a long list going on his computer. He'd heard from Landon already, so at least progress was being made on that end.

Grabbing a water bottle from the fridge, he cracked it open and gulped. Some spilled on his work shirt, but it felt good. Finishing off the entire bottle, he threw it in the recycling bucket, something Gramps had thought was a waste of time. Then he grabbed another and strode back to the front of the house.

Seeing a moving dust cloud in the distance, he stepped out onto the porch to see who was driving in. It shouldn't be Annette and Ed, and Cole and Lacey were spending the night out on Lake Pleasant with friends. When it was clear the vehicle wasn't a truck, he leaned against the porch post and waited for the stranger to reach the house.

The car windows were darkened, probably beyond the legal limits, and the sporty black vehicle was now covered in dust. Was someone lost?

The wide door of the two-seater car opened and a tall man stepped out.

"Fuck." Every alarm in Wyatt's body went off. He refused to move. "What do you want?"

The thin man took off his dark shades. "What kind of greeting is that for your dad."

"Biological father. There's a difference." He crossed his arms, gripping the full water bottle and tamping down the urge to throw it at the fake smile on the man's face.

"Kid, aren't you ever going to let that go? It's been over twenty years since I gave you life."

"Thirty. Over thirty years." That the man didn't recall how old he was, was no surprise. "What do you want, Dennis."

"Hey, show some respect for your elder. Didn't the old man beat that into you?"

Bringing his grandfather into the conversation wasn't smart. "I haven't respected you since I was six years-old when you told me you were coming to take me to a spring training camp ball game and never showed."

Dennis frowned. "You're making that up."

The situation would be laughable if it wasn't so pathetic. "No, I'm not. You don't remember because you killed that brain cell with alcohol or drugs or who knows what."

"Don't forget the women." Dennis grinned, his smile too close to Wyatt's own for comfort. "But there's never been a woman like your mother." The man actually had the gall to wiggle his brows.

Wyatt shook his head. If Dennis expected to start a fight over his mother, that wouldn't happen. *Big men never have to fight, only little men do, boy.* His grandfather's words rang true, particularly in this instance. He'd meant *little* in both physical stature and in their hearts. His biological father fit both criteria.

Studying the man, it was hard to believe he wasn't even fifty yet. He looked about seventy. The wrinkles were pronounced on his skinny frame, and his pale skin was blotched with scars from bar fights. His dark hair was slicked back with who knows what. "How'd you find me?"

Dennis smirked. "A little birdie told me old Abel died, so I went to the ranch to offer my condolences. Imagine my surprise when I found it deserted. I thought for sure he'd leave the whole thing to you."

Wyatt didn't move a muscle. His gut telling him that's what Dennis had banked on. His father's tactics were far too predictable.

When he didn't respond, Dennis' smirk faded. "One of those men who worked for the old man was in the Dusty Margarita and heard me ask the bartender about the place. He told me last he saw you, you were headed here with your horses. You got more than one? If they are a good breed, I hear you can get a good chunk of change for them."

Obviously, nothing had changed with Dennis. "You didn't answer me. Why are you here?"

The thin man strode forward and leaned against the front of the sports car. "I came to see how you were doing." He scanned the area. "Looks like you landed on your feet pretty damn good. What's this place worth?"

The hair on the back of his neck stood at attention, and every nerve was on high alert. He forced himself to shrug. "I have no idea. It's not mine. I just work here."

"I told you a long time ago, Wyatt. You don't want to be the workman. You want to be the man at the top."

He snorted. "Like you?"

Dennis crossed his legs. "As a matter of fact, yes. I'm doing pretty good right now, as you can see." He patted the car hood. "Bogus insurance claims can really pay off with the right legal team. I may not have anyone under me, but I'm in charge of my own destiny."

He raised his brows. "Don't you mean the drugs and alcohol are in charge of your destiny. What's it now, meth?"

"Don't be a fucking smart mouth to me, kid." The turn in tone was fast and furious.

Wyatt expected it. If the man kept to his pattern, cajoling and threats were sure to follow.

"I've got me a racket now." Dennis looked around the ranch again. "In fact, I'm staying in town for a while to see if I like it." He pointed his finger. "You've got it good out here. I didn't see a sheriff or cop in twenty miles."

Fuck, just what Canterbury didn't need.

Dennis was back to grinning. "I heard in town you got yourself a sweet schoolteacher all to yourself. I never pegged you for a schoolteacher. Your mom said you hated school."

At the mention of Alyssa, his whole body started to sweat. Anger swept through him like an afternoon monsoon. All his protective instincts sent his blood pounding. He uncrossed his arms and glared at the man who gave him life. "You—"

Dennis waved him off and put his shades back on. "Don't go getting your undies in an uproar. I got my own piece. She's a beaut and energetic, if you know what I mean." He turned his back and walked to the driver side door. Opening it, he took inventory of the ranch once again. He nodded. "You do know, this whole spread could be yours, but if you want it, you'll have to come to me. I've got the know-how. You can find me at the Open Road Motel in Wickenburg. They got a pool."

The man started to bend into the car but stopped. "And Wyatt. I know you're excited to see me, but you didn't have to pee yourself." Laughing, Dennis dropped into the front seat and closed the door.

Wyatt looked down. The crushed water bottle in his hand had sent water running down the leg of his jeans. He dropped it as if it were on fire.

The sports car made a quick circle in the dirt and peeled

out back the way it came, leaving a cloud of dust in its wake and Wyatt shaking with frustrated anger.

There was no law that said Dennis couldn't hang out in Canterbury, but he needed to find a way to get rid of him. He didn't like the insinuation that Annette could lose the ranch to a man like him. He also didn't like the idea that Dennis knew about Alyssa. There were definite disadvantages to living near a small town.

His mind immediately started searching for ways to drive his father out. Maybe there were bench warrants out on Dennis. That would be a good place to start. And if there weren't, what then? He found his hands curling into fists again and then his stomach growled. *Doing anything on an empty stomach is a fool's decision.* His grandfather's practical advice helped him relax.

Picking up the plastic bottle, he moved back into the air-conditioned house. The coolness on his now wet leg had him taking the stairs two at a time. Quickly stripping off his clothes, he headed for the shower. He'd brainstorm some ideas for getting his father to move on then confer with Alyssa and her dad in the morning.

Chapter Fifteen

The darkness opened up, and Wyatt froze at the sun on his face. "No." He knew this landscape. The open fields of bright green grass on the edge of the jungle where he stood. Feeling eyes upon him, he looked up and to his right.

The large gelatinous caterpillar over three stories high sat upon a horse-shaped mushroom. "Big men don't have to fight. Only little ones like you." It pointed one of its six hands at him then took another puff from his hookah.

Heavy breathing had him turning around. A giant White Rabbit shucked off its red coat and dropped it on the ground before jumping onto it and rubbing it in the mud. Then it opened its mouth of fangs and scrunched up its nose.

Rage filled him, rising from his feet, up his legs, through his chest and up into his head, his skin turning bright red with it, as red as the Rabbit's muddied coat. He fisted his hands and raised them. He was tired of being bullied. Tired of doing what he was told. Tired of not having his own life.

The giant Rabbit moved to the left, revealing a blonde woman in a blue dress.

Alyssa. The name whispered through his mind. She was everything that was good and right. She was worth fighting for.

The caterpillar whispered. "You can make it all go away." He held two hands out to his left.

Wyatt turned to find the Mad Hatter holding out a plate with a sleeping mouse on it. Its tail was wrapped around two pills.

"Come, Wyatt. Take the pills." The Mad Hatter gestured to the Rabbit. "And all this will go away."

The mouse woke up and yawned. Uncurling its tail, it sat up and blinked. "Forever."

He glanced back at the Rabbit, who raised its front paws revealing long, sharp claws. "Forever?"

"Yessss," hissed the caterpillar.

Grabbing the pills off the plate, he swallowed them.

The rabbit straightened, looking perplexed.

"You are no longer here, kid." The Mad Hatter's voice sounded like his father's. "But she is." He pointed beyond the rabbit.

Wyatt snapped around to see the Rabbit advancing on Alyssa. "No! I'm over here."

Alyssa smiled at the Rabbit and encouraged it to come to her.

A large Queen of Hearts card the size of the Rabbit appeared. "Off with her head."

"No!" Wyatt ran after the Rabbit, but his steps were too small. "You must stop it!" He yelled at the Queen. The Cheshire Cat's head appeared on the Queen's shoulder and smiled. "Poor Alice."

Alice? He watched in horror as the Rabbit swatted Alyssa leaving a trail of blood across her face and her dress. She stared at the Rabbit in confusion.

A stream of red blood started to flow toward him.

"Oh, enough of this croquet. Off with her head. She stole the tarts." The giant Queen pointed. "There's the proof."

This couldn't be happening. It had to be a dream. He just had to wake up, but he couldn't bet on it. He continued running to protect the woman he loved, his steps becoming slower.

"One pill makes you faster. One makes you slow. Guess you chose the wrong pill, kid." The Mad Hatter walked by him, gaining ground far faster.

"Save her."

"You gotta come to me, kid."

The Rabbit picked Alyssa up and like a child on Easter morning, bit off her head. Her blood rained down on him like a thunderstorm, filling his lungs, making it impossible to breathe.

Wyatt jolted up in bed gasping for air. Grasping his chest, he fought the constriction, but less and less filled his lungs. Lights floated before his eyes as he willed himself to stay conscious.

Breathe slowly. Alyssa's voice crept into his mind. *In…and out. In…and out.* Instinct had him following her instructions. He slowed his panicked breaths, focusing on her soothing voice in his head and taking air into his lungs slowly. *Good. You're doing good. Keep going. In…and out. That's it.*

Finally, the sight of his room overtook the flashing lights in his eyes. He dropped his hand from his chest as he continued to concentrate on his breathing. Now, he reached for long deep breaths, feeling his muscles relaxing.

"What the fuck?" He rubbed the back of his neck. Alice. Alyssa. The similarities were beyond eerie as was the fact he hadn't even noticed. Throwing his legs over the side of the bed, he rose. The urge to see her was strong. He glanced at his phone. Despite his need, part of him understood that showing up on her doorstep at four-thirty in the morning would not be welcomed.

He threw on a pair of jeans and headed downstairs in his bare feet. He opened the front door, intending to sit on the porch and let the cool air cleanse him of the nightmare.

Stepping out, he stilled. Something was off. He peered into the darkness of the moonless night and thought he saw movement where there was none. It might as well be a continuation of his nightmare. As his body tensed, almost expecting to be attacked by man or animal, a whinny sounded in the darkness.

Every one of his senses was focused on where the sound had come from. Either a horse was warning him or afraid for itself. Not moving, he stood completely still. Minutes went by with no new noises.

He should go into the house and grab a flashlight and his boots. He turned, opening the screen door, when the whinny sounded again. This time he was certain it didn't come from the barn or north corral. Had a horse escaped? Had Cyclone busted out in the middle of the night?

Quickly, he ran down the steps and padded across the yard toward the entrance to Last Chance. The slightly darker shadow of the sign was his guidepost. He was almost there when the whinny sounded again to his left.

Turning he saw the horse, only because its white coat reflected what little light there was in the dessert in the early morning hours. He approached carefully. Without a light, he couldn't see much, but the rope that held the horse to the rail designating the outside of Last Chance was almost as white as the horse. "Hey, fella. He looked toward the horse's end quarters but couldn't see anything. "Or girl. What are you doing out here?"

The horse nodded and moved closer to the rail, bringing its head over into his space.

"You seem friendly." Meeko had conditioned him to be extra careful. "Are you friendly?" Carefully, he raised his hand to let the horse smell him, but it just butted its nose under his hand.

Okay, that was pretty friendly. He gave the horse the attention it wanted. Obviously, someone had decided to drop it off as a rescue. His guess was the kids who had visited on Friday had told everyone and their brother about Last Chance, so someone decided this was a good place to dump a horse. In essence, it was.

Climbing between the rails, he untied the rope, which took a while. Whoever left the horse cared enough about it to not want it to wander off. Finally, he was able to guide the horse around the fence and onto the property.

"Ouch." He stepped on a sharp rock on the way into the yard. This had to be the stupidest thing he'd done in a long time.

Not willing to go into the barn in case the horse had a disease, he brought it to the south corral and let it loose. It didn't move away from him. "Listen, I have to go." The need to see Alyssa still burned in his chest. "At least you're a white horse and not a white rabbit."

The horse chuffed but didn't move.

"Do you need a lullaby?"

A nicker from the north corral told him that Meeko was awake and obviously didn't think much of his singing. He turned toward the north. "A lot you know."

"Okay, but just one song." Golden Slumbers seemed appropriate, so he sang. When he finished, he gave the horse a pat. "I'm going to call you Ghost for now. We'll get you checked out in the morning."

The animal seemed to be happy with the song and reassurance. Either that or it was happy to have company. Despite Meeko's snort, he'd come to his end of the north corral to listen.

Predawn light started to glow in the east. He couldn't wait any longer. The need to see Alyssa, make sure she was okay, overrode everything else.

Quickly, he ran into the house and took the stairs two at a time to dress. Within minutes, he was grabbing his keys and jumping into his truck.

The morning light spread across the sky behind him. What day was it? Would she be awake? He tried to think beyond the need to see her.

It wasn't until he'd hit the second stop light in town that he remembered it was Sunday. By the time he pulled into the apartment complex, the sun had risen and the day was starting. He pulled into a space before her apartment. She might not even be home.

Still, he got out of his truck and headed up the stairs. He had to know. The vestiges of the dream still holding onto his psyche tenaciously. Without hesitation, he knocked.

Silence greeted him. The entire complex was still asleep. Maybe she wasn't home. She could be at her father's. But maybe his dream meant she'd never made it home due to an accident.

Near panic set in. He knocked again, then listened at the door. Was that a door he heard? If so, she was up, and he'd just make sure she was okay. That and warn her about his father. And—

"Who's there?"

Relief filled his soul. "It's me, Wyatt."

The latch turned and the door opened.

She stood there in a furry bathrobe, her blonde hair falling to past her shoulders in an unorganized mess. He'd never seen anything so beautiful. Stepping in, he kicked the door shut with his foot and wrapped her in his arms, holding her tight. Reassuring himself she was alive, real, his.

"Wyatt?" Her muffled voice came from his shoulder.

He forced himself to loosen his hold and cupped her face in his hands. "Are you alright?"

She frowned. "I'm fine. I think the question is are you alright? It's six-thirty in the morning. On Sunday."

He dropped his hands, realization dawning. She had it right. He was obviously the one with a problem. Embarrassment flooded him. What was he supposed to tell her? "I apologize. I should go."

He turned to leave, but she tugged on his arm. "Oh, no, you don't. You came here for a reason, now come sit down. I'll make us some coffee."

"But you could go back to bed."

She tugged him over to the couch. "Not a chance. Now sit." She shuffled over to her open kitchen and went about measuring out coffee and pulling two mugs out of the cabinet. Once the coffee started heating, she leaned her butt against the counter. "Now, tell me what—" she held her finger up. "Wait, hold that thought.

Puzzled, he followed her with his gaze as she rushed into her bedroom and closed the door. Her voice floated through to the living room, but he couldn't make out the words. When she reappeared, her hair was brushed and pulled back in her usual ponytail, much to his disappointment.

"Okay, Snowdrop is locked in the bedroom, and I think the coffee is done." She poured two cups and brought them over. "Here. I'm sure I need this more than you."

In his rush, he'd forgotten about her rabbit. Unfortunately, that brought the images from his dream rushing back.

She sat down next to him and held her cup with two hands to take a sip. She sighed. "There's nothing quite like the first sip." She placed a hand on his thigh. "It's even better having that sip with you."

He placed his hand over hers, thankful she didn't think he was crazy when he was starting to believe he was.

"Now, tell me what sent you to my doorstep at such an early hour to ask if I was okay?"

He tried to look at her but couldn't. "I woke up not being able to breathe."

"Oh, no. You obviously managed to get your breathing back in order."

He nodded. "The reason I woke was because of a nightmare where you were hurt." He couldn't bring himself to even think about what happened at the end. "I had to know you were okay."

She squeezed his hand. "I'm fine. It was just a dream." In his peripheral vision, he saw her coffee cup move upward as she took another sip. "My question is why last night? What caused the dream?"

He rubbed the back of his neck. "I don't know. Yesterday I worked on the ranch all day alone. Then my father showed up as he's wont to do once in a blue moon, and I went to bed."

"It sounds like your father's visit triggered your dream. But I don't know why I would be in it unless you are always dreaming about me anyway."

He heard the smile in her voice and finally looked at her. She was everything he wanted, but something was seriously wrong with him. "I think about you all day and dream about you at night."

Could it be that simple? Pieces of his conversation with his father came back to him, and he tensed. He'd mentioned Alyssa specifically. He'd been in the dream too, as the Mad Hatter. Wyatt set the coffee cup on the side table and rose. More of the dream connecting to his reality.

He walked to the small island in her kitchen before facing her. "My father knows I'm interested in you."

She took another sip of coffee and shrugged. "That's no surprise. If he's been in town for more than two hours, he probably knows at least half the gossip.

She didn't understand the threat his father was, especially to himself. The image of the Mad Hatter offering him the pills flashed through his mind. "Damn."

"What is it? Did you remember something else?"

He wanted to lie, but that capability was beaten out of him by Gramps. "I did."

"Tell me." She set her coffee cup down and held out her hand.

He wanted to take it, but he couldn't. If he touched her, he'd never tell her. Now, he understood that she had to know everything. And if she did?

"Wyatt, tell me about your dream."

A chill raced up his spine. "In my dream, there is a giant White Rabbit with claws and fangs. It's taller than your apartment. So is the Caterpillar and the Queen of Hearts. But you and me and the Mad Hatter who had my father's voice were small."

She put her hand in her lap. "So we are all powerless in this unreal world."

At her observation, he understood now. "Yes. But the Mad Hatter offered me two pills and promised if I took them, it would all go away."

"Did you take them?"

Her almond-colored eyes held his against his will. "I did."

"Is that when you couldn't breathe?"

"No." He looked away, anywhere but at her. "I vanished as far as the Rabbit was concerned, so he turned toward you."

"I think I know where this is going."

At her serious tone, he moved his gaze back to her. Her face was far more serious than he'd ever seen it. "Where do you think it went?" Despite his dread, he had to know.

She clasped her hands, much like she had the first day he met her at the vet's office. He didn't like that observation.

"In your dream, you take the pills and you lose me to the Rabbit, correct?"

He nodded, his throat tightening.

"Is that what happened before you were arrested? Did you take the pills and someone was…hurt?"

Realization dawned like lightning, flashing in the night sky. "Oh, fuck." He turned his back on her. How had he not seen it?

"Wyatt, tell me what happened that got you arrested."

Her stern tone brooked no disobedience.

He looked up at the ceiling as if he could find the strength to endure her disappointment. Finally, he faced her. "Yes, you need to know."

Though her gaze held sympathy, her body was stiff. He already knew her that well. "I was almost sixteen. As I told you, friends had offered me oxycodone. I didn't have enough money for all twelve pills. I only had enough on me for one, so the dealer told me to meet him back at the auto repair place the next day with the rest of the money."

He folded his arms as if he could protect himself from her judgement. "I thought myself pretty smart. I decided I'd just take one pill and give the rest back the next day."

"That didn't happen."

He shook his head. "No. I took the pill that night and felt free of my family, my life, my resentment. I floated in a strange world, but one that made me happy. So the next day I didn't meet the dealer."

He took a deep breath. "I started getting paranoid that the dealer was going to find me, so a few days later I swallowed another pill. The relief was complete. My life was good in my mind. But by the time my worries got the best of me again, it was the end of the week and everything I feared, and more, came to fruition."

He'd never told anyone what happened that afternoon after school. No one but the police. "My mother was at work, so I was home with my sisters. Shaine was eleven and Madison was only three." His chest tightened as the memories flowed. "The dealer knocked on the door and Maddy opened it. I was in my room, just coming out into the living room because I heard the knock."

"He wanted his money, didn't he?" Alyssa's right thumb rubbed against her other one as her hands remained clasped.

"Yes. And he wasn't leaving without it." He took a deep breath. "The dealer grabbed up Maddy and put a gun to her head. He told me if I didn't give him the money, he'd blow her head off."

Alyssa gasped and her hands flew to her mouth.

"The dealer was definitely high, which scared me even more. I ran to my room and grabbed the pills that were left, but I still needed fifty dollars to cover the two pills I'd taken. I only had ten, so I rummaged through my mother's room, looking in drawers, the closet, even under her mattress. I found fifty dollars."

He lowered his head and looked at his hands. "As I held that money, enough to satisfy the dealer, I still wanted more. If I could just find fifteen more dollars."

"You wanted another pill."

The disappointment in her voice had him keeping his head down. "Even in fear of my little sister's life, I was ready to raid Shaine's piggy bank just so I could have that one more pill."

"Oh, Wyatt."

"I know. I even headed for the girls' room, but Shaine stopped me." He looked at Alyssa again. "She's a lot like you. She's strong and takes no one's shit. I offered the dealer the pills and the fifty dollars if he'd let my little sister go. When he saw there were still pills, he released her and grabbed the pills then took the money and left."

Alyssa's hand came to her chest even as a tear slipped from

the corner of her eye. "I'm so relieved no one was hurt. So how did you get arrested?"

He grimaced. "That was Shaine. She called the cops and told them everything that happened. Next thing I know, child and family services is calling my mother, talking to my sisters, and the cops are taking me away for stealing since they had no evidence of any drugs. I broke up our family single-handedly."

"Mom refused to get me that evening. In juvenile detention is where I had the first nightmare. The next day my mother picked me up, but she didn't say a word. She'd packed everything in my room and had it in the trunk. She drove me straight to High Mountain Ranch and told Gramps she didn't care what happened to me. She said she didn't have time for a problem child."

Alyssa rose. "Wyatt, I'm so sorry. You were just a teenager who made a mistake."

He shook his head. "No, she'd raised me better. I was just too selfish to see. And even then, I wanted a pill to make it all go away."

She shuffled to him in her bunny slippers. "Do you think you were addicted after two pills? You don't want one anymore, right?"

He couldn't look at her. "Gramps always kept me on the straight and narrow. I know that if it wasn't for him, I'd have found a way to escape life again. That feeling of all my troubles disappearing was so tempting, even after moving in with Gramps. You say he was abusive, but it was his strictness that kept me from falling down the rabbit hole again."

She wrapped her arms around him. "You don't need your Gramps anymore. You are a grown man and you have a good life."

She was right, but the dream had left him shaken. His fear

of seeking out oxycodone again looming too large to ignore. Desperately, he grasped her arms and looked into her eyes. "I need you to tell me you'll leave me if I fail to stay away from those pills. You must threaten me and mean it."

Alyssa pulled out of his arms. "I most certainly will not. I'm not going to emotionally blackmail you. I'll love you and support you. I'll help you find professional help if that's what you need, but I absolutely refuse to threaten you. I'm not your grandfather. I'm the woman who loves you."

His chest tightened. No, she wasn't Gramps. She was Alyssa, the woman he loved who deserved so much better than a man who was afraid he'd escape life with a pill the minute things got tough. He'd leaned on his grandfather like a crutch and now he wanted to lean on her the same way.

The enlightenment devastated him. He stared at her as his chest tightened and his body reacted to what his mind had determined.

"Wyatt, what is it?" She stepped forward to put her hand on his chest.

He grasped it before she could touch him. "No. You're right. I can't depend on you. I can't depend on anyone. I have to face this fear on my own. I have to know in my heart that I will never reach for a magic pill again. I don't know that. I don't know if I'll ever know it."

"Are you sure you're not looking at this still through the eyes of a teenager and not the eyes of the man you are now?"

He let her hand go and stared into her eyes. "My nightmare was crystal clear."

"There are professionals who can help." She gave him a tremulous smile.

"Yes, I know that. What I don't know is if they can help me." He raised his hand as she opened her mouth. "You know this is something I have to do…alone. Gramps always said, 'You gotta go cold turkey, boy.'" His resolve grew hard as steel.

"You don't need your Gramps telling you what to do. Think for yourself. You're a man now, not a teenager. There's nothing wrong with having support."

She deserved a man who was whole, not broken with self-doubt. "I will find what I need."

Her eyes began to water. "But what about us?"

He swallowed the lump in his throat. All he wanted to do was take her in his arms and tell her he would be strong for her, but he didn't know if that was true. He needed to conquer his fear for him to be of any use to anyone. He shook his head.

Surprising him, she nodded, causing the tears in her eyes to fall down her cheeks. "I knew that. I just hoped that when I finally found my person, the man I could see having a family with and growing old with, that he would be willing to fight for me. I never thought he would need to fight for himself."

That she could see so clearly what he hadn't raised his frustration. If only he'd seen it first. Why didn't he?

Gramps.

Betrayal rifled through him, but he squashed it. He couldn't blame his grandfather for setting him on the right path. He'd been the one who used the man as a crutch, never confronting his own fear. The nightmares had been his conscience trying to tell him, but he was so stuck in his youth, he couldn't see it. And now…he'd tried to replace Gramps with Alyssa.

He rubbed the back of his neck, letting his shoulders fall forward in defeat. "I want to be that person, Alyssa. I want…" He wanted so many things. He wanted a life with her. He wanted a future. Frustrated, he dropped his hand. "I can't be the one for you. There's a better man out there for you." Even as he said the words, every fiber of his being screamed at him.

"I think you should go."

Her voice, so soft and broken, cracked his resolve. He hesitated, his mind searching out some way to save them, but it was fruitless. She deserved someone who was whole, who could fight for her, who could love her knowing that he'd always be there, not in some manufactured dream world. He finally nodded, and stepped forward to hug her goodbye.

She held her hand out in front of her, shaking her head. "Don't. Please."

The anguish in her heart filled him with self-loathing. Gazing at her tear-streaked face, he accepted the fact that he had done this to her, to them. He'd failed them. This was his fate.

But even as he turned toward the door, he hesitated. The selfish part of him told him he was a fool, but that voice in his head sounded too much like his father to trust it. Finally, opening the door, he stepped out of Alyssa's life, closing the door behind him. Closing the door on his heart.

Chapter Sixteen

Alyssa stared at the closed door of her apartment. Her broken heart bleeding inside, causing her chest to hurt. Numbly, she walked back to her couch and sat, her brain trying to understand how everything went so wrong so fast.

Even as she reran their conversation over and over in her head, she came to the same painful conclusion. If she stayed with him, she'd be his crutch. She didn't approve of his grandfather's methods, but hers wouldn't help Wyatt either.

Maybe she just needed to accept the fact that she was meant to be alone. She'd just have to accept that...hopefully by the time she stopped crying. Her hands were wet with falling tears and her nose ran.

Didn't it just figure when she wanted to wallow in her misery, her body made her get up and find a tissue. Walking to the kitchen, she grabbed one from the box and blew her nose. A thump against her bedroom door surprised her. "Snowdrop."

She carefully opened it, sure that the poor bunny was confused since he had the run of the place all the time. Picking him up, she grabbed the tissue box and sat back on the couch. Snowdrop settled in on her lap.

Now she had everything she needed for a good cry, but the tears had stopped. "Snowdrop, you are a miracle worker." She stroked her companion of the last five years. He was the one constant in her life.

No, that wasn't true. Her dad also was and had been since she was born. This cinched it. There was no longer any reason not to move in with her father. She would always be alone except for him, so she might as well enjoy his company while she had him.

The thought of buying her own home just didn't seem important anymore.

~~*~~

"No, I won't let you move in now."

Alyssa stared at her dad in shock, her pecan pancakes forgotten. "What? You've been begging me to move in since the day I moved out. Now, you don't want me?" Her broken heart was teetering on the brink of extinction at the unexpected rejection. Two in one morning was too much.

Her dad put his hand on her shoulder. "Allie, it's not that I don't want you to move in. I still do, but I want you to make this decision when you have a clear head. Right now, you're hurting and if you move in for emotional reasons, you may resent me later."

"What? That makes no sense at all."

"Eat your pancakes." He pointed to her half-finished plate. He'd already cleaned his while she managed to tell him the gist of what happened earlier.

"Eat my—no, I will not. I want to know the real reason why you don't want me to move in. Is it Ms. Davis? Is that why you didn't need your truck on Friday?"

A flush spread over her father's face from his chin to his forehead.

"That's it, isn't it."

He shook his head and leaned back in his chair. "No, that's not it. Yes, Belinda came over Friday, but that's not why I don't want you to move in."

She threw her fork on her plate. "I understand. You want your privacy. I get that. Just don't start lying to me just because you have a girlfriend."

"I don't have a girlfriend."

"Dad, it's okay to have a girlfriend. I have no problem with that. You're alone and you don't want to be anymore. Who knows, some day that may happen to me, too. There's no age limit on liking someone. It's probably nice having someone your own age you can—"

"She dumped me."

"What?" She stared at him. "How could she dump you? She doesn't even know you yet."

He stood, his plate in hand. Walking away dishwasher then leaned on the peninsula, he stopped at the kitchen sink. "She didn't want to know me. She said it's called friends with benefits."

She rose. Since when did fifty-year old people adopt that concept? "I'm so sorry. Here I've been blabbering about not being with Wyatt anymore, and you went through the same thing." She started to walk over to him to give him a hug.

"You sit down and eat my damn pancakes." His tone brooked no disobedience. "And if they've gotten cold, there's the microwave." He pointed to the one on the counter.

She went back to her seat and took a bite. Even cold, they were delicious. Dad had mastered two areas when mom died, cooking breakfasts and cooking pasta and sauces. As a child, she was happy to live on those. But he'd attempted other meals, which she ate, mostly. Having odd animals around had come in handy though for getting rid of inedible food.

"You can't equate your relationship with Wyatt to my two dates with Ms. Davis. If you loved him then you can't think straight right now." He added his plate and cup to the dishwasher.

If she loved him? "I did love him. I do love him."

Her father nodded. "I know."

Now she was thoroughly confused. "What do you mean, you know?"

He closed the dishwasher then leaned on the counter peninsula to talk to her. "When I picked you up this morning, I knew it was love. With your other splits, you were either angry because your ego was hurt or you were fed-up and you dumped them. This," he pointed to her with authority. "This is heartbroken. And if I ever see that cowboy again, he's going to see the wrong side of my fist."

That brought tears to her eyes all over again. How could she have made it this far in life without her dad protecting her. He was forever her safety net. "Thank you. That means a lot to me."

He gave a single nod then wiped the kitchen counter.

She understood what he was saying now. It was like when mom died. She remembered people at the wake asking her father what he was going to do. He kept telling them nothing different for at least a year. But it was different the minute her mom fell. Dad had stepped into mom's role in addition to his. "Fine. I still have another month before I have to either renew my lease or let it lapse." Though she would have liked a year, just as her father had said.

He started pulling meat from the freezer. "You done with those pancakes yet?"

Quickly, she took a big bite and spoke with her mouthful. "Awmoth."

When his head snapped up to scowl at her, she grinned.

The act of lifting her lips felt odd, but good. Leave it to her dad to get her to smile when she felt the worst she'd ever felt since being an adult. It was eerily like losing her mom. She'd lost something that had just begun. She took another bite of the pancakes.

"You better finish up so we can go car shopping?"

The statement startled her. "I can't. Wyatt…" Fudge, Wyatt wouldn't be going with her now. "I mean, you said you wouldn't go with me."

He shrugged. "Consider it a break-up gift."

She rolled her eyes. "I suppose it's time. But it's Sunday."

"Joe's and Edie's is open every day but Monday. Smart business couple. You won't go wrong there. Not only are they local and can let us know who sold them the vehicle, but I'm the foreman on Joe's mom's new house in that new fifty-five and over development near Constellation Park. He won't steer us wrong."

She swallowed. "Is that a threat or a got-your-back kind of thing?" She stuffed the last pieces of pancake into her mouth. What could be better than shopping after having her heart broken.

"I'm ashamed of you." He scowled, then broke into a grin. "With Joe, it's a little of both. And he'll have to deal with me since I'm buying."

She'd just risen to rinse her plate, when she halted. "Dad, I can't let you do that."

"Yes, you can. I've been saving for your kids' college education. I figure, you being a teacher and all you'll probably make them go to college."

Her heart tripped at her dad's forethought.

"But since you say you'll be alone for the rest of your life because Wyatt needs to get his act together and he was the one you loved, we might as well buy you a used car so you can start house hunting. I'll go get the keys."

He strode out of the room before she could process everything he'd said. Was he testing her to see if she really didn't plan to have a man in her life ever again? Son of a biscuit. She'd gone from men in Maricopa County to men in either Canterbury or Wickenburg and now to no men at all.

That didn't mean she couldn't have a child. Who was she kidding? What she wanted was Wyatt, children, and a sprawling ranch.

She put away her plate and grabbed her purse. She was going to do what she'd done after mom died, focus on her day-to-day and her dad. And pretend she wasn't devastated.

~~*~~

Two Weeks later

Wyatt took his hat off and wiped the sweat off his face before putting it back on. One more stake and the entire fence would be marked out.

He stood at the end of the valley looking back toward the house. The fluorescent pink tape he'd attached from stake to stake could be seen halfway up, the rest too far to see. Sticking his bandana into his back pocket, he grabbed the last stake and mallet from the four-wheeler and measured the space between the last stake he'd put in and the one from a week ago.

"Perfect." Pleased, though not surprised, he found the midway point which matched the spacing between all the other stakes exactly, and pounded in the stake. Attaching the two ends of tape to the stake, he laid the mallet back in the ATV.

One major task accomplished. Next would be putting

in the posts. Since Lacey had agreed to an auger machine for digging the post-holes to delay hiring more hands right away, he'd go back to the house and research the best one and where he could buy it. The last thing he wanted was a day off.

Climbing on the four-wheeler, he headed back. Working from dawn to dusk helped him to sleep at night and avoid any more dreams. Riding Tundra though, kept Alyssa in his thoughts. He tried to avoid thinking of her, even though the psychologist said it was okay.

He grimaced. He could hear his grandfather in his head. *Spending money on a shrink is a waste of hard-earned cash. You put your back into your work and you won't have any time to think.* That was just his grandfather's way. Talking to the psychologist had helped him come to some new conclusions about his grandfather.

The old man was definitely stuck in a bygone era. The fact that he thought women were only for pleasure, cooking, and kids, was a testament to that. Things like recycling, "shrinks" as he called them, and equal rights were far beyond his comprehension. What the old man would say about him talking with a Latina psychologist was better not to contemplate.

Despite his two sessions with her, they had yet to touch upon his nightmares and fear, except for her diagnosis though that he wasn't an addict. Instead, he had a fear of becoming one. He didn't even know that was a thing.

As he drove behind the north corral, he looked for Meeko. Letting Alyssa go hadn't just broken his own heart, but according to Whisper, Meeko's as well. Whisper was so pissed at him after visiting Meeko last week that she refused to step foot on the ranch when he was there, so he'd absented himself from the Sunday dinners, usually by going to Cole's, to let the family gather.

He'd also left the ranch so Whisper could meet Ghost, who

was a mare. According to Trace, who gave him the story based on Whisper's findings, Ghost had been well cared for health wise, but when the children she'd been given to got older, they lost all interest. According to Whisper, the only daily human interaction the horse had was with a man who fed her but was afraid of her. The family owned no other horses, so Ghost was extremely lonely.

Glancing over at the south corral, he smirked. Ghost, Lady, Sadie, Macey, and Lucky had gathered into a tightknit group. Ghost was definitely making horse friends in addition to human ones.

He halted at the north corral, checking Meeko's new spot. Sure enough, the horse stood beneath the shaded area. His concern was that it was the exact spot Meeko was in when he'd gone to work in the early dawn hours.

Driving around to the front of the corral, he checked the feed bucket. Some of it was gone, but not enough. He was ready to irritate the horse just to get it to eat. Getting back on the ATV, he headed for the barn, but the truck in the yard had him stopping.

Alyssa?

His heart leapt, even as his brain told him if she was there, he shouldn't see her. Driving up to the porch, he turned the machine off and strode into the house. He checked the kitchen first, but no one was in there so he went across to the living room.

Roy Parker and Annette were studying a map. Roy looked up from it, his brows lowering into a glare.

Wyatt cleared his throat. "Excuse me, I was just coming in for some food." Before Annette could say anything, he turned the corner and stepped back and into the kitchen.

He should have known. He'd recognized the truck but had assumed it was Alyssa. He was an idiot. Grabbing a water and a container of leftover chili from the refrigerator along with a spoon, he escaped back outside.

He didn't blame Roy for being pissed at him. He was pissed at himself for being the train wreck that he was. Walking into the barn, he drank half his water then sat on a sawhorse and ate his late lunch.

He had to go back to thinking about the ranch. Thinking about Alyssa made his heart hurt, but worse, made him feel like he did when he was sixteen and worthless. He'd started working on a yearly budget with Lacey. He could pull that after dinner. He'd also wanted to talk to each person who worked on the ranch to find out how much they wanted to do so he could determine how many hands he might need. Keeping family for filling in would work best.

The truck outside started up.

He didn't want to think about Roy and Alyssa. He needed to stay focused. But as the truck headed out down the dirt road, he could see it in his mind heading into town. He could picture Alyssa driving home to her cube in it.

"Fuck."

One of the horses responded with a whinny.

He finished his lunch and rose. "Since when do you take objection to a little swearing?" He waited for a response and got one. Cyclone.

Shit, what day was it. The last thing he needed was for Cyclone to start kicking down the stall because he'd forgotten to take him out for a drive.

"Wyatt?"

He turned around to see Annette sticking her head around the barn doors. "Yes."

"Could you come inside, please. I want to talk to you."

"Of course." Quickly, he thought back to the last time

Cyclone had pulled the wagon. Riley had taken him out the day before yesterday. That gave him one more day.

Relieved he hadn't shirked his duties, he made a mental note to add that to his schedule.

Grabbing up his lunch mess, he headed into the house.

Dropping his hat on the hall table, he entered the kitchen to find Annette standing with her butt against the counter. She wore her usual button-down shirt and blue jeans. No doubt she planned to ride Sadie when the temps came down a bit later. "Do you need me to help you with something?"

She nodded. "Please sit."

He did as instructed. He wanted to ask why Roy had visited, but part of him didn't want to know. Staying away from Alyssa was a daily struggle.

Annette reached behind her and slammed a pile of paper on the kitchen table. "Charlotte found this on the coffee table in the family room."

Startled, he scanned a couple of the pages laying on the flat surface. "It's the personnel policies. I apologize for leaving them out. That must have been the night I fell asleep on the couch." He started to gather them.

She slammed her hand down on the pile. "What are you doing?"

Confused, he looked up at her. "I'm just getting prepared for when Cole wants to hire more people. Is that a problem?"

"Not the policies." Something like a growl sounded in her throat.

He sat back, recognizing her pique. "I'm not sure what you mean."

She threw her hands up. "I'm talking about Alyssa. She's an amazing woman, and I had to hear from Roy that you are no longer seeing her? What are you thinking? She's perfect for you."

His stomach knotted. "Yes, she is. She's everything I could want in a wife."

"Wife?" Annette's brows rose. "So that's why you suddenly end it?"

He straightened. "It was a mutual agreement."

"Why?" Annette moved to the chair opposite him and gripped the top rail of it. "Why would two perfectly good people end a perfectly good relationship?"

Always tell the truth, boy, or it will come back to bite you in the ass. He shoved his grandfather's voice out of his head. As he'd come to realize, the old man wasn't right all the time. He rose. "There's something in my past that caused a problem. I'm not happy about this either."

She opened her mouth, but he held his hand up. "That's all I'm going to say about it."

She straightened. "Is that why you've been working yourself from sunup to sundown every day? It's not just to make the ranch the best it can be, is it?"

He shook his head.

"You're trying awfully hard to keep her out of your head. I'm here to tell you it won't work. You can work yourself right into the hospital with heat stroke, but it's not going to make what you feel for her go away."

Her words were like punches to his gut. She'd read his mind and told him it was hopeless. His frustration had him raising his voice. "What am I supposed to do then?"

She grasped the chair again hard and leaned in, pointing her finger at him. "If you love her that much, you need to confront this thing in your past, and you need to do it now."

"It's not that simple."

She pulled back and glared at him. "Then make it that simple."

He stared at her, his mind racing. Something about her confidence in her own advice had him doubting himself.

"And Wyatt. Don't wait. This isn't something where all the T's have to be crossed and the I's have to be dotted before you act. This is messy. What's important is that you stop hiding behind your work and act."

"Right." Her absolute surety had a small drop of hope sneaking into his heart. Make it simple. Confront his past. But his past was part of him and with him.

Insight floated into his mind like an eagle catching the updrafts. Not all of it. There was a part of his past he could confront and get rid of, and it drove a black sports car.

~~*~~

Wyatt pulled into the parking lot of the Open Road Motel. It wasn't hard to figure out where his father was. The black sports car was parked in front of room eight. He had half hoped that Dennis would be long gone. He strode up to the door and knocked.

On his way over, he'd come up with a plan to get his father to leave town. It wasn't perfect, but as Annette said, it didn't have to be.

He waited but no one answered the door. The car was right there so Dennis had to be around somewhere, most likely getting high. Walking past the other rooms looking for a few men gathered together, the sound of kids yelling in fun floated to him from out back.

The pool.

He found an open-air hallway between two rooms and strode out back. There were a number of kids playing in the pool, but his father and a woman lay on lounge chairs drinking beers in front of sliding glass doors, probably their room.

Striding forward, he was upon them before they saw him coming. "We have to talk."

Dennis squinted up at him before putting his sunglasses on. "Wyatt. Now this is a surprise. Jeanie, this is my son, Wyatt."

The woman, more his father's age from the wrinkles on her neck, thoroughly checked him out. "He's one strapping man, Denny."

Dennis sat up. "Isn't he?" He stood, almost losing his balance before righting himself. "What would you like to talk about, kid? My offer?"

Wyatt looked around. "I think we should have this conversation in private."

"Oh yeah, right. There are eyes everywhere." He chuckled. "Let's go to my room. I need another beer anyway." Dennis opened the slider on the room and stepped inside.

The floor was littered with clothes, take out bags, and dirty towels. Wyatt walked over them. Obviously, his penchant for neatness did not come from his biological father.

"You want a beer? I got some bourbon, too. The gin is for Jeanie. She loves her gin and tonics."

"No."

"Ah, come on. It will help you loosen up. You're strung tighter than my old guitar."

"I don't drink."

"Anymore, right? And I don't drink any less." Dennis chuckled at his own joke. "Have a seat." He gestured toward the unmade bed as he dropped into the wide soft chair next to the bed's end table.

"I'll stand."

His father took a swig and studied him. "Kid, you must have something pretty important to say because you're towering over there like the Empire State Building." He gestured with his beer. "I saw that once you know. I was right in the middle of Times Square on New Year's Eve."

Everything about Dennis disgusted him. That they actually shared blood embarrassed him, but that wasn't why the man had to leave. "You can't stay here."

"I can't? Why not? The room rate is pretty damn good, and the pool can't be beat. Besides, this is the closest place to that ranch you're working on. How am I going to teach you how to own it if I'm further away?"

Dennis smiled, showing a missing tooth. "I'll be a fuckin' monkey's uncle. You want me to move onto the ranch with you." He saluted with his beer bottle. "Now that, kid, is something to celebrate."

"No." Wyatt sighed. Had Dennis really killed so many brain cells he couldn't stay with a simple conversation? A buzz in his pocket told him he had a text. Lifting out his phone, he checked it.

Landon. He didn't have time to deal with that. He slipped his phone back in his pocket to find his father looking at him. Damn, he'd just done what his father had done to him. Changing his mind, he held up a finger and pulled out his phone.

"You got someone more important than me wanting you, kid? I hope it's your teacher."

The text was a simple question about the number of stalls in the barn. He quickly responded then put the phone away. "No, it's a teenager who works for me. He had a question."

"That's more important than our celebration?"

"Celebration? No, no celebration."

Dennis leaned forward and opened the end table drawer. "Of course, we gotta celebrate. Father and son finally living together." He set the beer bottle down and pulled out a plastic baggie.

Wyatt stiffened. It was filled with various pills.

Dennis pulled out two white ones and held them out on the palm of his hand. "I got your favorites. Here."

The Mad Hatter's voice in his head continued. *It will make everything go away.*

He stared at the pills. He didn't want to make everything go away. He liked his life. And even if he didn't, the last thing he wanted to do is end up like his father.

Taking out his phone, he took a picture of his father holding the pills. "Thanks, Dennis. Now, I just need to send this to Sgt. Valdez."

His father stared at him as he texted the sergeant.

"Who's this sergeant? A friend of yours? Hey, sarge. It has a nice ring to it. Are you taking these or not?"

Wyatt slipped his phone into his back pocket. "No. I don't take pills."

Dennis sneered. "Anymore, you mean." He popped them in his mouth then grabbed his beer and swallowed them. "You really need to loosen up if we're going to live together."

"Listen to me. We aren't living together. I just texted a picture of you and those pills to a sergeant on the Canterbury police force. I'm sure he or someone from the department will be here soon to arrest you."

The beer bottle whizzed by his head.

"You son of a fuckin' bitch! What kind of kid are you to rat out your own father?" Dennis ran a hand through his oily hair as he anxiously scanned the room. "I gotta leave."

"And I suggest you never come back." Wyatt watched as Dennis started grabbing up pills, liquor, and money that was stuffed under the mattress. Having seen enough, he let himself out the front door. Outside, he took a picture of the license plate on his father's car. Just in case he needed it.

Sgt. Valdez did work for the Canterbury police, but the motel was in Wickenburg. He doubted Dennis would realize that until he was long gone, or not at all. Still, it would be good for the Canterbury police department to know about Dennis, just in case he did decide to come back.

Getting into his truck, he headed out. It wasn't until he hit the Canterbury line that his actions at the motel sunk in. He slowed the truck and parked on the side of the road. He hadn't even been slightly tempted to take the oxycodone pills his father offered. He no longer wanted his life to be different. He wasn't that hormonal teen boy with a chip on his shoulder big enough to strike up a wildfire.

He sat there stunned, searching for his fear and finding it gone. When Annette had said to get rid of his past, he'd only thought of getting his father to leave. Now, he actually had his father to thank for his newfound comfort? If Dennis had never offered the pills, he would have never known. Who would have thought he'd be thankful his father did drugs? He'd always seen his father's drug use as his own path because if it hadn't been for Gramps, he'd have followed in his father's footsteps.

When he got home, he'd thank Annette as well for making him face his fear instead of hiding his broken heart. Could he mend that, too? That drop of hope that Annette had introduced started to multiply. What if he could win Alyssa back? Would she take him back? Would she believe his fear had left after a mere two weeks when he'd lived with it for fourteen years?

He had no answer, but he had to try. His first thought was to ask Roy, but after the look he'd thrown him earlier, he doubted the man would see him. Who else could he ask for advice? He knew she had a teacher friend named Marty, but he had no idea how to reach her, especially on a Friday evening.

Putting on his blinker, he got back on the road. Maybe he

should ask Annette. She and Roy had obviously talked. He was just driving by Canterbury Tails when it hit him. Quickly, he pulled into a parking space and jumped out of the truck. Waiting for traffic, he hoped they were still open.

He crossed the street and bounded up the steps. He tried the doorknob and it turned.

A voice he knew came from down the hall. "I'm sorry. We're closed. You'll have to—you!"

He cringed, but his mind was made up. Taking off his hat, he gave Connie Richards a quick nod. "Yes, Ms. Richards, it's me, and I need your help to get Alyssa back."

The woman glared at him for a moment, then handed him the boxes she'd been carrying. "Well, if I'm going to help you, then I better lock this door so no one else comes in."

Relief poured through him.

"Just put those in the closet in the bathroom. I'll be right with you."

He found the closet and added the boxes of tissues to the second shelf where one box remained. He'd never thought how many times tissues might be needed in a vet's office. Coming back out into the waiting area, he found Ms. Richards already seated and two bottles of water on the little coffee table.

Sitting in the chair catty-corner to her, he opened the bottle and took a swallow.

She did the same then capped hers again. "There's one thing I need to know first. What are your intentions toward Alyssa?"

He didn't even have to think about it. "I want to make her my wife."

The woman grinned before rubbing her hands together. "Then we better get started. If you want to get the sweetest woman in town to take you back and marry you to boot, you're going to have to forget about all the typical things. Alyssa Parker is going to need something personal and convincing if you ever expect her to become Alyssa Ford. Tell me what you know about her."

Chapter Seventeen

Alyssa walked into the Black Mustang with Marty. Three other ladies waved to them from a table front and center of the small stage.

Great, just where she wanted to be, in the middle of all the fun — not. She'd claimed she was sick last weekend, but she didn't feel comfortable lying again. Though it wasn't that much of a lie because she really did feel like shit. Emotionally sick was just as real as physically sick, in her opinion. Getting over Wyatt was going to take a long time, if it was even possible.

They sat down with the other women, one from the school and the other two were people they'd known since high school. At least she'd made a deal with Marty. She'd be the designated driver only if Marty didn't try to get her to sing.

"Root beer for you?" Marty grinned as she stood to get their drinks.

"Of course." She tried to smile, but knew she failed when Marty's grin faltered.

At least this weekend she had her own car. Though her father had offered the money he was saving for his future grandchildren, she couldn't let him pay for it. It made her defeat too permanent, so she'd written the check she hadn't wanted to write and bought her new used sedan. Nothing fancy, but it ran, had low mileage, and had been well taken care of by Mrs. Sanderson before the MVD had refused to renew her license. The woman was in her nineties and couldn't see much past the hood of her car.

That her father had already started saving money for her future children had hit her hard. Nursing her broken heart, she hadn't thought about how her giving up on love might affect him. Now she felt a certain pressure, which is probably why he never told her.

But on Tuesday, after school when Lieutenant Clark had come to the school to go over his fire safety presentation with her, all she could think about was what Wyatt had done for her class with the fire truck. And when she looked at Lieutenant Clark, she didn't feel the excitement at talking to him that she had before she'd met Wyatt. As far as she was concerned, her heart was just too broken to ever heal right.

And it didn't help that not a day went by that one of her students didn't mention what they learned at Last Chance. Now she was the one who couldn't wait for recess to avoid any talk about the ranch. She hoped they had found a new home for poor Meeko. Had Kentucky stopped licking at his wounds?

"Here you go, chica." Marty set a root beer down in front of her.

She lifted the bottle. "Cheers to a fun night."

Marty clinked her glass of red wine to the soda bottle. "Now that's the spirit."

She took a swig of the soda. A little distraction from her heartache couldn't hurt. It's not like it wouldn't be waiting for her when she got home and cuddled with Snowdrop.

Two men came over to chat with them. She and Marty let them focus on the three single women with them, though she was technically single herself, she wasn't on the market. Two of the ladies joined the men for a game of darts. That left the three teachers, so of course, talk turned to school gossip and policies.

When some people in the crowd hooted, she turned to see the Karaoke Man, that was what he called himself, had switched on his equipment. He usually sang a few songs then had people come up. It meant they had about fifteen minutes before her ears started to hurt and about thirty minutes before Marty got up to sing. She wasn't a bad singer. At least she could carry a tune.

Alyssa took another sip of root beer. She recognized a number of people in the bar. It was a common hang out for both towns, so there was usually a mix plus a smattering of tourists. The bar was designed to look like an Old Western Saloon, complete with front board walk and inside wagon wheel décor.

Marty grabbed her arm. "Don't look, but Wyatt Ford just walked in."

Of course, her immediate reaction was to turn around. With her heart in her throat, she drank in the sight of him. Immediately, worry settled in. What was he doing in a bar? She glanced at one of the pool tables where she was pretty sure the men playing did drugs. Was he here to test himself? Or worse, had already failed?

Marty leaned in. "Don't look at him. Remember, you two aren't together anymore. For all you know, he's here to pick out a new girlfriend."

She frowned, giving Marty her best 'you're crazy' look. "You keep forgetting. We *mutually* agreed to end our relationship."

"That's what you tell me, but you never say why." Marty, who had only had one glass of wine so far, studied her far too closely.

"That's right. I didn't."

"You never kept your break-up reasons a secret before. That guy Ernest just didn't get rural life and wanted you to move to the city. The guy before him put his job over you. The one before that was more interested in sex than a relationship. The one before that wouldn't talk about anything."

Alyssa shook her head. "No, you have the last two backwards."

Marty's brows lowered as she tried to remember.

She took the opportunity to watch Wyatt stride over to the bar and order. She strained to see what the bartender put down in front of him, but another patron was in her line of sight.

"You do know you're staring, right?" Marty crossed her arms over her ample chest to make her point.

"Sorry. It's not like I can just turn off all these feelings like a light switch. I should have never decided to only date local men. This is going to kill me."

"I told you, just don't look. Hey, the Karaoke Man is about to start. Look at him."

Alyssa rolled her eyes. "The man is old enough to be my father."

"Exactly. Now you watch him while I get us another drink."

"I can get them." She pushed back her chair to do just that.

"Uh-uh, no you don't." Marty grabbed her arm. "You keep your butt glued to that chair."

"Fine." As Marty left, she had to agree with her. It was best to not see him. It just made it harder to forget that he had some issues to work out and thought she deserved someone better. The problem was, she didn't want someone better. She wanted him. She worried about him, which she was sure he would hate. Was he making any progress? Did he find it easier to concentrate on his issues and forget about her?

"Folks, we have a special treat for you tonight, a singing cowboy. He's dedicating this song to Alyssa. So Alyssa, wherever you are, take a listen."

She froze. He wouldn't.

Wyatt stepped up on the stage and took the microphone. He didn't stand behind the screen with the lyrics though. He stood right in front and looked at her.

What happened to 'he only sang to horses'? Part of her was thrilled down to her toes. Another part was worried he was going to embarrass himself. And the third part, her brain, was asking why he would come to the Black Mustang and dedicate a song to her.

The music started, but everyone kept talking because it was a bar and that's what people did. But she heard the first bars of the Beatle's song "Something." Then Wyatt sang the first phrase and her heart melted. His voice was beautiful. And as he sang every word, he looked at her.

Her eyes watered, but she couldn't look away. The room had grown quiet allowing his voice to fill her soul. As he sang the chorus, letting her know he didn't want to leave her, tears started to roll down her cheeks. She didn't want to leave him either.

By the second chorus, the whole crowd was singing with him. She only heard him. When he finished, the room erupted into applause, but he only had eyes for her.

He stepped down from the stage and came right to her. Taking her hands, he lowered his head to speak in her ear. "Will you talk with me?"

She nodded, her throat closed from the overwhelming emotion.

He led her outside into the warm night and pulled her to one side of the Old Western porch.

She searched his green gaze for answers, but she hadn't

asked the questions yet. She didn't know where to start. "I don't understand."

The night was quiet, the road deserted. The dark sky was lit with only twinkling stars. He took both her hands in his as he leaned his back against a post. "I'm not afraid anymore."

"What?" Her heart jumped, but her brain put on the brakes. "How can that be?"

He chuckled. "I had a lot of help. First, a psychologist who diagnosed me with the fear of being addicted."

She'd never heard of such a thing. "So not actually addicted or recovering from addiction?"

He shook his head. "No. Then Annette kicked my butt into gear and told me to conquer my past. Finally, and this is what I find ironic, my biological father, Dennis."

She cocked her head. "Dennis. This is the father that drinks and does drugs?"

"The very one. As I had told you, he's been in town, and I decided I didn't want him in our town, so I told him to leave. He thought I was telling him to leave the motel and come live on the ranch. To celebrate he offered me oxycodone."

"Oh, no." She stared into Wyatt's eyes, afraid of what came next.

"Oh, yes. It was the best thing he could have done. I looked at those pills and didn't want them, not then, not ever. He did for me what no one had ever done, made me face my fear. I'm not afraid anymore. I'm not afraid of becoming addicted. I'm not afraid of my past."

He lifted her hands in his and held them between them. "The only thing I'm afraid of is that you won't let me back in your life."

Her heart had started to beat hard in her chest, but she had to know. "And if I say I can't take you back. Will you search out your father or his pills?"

The anguish that came into his eyes, almost had her taking back her question. He lowered their hands. "Living the rest of my life without you is impossible to contemplate. But if it made you happy, I would accept that. And no, I wouldn't turn to drugs. Just like I didn't when Gramps died. I'm older and wiser now. I have no need of that crutch or any other. But I'm hoping that you would, in time, give me another chance."

Her heart soared. "How about now?"

"Now?"

She finally smiled. "Yes, now. How about if we take our second chance at love starting right now?"

Wyatt's smile grew wide as he pulled her to him. "I love you, Alyssa Parker."

She laughed. "I love you, Wyatt Ford."

He lowered his head, and she kissed him with all the love in her heart. Her whole world felt right. Happiness seemed to flow through her very veins. Her person had fought for himself and her. There was nothing else she needed.

Wyatt broke the kiss. "There is one more thing though."

"No. No more things."

He smiled. "It's a good thing, I hope."

"Okay." Had he bought a rabbit of his own? What would Snowdrop think?

He pushed off the post and backed her up. Reaching into his shirt pocket, he pulled out a box and knelt before her.

Oh, freak! She couldn't believe it.

"Alyssa Parker, will you marry me?"

She squealed like an upset Guinea Pig, and she didn't care. "Yes!"

Taking her hand, he placed a beautiful classic diamond ring on her finger. "Oh, Wyatt. It's beautiful."

He rose. "You are far more beautiful."

Clapping in the parking lot had them both turning.

Customers came up on the porch and congratulated them before moving into the bar.

She grinned. She couldn't help it. She was going to be Mrs. Ford, which meant she would be able to keep her handsome, kind-hearted, forged-in-fire cowboy for the rest of her life. Her happiness just couldn't be contained. "So exactly how many children were you thinking?"

He wrapped his arms around her again and hugged her to him. "I'd like to start with one and maybe have a couple more."

She murmured against his shoulder. "Perfect."

Another car pulled into the dirt parking lot, it's lights shining on the darkened lot. As Wyatt held her close, she recognized the woman in black getting out of the car. This time Mac wore a black tank top that showed off muscular shoulders and a pair of black jeans.

Alyssa pulled herself to Wyatt's side.

Mac strode up the stairs and saw her right away. "Hey, Lyssa." The woman's gaze swept over Wyatt.

"Hi, Mac. This is Wyatt. He just proposed." She held out her hand.

Mac stiffened and studied Wyatt again. "Did you get a good one?"

She'd forgotten that Mac wanted to be allergic to men. "I did." She looked at Wyatt. "This is Mac. She works at Poker Flat Nudist Resort."

To her surprise, he didn't even blink. "Then you must know my boss, Lacey Hatcher."

"You report to Lacey?"

He nodded. "I may run the ranch, but Lacey runs the whole operation."

Mac finally relaxed. "It's nice to meet you." She looked

at them both then pointed two fingers at them. "You two take good care of each other."

Alyssa grinned. "Oh, we will."

"Good. Now I have to go get drunk. Again." She turned and strode into the bar.

Wyatt squeezed her against his side. "You have interesting friends."

She laughed. "Just so you know, not all my friends get drunk on the weekend."

"If you say so."

"Oh, but I should probably tell Marty before she has too much wine. She'll blame me if she doesn't remember."

Wyatt frowned. "I'm not sure I understand."

"Well, if I don't tell her before she drinks too—Are those fireworks? There were lights reflecting off the cars in the parking lot. She looked to the sky.

They were getting brighter. "I guess people are celebrating our engagement."

Wyatt shook his head. "Actually, I think those are police lights."

Sure enough, the lights grew brighter and brighter. Eventually, a car pulled into the parking lot with a police vehicle right behind it.

He gave her a side squeeze. "Hey, just think of the story we'll be able to tell our kids about the night you said yes."

The policer officer exited his vehicle and strode past them.

She grinned. There was no way her kids were going to believe this. Once he'd received the requested documents from the other car he headed back to his vehicle. She couldn't resist. "Sgt. Valdez. What are you doing, working a night shift? I thought your seniority gave you days."

"Ms. Parker? How are you? I traded with my nephew whose

mother-in-law had surgery today, so he's with her tonight. Mr. Ford. Is that you?"

"Yes, sir."

"Well, isn't this an odd coincidence."

Alyssa couldn't contain her news. "Not really. He just purposed to me." She flung her hand out to show the sergeant her ring.

The sergeant's eyes widened. "You don't say? Congratulations to you, Ms. Parker. You got yourself a good one here."

She grinned. "I know."

"I better run this license before this driver gets impatient. Have a nice night."

As Sgt. Valdez returned to his car, she looked at Wyatt. "Are you ready to go back inside and celebrate with everyone?"

"Everyone?"

"Yes. This is a small town, and I'm so happy you landed in it."

He pulled her into his arms once more. "So am I."

After a too brief kiss they went inside.

Marty grabbed her right away, so Wyatt went to the bar to get drinks. "Is it true?"

She smiled. "It is. And it's very good."

"Squeee!" Marty gave her a bear hug. "We need to celebrate. You are going to have me in the wedding party, right?"

"Of course."

"I'm going to hold you to that."

Marty immediately took over. Drinks abounded, except for them, and they were pushed onto the floor for a slow dance. She wrapped her arms around Wyatt's neck and stared into his eyes. "Has anyone ever told you that you have the best smile this side of the Rockies?"

He chuckled. "I can't say that they have. Has anyone ever told you that you have the kindest heart?"

She shook her head. "No, but dad has said I have the biggest heart. I wasn't sure if he meant because I like to help people or because of my physical size."

He gave her a little squeeze. "You are the perfect size, for me, including your heart."

"And you are the perfect size for me, no which way about it."

He raised his brows. "Which way? I think it had to be your way."

She pretended to think. "No, I like Wyatt's way better. Because in the end, happiness is our reward."

"I couldn't be happier." The truth of his statement was in his eyes. "You own my heart."

Her own heart filled with joy at his words. "And you own mine."

He lowered his forehead to hers. "Forever."

"Yes." She tilted her head and found his lips, sealing the promise with a kiss.

Epilogue

"Wyatt? Come look."

At Alyssa's call, he left the kitchen. Having her living with him was a dream. Even he and Snowdrop were getting along. They added a gate to the top of the stairs and the rabbit loved having the entire upstairs for a playground.

He strode out of the house to find Alyssa on the porch. She wore a pair of jean shorts that showed off her ass and a half top that made it hard not to touch her.

"Look." She pointed at the north corral.

"Well, I'll be damned." Meeko was loving all over Roy who had come over to review the site for Annette and Ed's new house.

Alyssa's armed wrapped around his waist. "Meeko's found his *real* person. I think I was close, but it was Dad he needed."

He lifted his arm and wrapped it around her as they stood side by side watching the lovefest going on at the north corral. "Do you think your father would consider adopting him. It's not like Meeko needs other horses around." Not like Ghost.

"Do horses get along with Ostriches?"

He shook his head. "I've never heard of that. Didn't your father say ostriches can kill an animal by kicking them?"

"You're right. He'd have to keep them separate. The

270

ostriches aren't in the barn area, so that might work. I'm just not sure how he'd feel about owning a horse again."

He turned his head and kissed her cheek. "Why don't we ask him?"

She shrugged. "It can't hurt to ask."

He took her hand and they strode over to where Roy stood, Meeko's connection undeniable. "What do you think of Meeko?"

Roy turned to face them but continued to stroke the now docile horse. "I thought you said he was the mean one."

Since he'd addressed Alyssa, she answered. "He is, with everyone but you."

"That true?" This time Roy looked at him.

"Yes, sir. I couldn't even feed him for a while there without risking my life. He finally understood I was keeping him from starving and grudgingly lets me care for him."

Roy looked at Meeko. "Have you been an ornery son of a bitch, Meeko?"

"Dad, really?"

Her father shrugged. "I guess it takes one to know one." He chuckled.

Wyatt squeezed Alyssa's hand. "Would you be interested in adopting him?"

"Me?" Roy was definitely startled.

He shrugged. "Maybe you could think about it. It's not like we'll be able to adopt him out to anyone else."

"Why not?" Roy's frown showed he wasn't sure at all about the idea.

"Because every person he has been in contact with except you and your daughter, have been chased away by him."

Roy looked at the horse. "You're that much of a pisser, are you?" He turned back to them. "That's not a great selling point."

"No, but that's why this is a rescue ranch." And for the first time that truly sunk in. He wasn't a cattle rancher anymore. He was in charge of something even more important. "These animals come to us broken in some way. We prepare them for new homes, but every home is hand selected. It doesn't matter how much money a person has. What matters is their character because these are special horses."

He looked Roy in the eye. "You have what it takes to give Meeko a forever home."

"You think so?"

He nodded.

"Will you think about it, Dad. For Meeko's sake?"

Roy reached out and the horse immediately moved against his hand. "Let me think about it. Is there a time limit, son?"

Son. Wyatt's heart filled with contentment at the word. "No, sir. Take as long as you need." He paused, needing to express what he felt. "Roy, do you know you are the only man to ever call me that?"

"What do you mean?" Roy left off petting the horse and focused.

A little uncomfortable with explaining, he couldn't ignore the instinct to do so. "As you know, my father hasn't been in my life and my grandfather called me 'boy' because to him that's what I was, his daughter's boy. You are the only man to ever call me son, and I'm honored that in a few months I will be your son in truth."

"Well, shit." Roy's eyes misted as he looked to Alyssa. "You really found a good one, didn't you?"

"I sure did." Alyssa's smile made Wyatt feel as if he'd won the lottery on happiness.

"Hell, son. Give this old man a hug before I look like a blubbering fool."

With an open heart, he hugged Roy then stepped back, grinning like the boy his Gramps always called him.

"I guess this is as good a time as any then to tell you two what I wanted to give you as a wedding gift. Of course, you don't have to accept it."

"Dad, you know whatever you plan to give us for a gift will be appreciated."

"I'm not sure." He moved his gaze from Alyssa.

She let go of their clasped hands and took her father's. "Dad, what did you want to give us?"

"What I would like to give you is the world. I know I should have found another woman so you could have a mother, but I just couldn't do it. Your mother will always be my one and only love."

She shook her head. "Don't say that. I never wished I had another mom. She was my one and only mom. You made a great dad-mom."

Roy patted her hand. "I tried." He glanced at Wyatt. "And now you have a stalwart young man to take care of you. I want to provide you both with a home. But not just any home."

"Dad." Alyssa's tone was a warning.

Roy tensed.

Wyatt quickly stepped up. "Alyssa, I think we should be open to hearing about your father's gift."

She clamped her lips together and nodded.

Roy's shoulders relaxed. "Since I started working on the Benson's house, it got me to thinking. I could do the same on our property. I don't need all that space in the house I originally built for our family. I can build myself a little house and after I move out, I could renovate and update the one you grew up in to however you want it for your family." He smiled hesitantly. "I sure would like to be a grandpa that's close by."

Wyatt's heart raced. A home of his own? From his new father?

Alyssa's appeared as stunned as he was.

"Allie, I know you say I'd be too much in your business if you lived with me, but this wouldn't be living together. We'd each have our own new space, but be close enough to visit without getting in a car."

Whatever she decided, Wyatt would agree to, but his heart was hammering in his chest.

She turned her head to look at him and her eyes were filled with tears.

His stomach clenched. She would turn it down. Swallowing hard, he got out the words. "What do you think?"

Her broad smile released every tense muscle in his body at once. "I love it!" She turned to her father and gave him a long hug. "Thank you, Dad. That is the most generous, wonderful, amazing gift, but you will let me pay for materials for the renovation."

Roy widened his eyes and let out a whoosh of air from his lips, obviously very relieved as well. "I'm fine with that. I'm thinking all this building will at least keep me busy in my *early* retirement."

When Alyssa stepped back, she reached behind him and pulled his bandana from his back pocket. "I need this." Wiping her eyes with it, she blew her nose loudly.

He chuckled. "You can keep it." He gestured toward Roy. "How about coming inside. I'd like to get your ideas on a few projects I'm planning for Last Chance."

"I'm happy to give my opinion."

Alyssa snickered. "Be careful what you ask for."

As the three of them headed to the house, Alyssa updated Roy on some of the ideas they had. "And over there, we're thinking of setting up a petting zoo." She pointed to the other side of the barn. "It would be close to the entrance, so there would be no need for strangers to go further onto the property than the house and corrals."

Roy stopped and looked at him. "Is this petting zoo going to have rabbits?"

Wyatt flushed. Since the day he'd confronted his father, he'd had no more nightmares. Not even bad dreams.

"Daadd."

Roy gave him a light punch in the arm. "Don't worry, Allie. Wyatt can take a joke. Right, son?"

He nodded. "I can. But try living with Snowdrop and see how much a hurry you're in to be around rabbits."

"Wyatt! My Snowdrop is an angel."

He leaned into Roy and lowered his voice. "More like an archangel."

"I heard that." Alyssa grabbed his hand. "Come on, let's go inside, so you can tell Dad about all your plans."

He had plans for the barn as well, but he knew why Alyssa wanted to steer clear of that area. They had just moved her dad's retirement gift, an expertly made Memory cabinet, into the tack room and it wasn't covered. She had one more coat of stain to put on and then he'd move it into the house so she could add all the awards and life events to it.

He'd had no idea his schoolteacher was an expert woodworker. He actually looked forward to a lifetime of discovering all her facets. They had talked about things she could make for the ranch, but now maybe they could change their plans and think about what she could build for their new home.

Saying that in his head made it feel more real, even if it might still be a year off. It would probably take him that long to get used to the idea.

Once inside, Alyssa took over the conversation, showing her father the plans for the land as well as the new website Landon had up. He was still working on the online adoption application and interest form, but it looked a hundred percent better. The teenager had even come out a couple times to take photos, and starting next week, he would begin riding lessons. What was even more impressive was his grades were better.

Wyatt couldn't remember being happier. *A complacent man is one who doesn't know what he's missing.* At his grandfather's words in his head, he frowned.

Shut up, Gramps. I know when I've got it good.

You deserve it boy.

The phrase, so rarely heard from his grandfather, had him looking up. He shook his head. No, it couldn't be him. It was just a convenient memory.

"You don't think Dad's idea of allowing seniors to have field trips out here is a good one? Why not?"

At Alyssa's words, he refocused. "No, I think it's a good idea. Why?"

She frowned at him. "You shook your head."

He grinned. "Just thinking about all the chores I still have to do today."

"I think that's my cue." Roy rose. "Besides, I want to take my notes back to the house and update my plans."

Alyssa sighed. "Okay. We'll be over tomorrow for breakfast."

"You better be."

He followed his future father-in-law and future wife down the hall and out the front door.

After saying goodbye, he and Alyssa walked up the steps of the porch. On the spur of the moment, he grabbed her hand and walked to a chair and sat.

"What? I thought you had chores."

He pulled her onto his lap. "This is better than chores."

She looped her arms around his neck. "I agree." Then her mouth found his and his heart sighed.

Finally, he pulled away, knowing if he continued, no chores would get done at all.

"I think Dad's thought more about our wedding than we have."

"I don't. I think about marrying you every day."

She leaned back. "You do?"

He nodded. "I do. I would take you down to the courthouse, or whatever Canterbury has for that kind of thing, and marry you right now."

"Wow." She cupped his face. "You do know when you say things like that it just makes me love you more."

He laid his hand over hers then turned and kissed her palm. Moving her hand to hold it close to his heart, he stared into her kind eyes. "It's the truth. But I want you to have the wedding of your dreams."

"Would you mind if we got married at my dad's place?"

"Not at all. If you don't mind waiting until after Dr. Jenna and Logan tie the knot."

She frowned. "When will that be?"

He had to think. In the flurry of moving Alyssa in with him before her lease expired, he'd lost track. "It's the first week of November. They're having an outdoor wedding at their house."

"Oh, that's perfect weather. It would probably take me that long just to find a dress and ask Marty to be in the wedding party and…what about you? Do you have anyone you'd want in our bridal party?"

He'd only been to a few weddings and wasn't up on all the ins and outs. "I'd like to invite my mom and sisters. I'd also like to have all the Last Chance people there. They are my new extended family after you and your dad."

Alyssa's eyes started to sparkle with excitement. "I can't wait to meet your family. But even more, I can't wait to be your wife."

"Your students will have to learn to call you Mrs. Ford."

She shrugged. "Children are very adaptable. I can already hear Lydia correcting anyone who gets it wrong."

At the mention of the little girl with the back brace, it reminded him of their conversation. "That little girl is very smart. She's going to be someone important one day."

Alyssa nodded. "I agree. Sometimes her insights even astound me."

"She told me that Kentucky was lucky he was a wobbler because he would never have a rider telling him what to do. Instead, he could do what he wanted. I think I'm more like a horse than I realized."

She wiggled her eyebrows. "I certainly enjoy riding you."

He laughed. He never expected her sexual innuendos. "Thank you. But I meant that I used to be like Tundra, needing someone to guide me like Gramps. When he died, I became a wobbler like Kentucky. But it took you to help me see I could choose my own path in life."

She pulled her hand from his and tilted his head. "I'm glad you found your way. I'm even more glad you found me."

Looking into her eyes, he finally felt worthy of her, and he would spend the rest of his life making her happy. "I love you, Alyssa."

The End

For updates, sneak peeks, and special prizes, sign up to receive the latest news from Lexi http://bit.ly/LexiUpdate

Read on for an excerpt of *Christmas with Angel.*

Chapter One

Day before Christmas Eve

Cole Hatcher added two pillows to the makeshift bed of sleeping bags on the hay. He'd unzipped each and spread them out so he and Lacey could crawl in together. Maybe if they could have a little privacy, they could settle their Christmas issue.

He'd pilfered all the snowflake decorations from the tree inside and hung them from the beams. In his mind, he'd envisioned it to look like it was snowing, but in reality, it looked like plastic, glass and felt snowflakes hanging from beams. Lacey would get it though. She couldn't expect more than this from her cowboy.

Adjusting the garland around the stall walls, he pulled over the small table he used for grooming the horses and placed it next to the bed. With a rag he'd grabbed from the house, he wiped it off and placed a bottle of wine on it with two plastic cups. "That should do it." His Christmas Eve present was ready, though a few hours early.

Stuffing the rag in his back pocket, he turned the battery-operated lantern to low and set it next to the wine. "Perfect."

As he headed out of the barn, the six horses in residence paid him no heed except for Angel. Her wary eyes watched him until he was out of sight.

Giving Angel to Lacey had been the best thing he'd done for that horse, besides take her from her owner. She was so fearful of men that her bond with Lacey had grown strong.

Now if he could just get his fiancé onto the same page with him, life would be great again.

Cole strode across the dirt yard, the only sound to break the crisp night air, the two note call of a whippoorwill. The quiet beckoned him, but he needed Lacey to truly enjoy it. The house lights should have been welcoming but with his two cousins in residence, one baby, Billy and his grandparents, the four bedroom house was packed.

He took the stairs to the porch two at a time. Pulling back the screen door, he opened the heavy, ironwood front door. As he stepped in, he had to stop himself from stepping back out.

The baby cried upstairs while his two cousins, Logan and Trace argued. A door slammed on the upper level then Trace stomped down the stairs, yelling back over his shoulder, "I'll be watching the game with Grandpa if you come to your senses!" He nodded to Cole as he passed by.

Old Billy, who used to work and live at Poker Flat and had just spent two months in rehab for alcoholism, ambled through the front hall from the kitchen, a bottle of water in his hand and a smile on his face. The television in the living room clicked on just as Billy entered and the volume increased substantially.

Cole winced, the noise level and activity in the house was almost painful. Like Lacey, he couldn't wait for their own home to be completed, but it barely had walls and was far too incomplete for them to have the privacy and quiet they needed. Since Lacey had given up her casita at the Poker Flat Nudist Resort, they had nowhere to go…except the barn.

She was probably in their room where she always retreated

right after dinner to crunch numbers, do research, or iron clothes for work. He ran up the stairs, excited to show her the present he'd arranged, and opened the door to the bedroom.

Lacey stood next to the bed, her deep pink sweater fitting her like a second-skin, wisps of blonde hair escaping her long braid. Her maroon skirt flowed about her, accentuating her delicate femininity. He still couldn't believe this hot woman was his. She had a basket of laundry dumped out on their bed, clean clothes strewn over the quilt and a small pile folded to her right. He walked straight to her and wrapped his arms around her waist from behind. "I have a surprise for you."

She stilled then sighed. "Is it ear plugs?"

He kissed her neck beneath her ear, loving how tiny she felt against him. "Even better."

She dropped his fire department t-shirt and turned in his arms. "Better is good." She lifted her arms around his neck. "Don't get me wrong. I love your family. There just seems to be so many of them in this particular house. And now that Billy's here, it makes it very cramped."

He looked into her light brown eyes that reminded him of amaretto. "You love my family? Even my parents?"

She lowered her lashes and stared at his chest.

Damn, he needed to wait to discuss that. Talking about his parents only brought up what his mother had done to break them apart. That didn't set the mood he wanted. He wouldn't press it now. "So aren't you a little bit curious about my surprise?"

She lifted her gaze to meet his. "Is this my Christmas Eve present?"

His family had always exchanged gifts on Christmas day, but maybe he and Lacey could start their own tradition. "Yes, just a few hours early."

She looked over her shoulder at the clock sitting on the

nightstand. "Only three hours and seventeen minutes early. Should I wait?"

He started to grin but it turned to a grimace as his cousin's baby let out an ear-piercing wail. "You might be able to, but I can't."

At the sound of the baby's scream, Lacey buried her head against his chest. She lifted it to look up at him. "I could use a surprise right about now."

"Good." He kissed her on the forehead then let her go so he could take her hand. As he took a step toward the door, she resisted. "I thought you were going to give me a surprise."

"We have to go outside for this."

She pointed to the pile of clothes. "But I need to finish folding the laundry."

"Leave them. This is more important."

"Okay." She let him pull her down the hall.

When they got to the top of the stairs, he released her hand and stepped aside so she could descend first. Another screeching wail sounded from above, and they both picked up their pace. As he opened the front door, the television volume increased another decimal in the living room and from the corner of his eye he caught sight of Billy who had joined his grandfather and Trace.

Lacey stepped onto the porch and sighed.

No sooner had he closed the door than she placed her hand on his chest. "Do you hear that?"

He listened. The quiet was almost deafening until four hoots, sounding like a bouncing ball, broke the silence. "You mean the Screech Owl?"

She smiled slyly. "No, I mean the quiet."

He grinned. "Wait until you see my surprise." He took her hand and they walked down the steps toward the barn.

"I hope you didn't get me another horse. I'm very attached to Angel and I think she'd get jealous."

He shook his head. "No, it's not a horse. Luckily, I haven't had any calls this week. Maybe the Christmas spirit has people being kinder to their animals." He frowned at the thought of what else the Christmas season brought. "Now if we could just get Christmas tree fires under control, everyone could have a happy Christmas."

She squeezed his hand. "I've never understood the need for a live evergreen tree in the Arizona desert. It's so dry. If a person wants to smell evergreens, they can always go up to Prescott for the day or take a hike right here in our own mountains."

"You make the house smell great with those scented candles you use. I'm glad you found them in the glass jars."

She stopped at the entrance to the barn and looked at him. "Can you turn off the firefighter tonight and give me the cowboy who loves to save abused, hurt, and unwanted horses?"

He grinned sheepishly. "I'll try. Actually, your surprise is definitely from the cowboy." He winked.

Lacey's gaze roamed over him, and he couldn't help but count himself lucky all over again. To have found her a second time, at a fire no less, had been sheer luck. That she was just as dedicated to his horse rescue ranch as he was, was a bonus. Her wizardry with the finances had also improved their solvency. But to have captured her heart once more against all odds was the greatest luck of all. "If you keep looking at me like that, your surprise might have to wait."

She widened her eyes. "Like what?" She even batted her lashes.

He laughed and pulled her into his embrace. "I love you, soon-to-be Lacey Hatcher."

"I know." She stood on tiptoe to give him a kiss.

When she didn't deepen the kiss, he had to stop himself from lowering his lips to hers again. The open barn door was not the place to start making love to his woman. Reluctantly, he released her, but grasped her hand again.

After pulling the large door closed behind him, he led Lacey through the barn, passing the filled stalls until she slowed by Angel. He understood and let go, continuing toward the last stall, not wanting to disturb the bond between her and the rescued horse.

No sooner had Lacey turned toward the white Arabian, than Angel gave a soft nicker and walked to the stall door. Lacey pet the badly marred head, cooing to her like one would talk with a baby.

Cole never tired of watching their connection. He had almost given up hope that Angel would ever interact with humans again after the abuse she'd take from her former owner. That the horse came into his life shortly after he had found Lacey again made him think it was fate. Though the horse shied away from men, she completely trusted Lacey.

When Lacey finished, she walked slowly toward him, or was she sauntering toward him? Shit, his muscles tensed in anticipation.

She still wore her clothes from work, her long skirt swishing against her white cowboy boots. The sweater showed off her figure even if it didn't reveal even a hint of cleavage. It was hard to believe she worked at a nudist resort. He was thankful once again that the resort had a strict policy about employees keeping their clothes on during work. He would go insane if Lacey was supposed to work nude. On the other hand, because Kendra owned the nudist resort she was expected to be nude. He had no idea how Wade handled his fiancé being naked half the day. Cole couldn't do it.

284

But Lacey was sexy even with her clothes on, especially after a long day, when her braid had loosened and her messy wheat-colored hair made it look as if she'd just spent an hour in bed with him.

He watched her eyes closely as she approached. Her gaze was riveted to him and his chest puffed with pride. When she licked her lips, he had to force himself to stay still as every tendon pushed at him to move.

Finally, her gaze flitted to the stall behind him and her lips formed a pleased smile. "Oh Cole, it's the best present you could have given me."

He released the breath he'd been holding and opened his arms. "You like it?"

She walked straight into his embrace. "I love it."

"It might get a little chilly tonight."

She shrugged. "That's why I have you to keep me warm."

"Just to keep you warm?" He frowned. "I was hoping to start a fire inside you."

Lacey's short intake of breath had his cock taking notice.

She wrapped her arms around his neck. "You are as good at starting fires as putting them out."

"Only for you." He lowered his head and kissed her.

She pressed her body against him and pushed her tongue between his lips. He caught it with his own.

Every nook of her mouth was like new territory. He tasted the tartness of the wine she had with dinner and a flavor that was all Lacey. His hands roamed over her back, feeling her sweater slide against silk.

His cock hardened at the thought of what his Racy Lacey might be wearing underneath.

She pulled her lips away abruptly. "You have too many clothes on."

"I was thinking the same about you." He wiggled his brow. "I bet I can take my shirt off faster than you can." He let his arm go slack in anticipation of the race. They were always betting about sex.

She kept her arms around him. "And what does the winner get?"

"I'm thinking, choice of position." At his words, a shiver ran through her body, sending lightning straight to his balls.

"On the count of three. One. Two. Three."

No sooner had she dropped her arms than he reached back and pulled his flannel over his head. One button pinged across the stall, hitting the wood, as his face cleared the tail of the shirt.

Lacey had brought the sweater up over her head, but her face was still hidden.

Cole stared at the pale pink corset that cupped her breasts and accentuated her waist and hips. With her skirt still on, she looked like a saloon girl from the old west.

As she pulled the sweater free, she took a breath and her areolas peeked above their confines.

He swallowed hard.

"Are you admiring my new corset?" She smiled slyly, the vixen.

He shook his head as he traced a finger along the top edge of the satiny lingerie. "No, I'm admiring this." He pushed his finger inside the cup and flicked at the hard nipple beneath."

"But you like it, right?"

"I think it might require a closer inspection." He used his other hand to burrow beneath her other cup and lift the breast above the soft satin so the corset held it up for him to view her rosy tip. "Hmm, I'm liking it more and more." He performed the same readjustment on her other breast then stood back.

"Now that's perfect." He stared at her hard nipples held aloft. "I really like it."

"I'm glad." Her lips formed a seductive pout. "But I lost the bet."

He reached out one hand and brushed his fingertips across her hard nipples. "Yes, you did."

Her chest rose as she sucked in a breath at his touch.

He loved how responsive she was. "I think it's time you took off your skirt so I can decide exactly what position I want you in."

She cocked her head. "And that must be determined by what I'm wearing underneath my skirt?"

He nodded. His soon-to-be wife never failed to surprise him when they crawled into bed at night. Her love of lingerie had him anticipating their alone time even during dinner. He was definitely the beneficiary of that little fetish. It didn't take much to get Lacey hot, but in the house, she had to keep quiet when they made love, and that took something away from the experience for her. Tonight, she could let go completely with no one the wiser.

Lacey untied the bow at her waist and pushed the skirt down to the barn floor before stepping out of it.

He was too distracted by the movement of her breasts at first, to understand her smile.

"So what position would you like?" Her voice was teasing, a sound he hadn't heard in over a month.

This had definitely been needed. He lowered his gaze and raised his brows. "I can't decide until you take off that damn slip too."

She giggled, another sound he hadn't heard in a while. He needed to do something about that. The stress of building a house, working, caring for the horses with so much family around was too stressful for the only-child Lacey.

As she shimmied out of her slip, his jaw dropped.

Also by Lexi Post

Contemporary Cowboy Romance

Cowboys Never Fold
(Poker Flat Series: Book 1)
Cowboy's Match
(Poker Flat Series: Book 2)
Cowboy's Best Shot
(Poker Flat Series: Book 3)
Cowboy's Break
(Poker Flat Series: Book 4)
Wedding at Poker Flat
(Poker Flat Series: Book 5)

Christmas with Angel
(Poker Flat Series Book 2.5, Last Chance Series: Book 1)
Trace's Trouble
(Last Chance Series: Book 2)
Fletcher's Flame
(Last Chance Series: Book 3)
Logan's Luck
(Last Chance Series: Book 4)

Dillon's Dare
(Last Chance Series: Book 5)
Riley's Rescue
(Last Chance Series: Book 6)
Wyatt's Way
(Last Chance Series: Book 7)

Aloha Cowboy
(Island Cowboy Series: Book 1)

Military Romance

When Love Chimes
(Broken Valor Series: Book 1)
Poisoned Honor
(Broken Valor Series: Book 2)

Paranormal Romance

Masque
Passion's Poison
Passion of Sleepy Hollow
Heart of Frankenstein

Pleasures of Christmas Past
(A Christmas Carol Series: Book 1)
Desires of Christmas Present
(A Christmas Carol Series: Book 2)
Temptations of Christmas Future
(A Christmas Carol Series: Book 3)
One of A Kind Christmas
(A Christmas Carol Series: Book 4)

On Highland Time
(Time Weavers, Inc.: Book 1)
A Pocket in Time
(Time Weavers, Inc.: Book 2)
Come Viking Time
(Time Weavers, Inc.: Book 3)

Sci-fi Romance

Cruise into Eden
(The Eden Series: Book 1)
Unexpected Eden
(The Eden Series: Book 2)
Eden Discovered
(The Eden Series: Book 3)
Eden Revealed
(The Eden Series: Book 4)
Avenging Eden
(The Eden Series: Book 5)

Beast of Eden
(Eden Series Tolba: Book 1)
Bound by Eden
(Eden Series Tolba: Book 2)
Burning for Eden
(Eden Series Tolba: Book 3)

About Lexi Post

Lexi Post is a New York Times and USA Today best-selling author of romance inspired by the classics. She spent years in higher education taking and teaching courses about the classical literature she loved. From Edgar Allan Poe's short story "The Masque of the Red Death" to Tolstoy's *War and Peace*, she's read, studied, and taught wonderful classics.

But Lexi's first love is romance novels. In an effort to marry her two first loves, she started writing romance inspired by the classics and found she loved it. From hot paranormals to sizzling cowboys to hunks from out of this world, Lexi provides a sensuous experience with a "whole lotta story."

Lexi is living her own happily ever after with her husband and her two cats in Florida. She makes her own ice cream every weekend, loves bright colors, and you will never see her without a hat.

www.lexipostbooks.com

Printed in Great Britain
by Amazon